MW01136995

2050

KRISTIAN ZENZ

Archway Publishing books may be ordered
through booksellers or by contacting:

Archway Publishing
1663 Liberty Drive
Bloomington, IN 47403
www.archwaypublishing.com
1 (888) 242-5904

ISBN: 978-1-4808-7689-7 (sc)
ISBN: 978-1-4808-7690-3 (e)

Library of Congress Control Number: 2019904521

Print information available on the last page.

Archway Publishing rev. date: 4/22/2019

CONTENTS

Prologue.. ix

Chapter 1 1
Chapter 2 10
Chapter 3 15
Chapter 4 20
Chapter 5 26
Chapter 6 31
Chapter 7 35
Chapter 8 41
Chapter 9 48
Chapter 10 58
Chapter 11 68
Chapter 12 78
Chapter 13 87
Chapter 14 99
Chapter 15 110
Chapter 16 119
Chapter 17 130
Chapter 18 138
Chapter 19 147
Chapter 20 159
Chapter 21 170
Chapter 22 183

Chapter 23 196
Chapter 24 209
Chapter 25 220
Chapter 26 233
Chapter 27 246

Epilogue..265
About the Author 269

To Selena and Mandy

PROLOGUE

We started dying before the snow, and like the
snow, we continued to fall.

—Louise Erdrich

My parents were worried for me. I was worried for them. A crippling
blackout had wiped out the entire city. The power came back on
later that day—literally in a flash—but I needed to calculate the
damage it had caused for me when the electrical grid collapsed
from an overload of data. In truth, when one electrical system died
these days, all of them did.

The first two floors of my home were engulfed in thick,
burning winds of fire, which made a noise like it was crying our
names.

This had happened with the technological blackout and the
windstorms that hit us, with temperatures steadily increasing. A
blaze of fire had suddenly ripped through the entire house. We
were already huddled inside the nearly empty basement. I had
managed to escape, leaving my unfortunate parents behind in a
room filled with black smoke and dust, created by the fire that
carved a hole through the floorboards. I leaped to safety through
the tiny glass window beneath the first floor. When I was finally
free, I saw the area was entirely burned; black grass covered the
ground. I had scrapes, bruises, and burned skin. The important
thing, though, was that I was alive—and glad to be.

The more urgent matter was my parents. They were currently buried under the burning rubble and surely were either dead or dying. The local fire brigade, unfortunately, did not arrive in time to save them. In fact, they were nowhere close to doing so. The fire trucks were autonomously controlled by built-in computers that automatically set the vehicle to the exact speed limit, thus arriving nowhere near on time.

I had a different outlook on life after this tragedy, all because of a simple yet disastrous technological failure. From that point on, I had started a new beginning—a quite unnerving one.

The date was December 1, 2050.

CHAPTER 1

The men all played along to a distant beat. They rose and fell every second, moving along with the waves of the lake. Some said they were simply dancers. Yet others said they were diffusions of the common man. No one pointed out their casual moves, as these moves were cast with curtains open every day. No one ever spoke of the sounds they made, as those sounds blended in with the noises heard throughout the city.

The pounding of stone and disposal of rubbish became the subject of the artists' canvas. This canvas was as wide as the windows from which it was seen, as bright as the sun in the sky, yet as blue as the lake below. Darker and sleeker the world had become, yet that forsaken lake on the eastern edge was as bright as ever. The metamorphosis that had channeled the being of the inner eye couldn't be passed up, and these artists' crafty hands created something that would not stand out, yet everyone who saw it would notice it. The sun gleamed back into these eyes, just as it did for the lake.

They said I was dreaming. I was.

With my eyes open.

The view from the top floor was grand—a panorama of gray glass and scaffolding. The city was always progressing toward the next level. I wanted this level to be the last. The men were directed around cones and under steel poles as they were led to yet another new apartment tower under construction. They had become the signal of what the world once had been and now was: built by man and only for man.

This gleaming tower had a glass exterior cast with a formal tone of a darker blue. It was just enough to differentiate it yet familiar enough to blend in with the rest. It was as if the cream city was drained of its color.

This was the view I thought would never grow old. It contradicted the entire skyline that screamed modernity. I was never eager for a visual like this.

I had started to drift, nearly collapsed from exhaustion, along with the impatience of waiting for the workday to conclude. This was the case until the boss woke me up.

"You could at least pretend to be busy," Richard Clark, head of the company, said. "But you're good. Your shift is done for today."

I lifted my head with slight enthusiasm, gathered my belongings, and headed toward the elevator. The shaft was wide and free, yet the doors closed with the tightest of locks. The strong December winds had penetrated the shaft just a little, yet it flew down to the ground floor with a breeze.

The ground floor workforce had already cleared out to the street outside. I took a glance at the cafeteria to the right of me and thought about coffee for the walk home. But no amount of caffeine could erase my misery.

The snow never came. The trees were gray. The lights were faded. Yet I remained there, locked in the same space, hoping one day this earth could see change.

From what?

This thought got into my head at times, deservedly so. I looked in all directions while hoping that some force was alive to carry me home.

My God, it was dead outside.

December 15, 2050
Milwaukee, Wisconsin

My life has changed a bit in recent years. In spite
of the many misleading things they said would
come, our world has gotten worse and worse.
The only good thing that has come of this is the
experimental end of trash. It doesn't help. More
and more humans are being born. By now, we
should have at least a little common sense with all
the technology, not just those autonomous cars.
Something that could make our lives better, not
ruin them. Also, now there is little to no gasoline,
so we can't use the old cars, the kind we have the
ability to actually control. Also, gold isn't the most
expensive thing anymore. Somehow, electricity is.
None of our machines runs on gas. The ones that
do just sit there. They said coal was bad for our
planet, and it is—by getting rid of it. This is just
pure stupidity. I am not happy on any level.

I closed up my diary tightly and laid it on my bedroom carpet,
which was white but discolored from dirt. *Maybe that's the last
book I'll own,* I thought.

I then looked out my Park Lafayette Tower apartment window
to see the still-brightly shining sun, like I was a vampire. It wasn't
a good feeling—at least, not when I looked below. I let Prospect
Avenue do the talking. We humans had no control, whether it
was because of the autonomous cars or that no one needed a job
anymore because money was now a virtue. Everyone could have
everything they desired, from a mansion with electric windows
to an electric supercar with electric everything.

Sadly, I did not possess the attributes to own any of these

because I was a poor man. This was a strange concept, since I stated that money was a virtue. The government, which was the only source of control in our world, wouldn't let me have the rule of virtue. That was because ever since I had developed *my* theory as a child, I told everyone...all the time. But they didn't want to listen.

One would say, "Right. The world will end in just thirty-five years. Dream on."

Another would say, "Take your old-fashioned beliefs and move on."

I'd offered my opinion to the most knowledgeable adults, but even they didn't seem to listen. I rallied at protests, submitted commercials, and gave prime examples of how the world would end if it continued to grow.

Unfortunately for me and my colleagues, it felt like segregation all over again. They didn't care for my points. They banned me from protesting again and from leaving the city. For the government to do this was quite daring. They took my technology, which was actually quite ironic.

I then sat at my lonesome desk, which was tan with stains directly above it. It was the exact spot where I did my work and thought things through. I didn't own a laptop or a tablet; I didn't need one. I could live perfectly well, all by myself, with no digital distractions. In fact, not owning one made me happy. This differentiated me from the rest of the world and made me look smarter. It was the only thing on the current planet that made me happy. It reminded me of older, humbler times, when I was not depressed in my lost, gloomy hole of thought with such implausible ideas. That was my next point of view—a person could be perfectly happy without any digital distractions, although I was the only man on earth to support that belief. At my desk, I worked on the plans. I had to do certain things. I never bothered anyone in the slightest.

It was funny how much this crazy technology had been constantly berated from 2010 to 2025. Books, movies, and TV series made fun of the crazy technology that had started to wrap around us. They made it look horrible. Yet we laughed. Then why did we continue to use technology?

I wished the earth would listen to me, perhaps just once. Not one of the fifteen billion people on this earth agreed with me. The only way to do this was to force them.

No one ever felt bad these days, except for me. It was a fact that our lives had changed, and it seemed there was no way to fix it. The one great force, which otherwise was known as the government, would prevent a person from changing it because it was too good. I could not live with that seed planted in my mind. That was exactly why I was put on this earth.

People did not understand my point of view because it was quite the concept to take in.

The simple thing was that … well, if humans didn't take control, technology would do it for us, and eventually all species of life on the planet would die.

I would throw this ridiculous theory on paper, a short explanation to the entire population, which had doubled over the past forty to fifty years to a scorching fifteen billion people. I felt like the earth was about to collapse under my feet. The reason was that if the earth continued to grow and medicine continued to save lives, the world would have such an extravagant amount of people that it would simply collapse.

Why? Earth still had plenty of space, although it was not the space; it was the ever-growing pollution that was the problem.

That sounded oxymoronic—pollution, when there were electric cars, solar power, and other "green" inventions. This world was two things: people and oil.

People let out billions of pounds of CO_2 emissions every day, as everyone knew. The electric gadgets couldn't balance that out.

With all those electronic devices came the lack of oil usage. The Middle East powerhouse now had gone fully electric. That was where the stock market was, obviously, so oil became just a hazard that polluted the air. What should we do with it? No one could figure it out. We can't simply dispose of it.

But I feel like the whole planet is on the verge of doing so.

That is why I want to stop it.

Everyone thinks the world is great because they don't have anything to do but lounge and relax—the once frowned-upon American dream. Sadly, everyone now has an excuse to become obese because medicine will take care of them and will fix them up in no time, just to start the same redundant cycle all over again. It's grotesque. It's sickening. It's saddening, depressing—whatever you can think of. I can't stand it. It's wrong in my still useful mind.

Taking this into consideration, I now somehow thank criminal activities, such as murder, homicide, suicide, and the like. I never have wanted to thank such a horrible thing, but now why not? Because each and every death gives us the slightest help to sustain our planet. It is an extremely unusual thought, and I'm the only one willing to believe it. Do I thank God that world hunger is still around? That will also help the earth live on for a few more decades as we attempt to keep it in balance. Think of it like natural selection or population control. It seems wrong, but it takes courage, and it is, in fact, the greatest sacrifice known to man— to let others live. Hey, the Incas did it. Seems uncivilized now, on such a planet with sophisticated cultures and white buildings, tall and bland, that look like shampoo bottles stretching into the air. I attempt to sound realistic, but these days, sarcasm doesn't even do it justice.

All in all, I believe that the world will eventually die off *if* the government doesn't consider a new standard of lifestyle—ethereal, with some sort of technology wipeout, or pollution, whichever comes first. I guess you need a little technology to wipe it out.

Nobody listens to anyone anymore. The world has begun to fall apart in our hands, crumble within our heads, and destruct within our souls. The many men and women who live in this hell have watched like it was a pretty light show. A political debate. Laughing.

Funny.

Really funny.

You know, failure is funny to the sickened human. This made me laugh. Disgrace, as a mandate, starts when we're teens. Epic fails depressed them, and everyone laughed. This gave them the power they wanted. The arrow was shot through the wrong window.

It all starts with preteens. They get their first phones or appliances, and they have entrance to a little disaster called the *internet*. All their innocence is lost. They realize that the world isn't this happy-go-lucky place they thought it was. And that twelve-year-old thinks he knows everything now and tries to become more of a smart ass than his friends. And they become so rude, acting like people who have no life, posting videos on YouTube, and making themselves get a little more idiotic than they already are. It makes sense. Once they see the technology, they each become less of a person.

What else has this technology has done, and what has it given us? It's the bullshit nobody asked for. Everybody wanted the flying car or the helpful robot—something extravagant like that. Rather, we got this phone with no buttons. A car with no steering wheel. An excuse to become more of a lazy ass than ever before. Yet nobody's complaining; they're too busy texting to get their heads through anything beyond their level. People are cruel. The earth is cruel to itself. And it's only being brought down by the people who think they want to make it better.

Nobody has a care or a clue; it's too much work is all they know. The art is gone. The passion is gone from life. Art has turned from beautiful paintings to spots on a white canvas. Music has turned from musicians playing beautiful tweaks on an instrument to nobodies with no skill who want to make quick bucks with a synthesizer. A smog-filled universe has fallen through the sky and created an impenetrable dust that nobody can break. People made it. There was nothing left of what was better. Humans just can't stand to lose, can they? That is maybe why they can't win. Humans, in a few words, are smart enough to act even worse than they already are.

It is a simple plot: when you gain your knowledge, you lose your innocence. When you gain your power, you lose your knowledge. The more you absolutely have to find out, the more you are going down. When were you happier? When you were making money at a lifeless job, or reading with a friend at age seven?

I saw my friends trailing down the spiral staircase of death and fear, following what was at its peak, killing the roots they had just grown. I stuck to my roots, and I made it through the judgment that has whisked its claws at me for so many years. When your planet can't win or lose, you need the middle ground. A double negative is a positive, right?

That's what's going to save us.

That just gave me an idea.

That idea would eventually come out as ... ending the lifestyle.

Defeat technology in its source, back when it was still able to be controlled.

I will have to configure a plan as I go. It will work, no matter the flaws.

Night had fallen, another day of depression through the recklessness of my life and my dead-end job. I crawled into my loft, thinking, *How this will work?* It's sort of a feeling of nervousness, blended with confidence. It's a subtle feeling of strength.

I covered up my entire body under white sheets and turned the light off with a simple hand gesture—not really, there is a horrible hand gesture to turn out the light. I wish it was the middle finger. I had a plan. I was looking at the posters of *Back to the Future* and *1984*, plastered to the wall with glue. I shall prevail and teach the world its biggest lesson.

My name is Patrick Shields, and I will use 2050's technology to destroy it. I will create a better humanity by destroying ours.

I will keep the world alive, one way or another.

CHAPTER 2

December 16, 2050

Every day it seems the world is going to end the next day. Or maybe that is just my impatience. I heard on the news that the government has found a way to make viruses more powerful. We already have nuclear facilities. What would happen if this virus got released to the public? I mean, we're still trying to figure out how to get air onto other planets. Our president isn't doing any good. Now he is trying to pass a law that says we need more mines and power plants. Sarcasm doesn't even cut it these days. The only thing is, we can't think about it. We basically run on power. Our cars wouldn't work; they still fail occasionally. Neither would our water—or heat. Plus, video games, TV, even cooking utensils wouldn't work.

The next day was humbling for me, as usual. I crept out of bed and once again got ready for my only job at the office.

I washed my face at the dirty kitchen sink, splashing my face in water. I rode out of the bathroom and wandered through the halls of my apartment space. I then entered the kitchen, where I ate the same cereal, as usual, with the same milk. On my tablet, I read my virtual newspaper—paper copies are no longer available. I learned that, once again, another tablet was being released that was "bigger and better than ever."

I envied that, although it made me laugh.

After eating, I put on my black coat and walked out of my apartment building, which was tan on the inside and still brown on the outside.

Behind my apartment was a dark alley, where residents parked their cars, all of which were autonomous. In fact, that was the new government standard—to take away driving and make it "safer." Issued in 2037, it basically took over the aspiring minds of humans. Toyota sold the most autonomous cars as of this year.

I crept down the brownish steel stairs that were covered with spots of oil and dirt, waddled down to my car, and hopped into the backseat, which had tan leather throughout—no, leather isn't used anymore, only cushy plastic.

Before I could shut my door, my neighbor and best friend, Krystal, came running out of her apartment looking gleeful. She is technically on my side, but she's certainly not as perturbed as I am about it.

"Hey!" she said happily, walking up to me with a grin. "How are you today?"

"Oh, just heading off to my same old job," I replied, starting up the autonomous car with the standard press of a button. "Have to go impress the boss."

"Oh, right." Krystal leaned on the shining hood. "Give him an invention to improve nature as it is."

"He wants me to 'understand how great the world is' and make me adjust to the standards."

"I see. I personally agree with you; I just hide all of my attitude and store it in my head."

I set the destination into the infotainment system, which takes up the entire dashboard. "I have to run now. Wouldn't want the boss to blow up into bits."

"I understand. See you later today." She ran off into the distance.

My car automatically swerved, calmly, slowly, out of the parking lot and onto the same street that I traveled along every single day. It was made of concrete, with no signs in sight, no stoplights. It had no character; it was just a never-ending strip of boredom. No curves were needed either because if a hill or expressway was on your route, the road would just cut through, preventing both an accident and providing some fun.

I drank the coffee in the backseat, which was ironic—my parents had done that already forty years ago. The autonomous car was the new standard of the planet, but the entire idea had been lurking since 2015.

Traveling down numerous streets in this time, you would notice that the architecture of the entire planet had changed greatly over the years. Now, around two-thirds of buildings were clear glass. Glass molders learned to curve glass to the extreme so it curved around the entire bend of the building, like a blanket wrapped around you at night.

I was developing a plan not only because the earth had gained too many humans, but because the style of everything—from cars, to buildings, to lifestyles—was horrendous in my head, the heretic that I am. I could not stand it for even a moment. Even fifteen years ago, when this style first erupted worldwide, I nearly plotted suicide. Yet I changed this around, knowing that this planet could do so much better.

The buildings that everyone saw on the streets were white, gray, or clear glass.

Some called it modern- wasn't it interesting? Even the new outcroppings of suburban houses were modern. It started around the turn of the millennium, when designers started to lose creativity, or maybe they never had any.

It was a goddamn act of selfishness. Money over beauty. And it was everywhere. A house was supposed to be inviting, not a cold hell hole with blue LEDs for porch lights and soccer turf for grass.

Well, my crisis was certainly big enough, but there was no way they would let me, the supporter of a simpler lifestyle, get my hands on that. I had to plot a plan for *that* as well, most unfortunately for them.

Eventually, I reached my Northwestern Mutual Commons office tower, which was big and silver. It was awesome when it was first built but eventually was dwarfed by surrounding apartments. The parking lot was made entirely of concrete, which still laid smooth beneath a car's tire.

The building was around thirty-two stories—550 feet tall, short by today's standards. The driverless automobile parked itself in the lot, where it sat with other black, silver, and white autonomous cars, otherwise known as bland, boring, "mature" colors.

The car knew where it was by its advanced satellite navigation built directly into the panoramic sunroof. It shut itself off. I had to admit it was pretty cool for a while, but there was no self-control on the car—or virtually anything else for that matter. It was too much and needed to stop.

I got out of the car, shutting the back door softly. The car then locked itself as I walked away, straightening out my tie. Speaking of which, fashion sense either stayed the same or went downhill. For working men or women, style stayed the same but got more dynamic—a flash of everyone else's style. It was like a mix of the 1950s and 1980s, absolutely crazy, with flashy colors. It seemed odd, in my pit of despair known as earth, but I personally supported it because even though it sucked, it still showed a sense of freedom on the planet.

I crept into the big, bland building, where a scanner sat perched against a wall. It would scan my eyeball, analyzing the DNA in the cornea, so the whole building security franchise would know that it was me, a simple worker. It was as an excellent way to deter intruders. Interesting what they created to control security in any building of slight importance. Mostly trying to keep those away who would hack into the system.

I then entered the building through the scroll doors and got on the escalator that would take me to my floor.

Inside, a white tile floor lay beneath the standard black shoes everyone wore, most of them doing nothing; sitting at their clear table-top desks, sipping self-served coffee. It was somewhat like a lounge area. Actually, I am the only one who moves around here.

Up the stainless-steel escalator, I traveled silently, staring at everyone doing nothing. This whole building was like a warehouse of laziness; the only object that came out of here was carbon dioxide.

As the tall escalator finally reached the top of itself, I stepped off calmly and walked down Hallway 730 B; room 2 is where I work.

The hallway had gray carpeting; the entire wall to the right was completely glass, which glimmered in the bright sunshine.

Chapter 3

December 17, 2050

"Welcome aboard!" Richard said in a stern yet somewhat jubilant voice. "What do you have for me today?"

I said nothing but let out a slight sigh, an angry one. I walked up to the curved silver table inside the great white room and laid down my brown briefcase, ready to present my latest "creation" to Mr. Clark.

"Here you are, good sir," I said drearily. I was about to present an idea that would once again benefit the automatically controlled life of 2050. I held out my decorative, medium-sized poster. "This insurance plot will certainly be the lowest of any insurance company for autonomous cars. It covers all electrical issues and prevents hacks up to 15 percent or more."

"Wonderful!" Mr. Clark said merrily. He could barely get out of his brown leather chair with the size he had become. "This will certainly bring profit to the company."

I folded it up, put it back in my briefcase, and sat down in my clear plastic chair.

"I have a big assignment for you," Richard said, sitting down once again. "I need a big invention from you by next week. The holiday is in a week, and I need a big gift from you!"

"You don't even appreciate my work," I muttered.

"What was that?" Mr. Clark asked.

"Oh, nothing," I replied. "I see … I will have an idea by tomorrow for you."

"Excellent!" he replied happily. "Make it snappy! I mean it—by tomorrow."

I locked my brown briefcase with a click, stood up, and trudged out of the room like an elephant in a zoo.

I then headed to my office for the rest of my workday—mine already being short—where I usually would have planned another device for Mr. Clark. Instead, I thought of how to do the opposite. I went down the shining escalator to my office stall; I thought about nothing at that moment. The office area was something like thirty-five years old and one other thing that had not yet relegated itself to today's standards. Inside, the area was curved and very sleek, with laptops and tablets everywhere, since paper was gone forever.

I sat down in my chair, trying to think of a way to stop the progression of time. For a few moments, I had no idea how this was going to manifest; I had tried numerous other things previously. Thinking was painful today, with heat heavy on my skin; the black suit I wore didn't help the case. As long as I sat, no solution came to mind, not even a hint. I was too busy thinking of the consequences of all this progression rather than how to fix it.

Sun shone on me through the clear windows, lurking like a spy. But when I glanced at it, I realized something was up; something was actually wrong. The sun actually felt hotter, brighter. I became worried and knew something had to be done. I was the only one who could do so.

Then, worrying about time's progression, it came to me—a big idea that could virtually destroy technology. The invention would be a time machine. In capital letters—*A TIME MACHINE*.

I realized that a time machine would kill two birds with one stone. I could use it as my solution to the 2050 crisis, as well as the big invention for Mr. Clark's holiday. It had nothing to do with insurance, but in his free time, he was a technology geek. It was perfect. But how would I engineer a such a complicated marvel? Answer: with today's technology.

"All right, everyone, lunch break in the main office!" the voice on the loud speaker shouted. Everyone currently working at their office stations pressed a button. The mechanical system that would take the chairs to the main hall was somewhat like a slot-car system; it led the chairs on the hinge, moving them along the ground. It was quite clever, actually, but it took away the only type of exercise we had: walking.

"You don't believe in advanced technology like we do," a man next to me said sternly. "You are assigned to walk to your station."

"I would prefer to do so," I said calmly. I hopped out of my chair, seized my lunch bag, and walked to the main hall.

Inside the hall, the area was big, open, and spacious, with a huge clear table and sleek, tan-leather seats with glass supports, hinged to the glossy white tiles.

Everyone took their seats, lounging in them, as they set their gourmet lunch trays on the glass table. I was stuck with a paper bag. *I honestly don't give a damn. Sorry,* I thought.

I took my seat at the end of the table, just so people could avoid interacting with me. That's how varied our opinions were, but this time, I had something with which they would agree.

Everyone sitting at the glass table began to discuss their inventions and how they'd go about creating them. Oddly enough, I dived in and listened; no time machine was mentioned.

Right afterward, I began to rethink the whole idea of a time machine, two words that usually do not go together well. Could I make it sound plausible, or was it just another scheme pulled from a science fiction movie?

"Hey, everyone!" I said, somewhat worried.

Only one person noticed my nervous statement, saying, "Eh, it's him again." He attempted to dumb me down. "He's just ready to complain about how great the world is."

"Actually, I have been thinking and have decided to … well, simply agree with all of you," I said, as his jaw dropped in shock. "That's why I have a new invention to prove myself changed and for the sake of the world."

"Really?" He looked at me like I was crazy. "How did you change your opinion suddenly?"

"I figured I'm a person who is open to new things," I proclaimed, laughing inside. "So again, I got an idea."

"What is this invention?"

"A time machine," I replied, gaining both confidence and anger steadily.

No one said anything for a few moments. Then, someone said enthusiastically, "Holy crap, that is excellent. That's the one exaggerated invention that was missing."

"I love this!" a woman shouted from the other end of the table. "So many possibilities could happen with this marvelous invention—well, if it turns out."

Everyone at the glass table then rejoiced happily about my idea. It was in the bag, as everyone who had frowned at me moments ago now directed smiling faces at me. It felt unusual for me, since the last smiles I'd received were from my parents, right before they died in the incident two weeks earlier.

Right afterward, work time was finished; it was time for everyone to relax again but back at home. I was going to do the complete opposite by planning my time machine to save the world from collapsing. I was under a canopy of happiness now and was about to change it as well.

As everyone still talked about my invention, I walked back to my office, picked up everything I needed, and walked out of the white office building. I was confident, but I had to make Richard feel that confidence as well.

I started to rethink the whole thing again—the idea of a time machine. I had to make it first. I had to make it right.

CHAPTER 4

December 18, 2050

The journal entry I created today was actually my plan B. How was I to manage so much, I wondered. In the end, I probably would just focus on the time machine.

The biggest issue I had with the time machine project was that it was a *time machine*. I could create just about anything, but to travel back in time … was it physically possible?

That was on my mind during the entire drive back to my apartment. I had to ask Krystal.

The autonomous car took me to the parking lot behind my apartment, where the smell of asphalt still was present. The car then parked itself in the lot, right behind the same stairway I used every day.

Then, as usual, Krystal came in, as her car parked itself in the lot as well. She hopped out happily and came running to me.

"Hello," she said, leaning on the hood of my car. "How was work today?"

"Like always," I replied with a sigh. "But today had one difference for me. I plan to kill two birds with one stone. I'm going to solve a problem, do some population control, and impress Mr. Clark with an invention I have thought of."

"Really?" Krystal said. "What could impress that dimwitted man?"

"A time machine," I said with confidence.

Her eyes widened. She seemed to not know what to think of it. "Oh, wow," she said, with a hint of sarcasm. "I don't think time travel is physically possible. Do you have a solution for this?"

"Yes, I guess," I said softly. "If we could somehow invent a generator that could separate our molecules, transport them to a different time, and then assemble them back together once we have reached our destination, that would be the only possible way to time travel. The variables would correspond to quantum physics—time stops at the speed of light, to correspond to the actual time in the area."

"That's unusually logical," Krystal said with a shrug. "Is it painful?"

"Probably," I admitted. "Many molecules in our bodies would be ripped apart for time travel."

Krystal nodded. "I see. Let's start building and researching tomorrow."

"Plus the day after; I don't work," I said happily, "so we can work on it."

"Excellent! See you then!"

"Okay," I replied, but I was somewhat distressed at what I just had said to her. I still was uncertain about how a time machine would work—or would it fail? Would it send me to a time without electricity to generate? It would be tough to get this right, but I had to tell Mr. Clark first, before any of that could begin.

I walked up the stairs and entered my apartment, which usually seemed dreary and boring. But I had high hopes today with the time machine plan and all of that. It was useful; it would save the world.

It was time to get cracking. I swooped up the stacks of paper by my printer and ran frantically—yet happily—to my desk. It was time to draw a prototype—multiples, actually—to eventually present to Mr. Clark.

Things were looking more shaky for this contraption; it would have to be strong and resilient in all weather conditions, but it also needed the ability to be pulled apart during the molecule separation of time travel.

Things then got even more sketchy. Oddly enough, unlike all of the boxlike concepts back in the day, this had to be as aerodynamic as possible so that it could travel quickly into a different time. Physics still existed in the physical movement of beings.

One side of the time machine would be curved; the others would be rounded off but still square. The entire time machine had to fit two people, extra components (in case a problem occurred), and all of the electronic parts, such as the date setting, the propulsion into time, and more. Even more, I had to develop a material that could be disassembled during time travel and then be brought automatically back together when we reached our destination.

I realized that metal, such as aluminum, could be ripped apart in seconds under strong heat—heat generated by the speed of light. That would consume the beings inside the machine as well. Because molecules inside the human body have the ability to disassemble, I needed to plant DNA in that material.

Now, I realize that time is just a number. It is not physical. Quantum physics is physical—basic cause and effect. We chose how long a year was. We chose how long a month was, a day was. Time was invented to keep track of the growing season for the Mesopotamians. With that in mind, I would have to reverse the pure quantum physics. I needed to do a little more research on the apparatus.

10:30 p.m.

You can easily reverse something by doing the previous action again. Something that was in the past. Again, time is a number. You can't make time happen again. You could copy it or act it out, but it wouldn't be precisely the same.

It seemed that if I were to go faster than the speed of light, which could be covered by today's extravagant electric motors, then I could go back in time. If I could, there would be no time to travel via a linear path—this allowed for another direction to go back in time.

The future would be much simpler than that because I would be fast-forwarding the same linear path we are all on, which would carry out a previous action in the past. It would not cause me to multiply because although we may be on the linear path, there is no trace of our past selves. The shadows do not stay.

Another of my theories was that if I did something in the past, but before that, someone wanted to see me in the past—but before the time travel *I* did—that first action would have been already carried out the in the second and third.

An example: Let's say I wanted to meet some Romans and traveled to the year AD 360 from the present. But before I did that—let's say a day earlier—someone time-traveled to see me before the year 360. They would have known I already had done that, since it occurred both times—inside the head of the guy from the present and me, from the year 360.

I wrote this all down, just in case someone wanted to make it an official theory.

I had the time travel figured; now I just had to design a sleek, aerodynamic time-travel capsule.

I designed several concepts, good and bad. Some even had cupholders. I took my best one, scanned it, and created a convincing PowerPoint presentation. I was ready for Mr. Clark tomorrow, and I certainly had a promising machine ready for him. I dimmed the apartment lights and headed off to bed for a good night's rest.

December 19, 2050

The next morning was once again unusual for me—I was actually happy to head off to my bumbling job. But I had to get there.

I dressed in my normal work clothes and headed down the stairs and into my autonomous car, starting a more fast-paced drive to the sleek office building.

As I walked in, things were quite the same—everyone was doing absolutely nothing or just iPhone work. Unlike the rest, I was on a run to save the population.

I walked in with confidence—much more than usual—to Mr. Clark's emporium of an office and met him there; he stood silently like today's average entrepreneur.

"You look … happy today," Mr. Clark said, glancing at me. "What do you have on your mind?"

"Oh, just an idea I whipped up for you last night," I said happily, laying out my poster.

"Sounds promising," Mr. Clark said. "What might it be?"

It seemed like I had this in the bag. But even though Mr. Clark was cynical, he still was smarter than the average boss. All I could do was hope.

"The idea is this," I said, flipping over my poster on clear table. "A time machine."

I cringed at what I expected he would say, but—like the inconspicuous coworkers—he at first did not say a word. Then he gulped, looking utterly surprised. "Wow, I absolutely adore this idea! This will come in handy when I forget to get my coffee all the way downstairs!"

Even though I would have preferred to both punch him and laugh at what he'd just said, I contained myself, knowing that I was in the clear and almost was ready to verify my plan. I rejoiced as he studied the numerous concepts.

"You have made my holiday," Richard said happily as I walked out the door. "Thanks!"

After walking out, I realized something—that was the first time he had ever thanked me. My fate appeared to be dramatically changing.

I happily walked out of the office and through the scroll doors, but I heard something unusual. I ignored it, thinking it was probably someone getting out of a chair. I walked back to my autonomous car, and it took me home.

Chapter 5

December 19, 9:00 a.m.

After developing my plans for the time machine, I was ready to start building it. It would be hard, but my plans were convincing for everyone who was under my wings. Mr. Clark believed in the premise; so did my numerous colleagues. Almost every formidable problem was solved for everyone who supported the distressed nature of 2050. Now that everyone who could make my plan vulnerable was out of the way, I could build it, take my plans, and solve the crime of the year. But I had other plans as well.

For now, two more power plants had dropped, and the temperature was hotter than the day before, at 66 degrees. This was very warm for December 19. Something was destroying the ozone layer, bit by bit, but much faster than thirty years ago. It was now time for my plan to get rolling.

***

A coworker known as Jim had read something he'd found on the floor. He'd decided it was of extreme importance when he saw Patrick Shields's name slapped all over it.

"Hmm," he said as he finished reading. "This appears to be Patrick Shields's diary entry." Jim ran from the spot where he'd found the diary entry, hugging it like a bear. He ran through the hallway as fast as he could until he reached Mr. Clark's office, which was one story below and down a deep, dark hallway. Jim let himself into the office, opening the wide, clear door, and entered the room.

"Excuse me," Jim said to Mr. Clark and the professionals who surrounded him. "I have found evidence in an important case."

"Which case?" Mr. Clark asked. "There hasn't been any trouble in the silver office for a while."

"Let's talk for a minute," Jim said, as Clark's secretary, Jen, watched silently in the background. "I believe Shields is up to total crap—again."

"Really?" Richard said. "Explain." He rubbed his chin in grief but with a slight smile.

"When Patrick said 'time machine,'" Jim said, "he didn't mean it in a good, helpful way." Would Mr. Clark burst into a fiery ball of rage, or would he just collapse all together?

As it turned out, neither happened.

"I can see that completely," Mr. Clark said, slightly more subtle than previously and shockingly calmer. "That's not the first time he has faked an agreement. What does he really want to do?"

"He wants the population to decrease down to just seven billion. He thinks the world will collapse if it becomes any more polluted by humans and the production of our needs and wants."

"Right," Mr. Clark replied, startled yet still calm. "I have always had my suspicions about him. He's changed his personality to an entirely new one."

"He likely doesn't know that he dropped his journal entry,"

Jim said, giving an evil look. "We now can track him down and destroy his plan."

Richard listened and then took the paper in his hands. "It sounds convincing at first," Mr. Clark said as he read each word, "but to kill … virtually everyone? God above, the man is horrifying.

"According to his fan blog, no one reads." Jim pulled out an eight-inch tablet.

"Good for him," Mr. Clark said sarcastically. "He won't last long. I might force him into jail or even the death penalty if he keeps up this crap." He turned to his secretary. "Jen, go make arrangements for the tools to stop him." Clark said and then ordered everyone out of the sleek room. "Jim and I will handle the bits in between."

"I will make plans later, but this is just excellent!" Jim shouted. "We could become the saviors of 2050."

"Heroes of a convoluted plan that has not even been put into motion yet," Mr. Clark said, looking in the other direction.

Jim walked out the sleek, curved glass door, his face stern and his hands tight, leaving Mr. Clark by himself.

***

Shield's apartment complex, Park Lafayette Towers, Milwaukee
After I assessed my plan, I would become the savior of 2050. Although I was in the clear, I still couldn't build the time machine entirely by myself. That was why I needed Krystal.

She still wasn't home but probably was on her way. She knew that I needed extravagant amounts of help, and in less than two days, the time machine needed to be complete, ready for Mr. Clark.

I patiently watched out the window, staring toward downtown

from my apartment complex. As the moon shone on the tallest building, I couldn't but think, *Where did the world go wrong?*

No matter, though. I had justified my plan enough to everyone; it was time to build my solution to even greater heights.

While I was waiting—more desperately than ever—for Krystal, I checked my blog on my laptop as I sat under dim light in the kitchen. According to one fan of mine who lived on Mars, my idea and I were in the *Daily Herald* newspaper. This was a huge step for me, but I wondered if it was a good one.

It was said that my time machine could go into production, based on the needs of Mr. Clark, of course. Even though this hype was good for me, and the whole burden fell to me, I was starting to rethink that as well. What would the world do with such a device? They could destroy the world with a click of a button, like the virus. Along with that, absolutely no one would read the 250-page manual included. It was looking like I'd have to destroy my own invention after I solved the project.

Krystal eventually showed up to my apartment, placing her autonomous car in the same designated spot as usual. She came out as fast as she could; I watched from the wood-framed window above.

I rushed down the stairs, reaching her as quickly as possible. I opened the door, and she was standing there, still looking happy.

"Hello!" she said cheerily. "How were things with the boss?"

"Oh, actually pretty good. For now, he is out of the picture. We are clear to finally make the time machine."

"Excellent," Krystal said confidently. She came through the door, and I shut it tight. "Now, first thing on the agenda …" She pulled out a laptop and pushed the "notes" icon. "Components?"

"We will develop each and every component through my assortment of 3-D printers," I replied, pointing to them on the desk. "It will be an assortment that can rip up in great heat."

"Okay," Krystal replied, seeming unsure. "We should get started, then."

I went to my desk, grabbed some piles of paper, and inserted them into one of the 3-D printers. The laptop connected to the printer had a digital diagram of the first component, around fifteen feet in cubic volume. The printer would print out that exact shape.

As it was happening, Krystal and I decided to draw up the next components on our laptops.

"Should one or both sides be aerodynamically swooped?" Krystal asked.

"Just one," I said confidently. "You see, it needs to flow through just one direction, since we would be traveling faster than the speed of light through time into time.

"This whole idea sounds quite complicated," Krystal said.

"It always has been." I turned my head, noticing that the first component, the control box, was complete, even though it was just a frame. "First component of my fifty-two proclaimed is finished," I said to Krystal, who seemed to be nervous. "Next is to install the gears, wires, and dual clutch into the area frame."

Krystal tried keep her cool as she took a deep breath. "All right," Krystal said. "This better work."

I walked back to my laptop and started to develop the first parts and dual clutch for the time machine.

Chapter 6

December 19, 2050, noon

After completing numerous drawings of every last component of the time machine, it was time to design the rest of them in the five 3-D printers. I'd been waiting for a moment like this.

"Next part to process through each 3-D printer is the entrance to the interior capsule," I said, sorting out the numerous drawings that were ready to be inserted. "This will be done in around fifteen minutes."

Krystal was extremely confused by my drawings, wondering which part went where. "What about the frame first?" Krystal asked, walking around the entire white room. "The frame is supposed to joint all of the body work together."

"The frame slips inside each body panel," I explained, still hard at work. "It supports the roof, like an autonomous car or a house."

Krystal then lost it right in front of me. She abruptly threw the papers on the ground, as well as the laptop. "Man, this is just dreadful, absolutely dreadful," she sputtered. "I am leaving this joint."

I gasped. "What's wrong?" I asked, confused but also a little pissed. She'd had slight little outbursts like this previously.

"I know this important to you, but I just can't handle this," she replied, on the verge of tears. "This is far above my level."

I thought for a moment and then said, "Is it that you can't do this, or do you not want to?" She seemed to be about to leave. "I assume you don't want to do it."

"I … don't want to," she said, setting down her briefcase. "Completely out of my comfort zone." She left the apartment, shutting the door tightly.

I needed her help, so I had to get her back. I burst out the door and saw her running back to her apartment complex, down two from mine.

"You just go and leave me empty-handed?" I shouted, as she stopped to look back at me. "Even though I am most certainly independent, I can't take a chance with this experiment to save humanity."

"I can't do it," she said firmly, calming down. "If I mess up this for you, you will then have no chance at this project."

"But I probably can't do it at all if you don't help," I said. "You know how dearly important this is to me."

"I do know that," she said, edging out of my sight. "That's why I'm trying to leave."

I stood there, feeling disgusted, in the bright, increasingly hot sun. "All right, fine," I said, trying not be negative to my best and only friend. "I will once again proceed alone."

I watched her run to her apartment, probably disappointed by how angry I was and because she didn't possess the means to help me configure the time machine. But that was on me. I was strictly independent and would get this done sooner if I worked alone. I walked up the stairs to my loft area, seeing that the time machine was surprisingly halfway complete, even with the fracas.

Krystal was no matter; I knew I could get this done.

I picked up a laptop and found that the left-side exterior shell was ready to be constructed once again.

"Ah, yes," I said to myself, pressing the upload button to send the computerized drawing it the 3-D printers.

As that printed out, I designed the next part of the time machine—the left side, of course.

Things were not that complicated from then on. We only needed a few panels on the body. In the fourth one, the dual-clutch transmission was still being prepped and designed; it would be imported into the front area, somewhat like a car.

Dual clutch was finished. The 3-D printer said it was done and oddly spewed out smoke when I opened up the sides. I didn't have to lift it out; automated robotic hands imported from a Honda robot were planted on either side and lifted out the dual clutch.

I kept some technological components secreted in my apartment. The components were very sharp and extremely hot, so when in such a rush of a process like this, robot arms could be useful.

The time machine was at the end stage of construction, surprisingly. All that was needed was to be fit and finished, made tight so no light would be let in during time travel.

The component turned out to be quite large and quaint, with an aerodynamic shape and tons of buttons and navigation screens at the control panel. I thigh-tried the bolts, adjusted the buttons on the front inside, and checked every single part as if I was working in the automobile industry. But I couldn't just let it fly apart during time travel, which is exactly twenty-five miles an hour faster than the speed of light, according to Krystal. Don't know where she got the number. Nobody knew yet.

Even though the time machine and the Backwards Era plan was extremely arduous, I still prevailed and somehow finished the time machine.

And what a beauty it was—such prodigious and avant-garde work.

At least it was beautiful through function, because from a

distance, it looked like nothing more than an aerodynamic cheese grater—though seriously, its shape was to correspond to the speed in excess of light.

As I put a tarp over it, letting it cool down, as it had come out entirely from a 3-D printer. It was now time for me to rest my joints and update my blog. I went on to do so, leaving the 3-D printer out in the open.

What to do next? There was nothing else but to call Krystal and alert her that the time machine project was finished, and the Backwards Era project was a go. I grabbed my cell phone, cheap in character, and dialed her number as quickly as I could.

She answered.

"Hello?" I said, nervous that she would be upset.

"Hi!" she said happily.

Oh, thank God, I thought. "I'm glad you're better. I just wanted to alert you that the time machine is complete and is now ready to travel." I cringed at what her response would be.

"Excellent! I knew you could accomplish it in the end." She had apparently forgotten about the incident earlier that day, which was good for me. "Can I come over and check it out?" she asked, almost begging.

"Tomorrow you can," I said, as calmly as I could. "I promise."

"Okay, great," she said, seeming impressed that I'd actually finished it. "See you then."

"All right," I replied. "Until then."

I hung up the phone and began to work on my blog. The time machine stood proudly in the background, behind the laptop.

Chapter 7

More news—temperatures have increased by an average of half a degree over the past two weeks. That's scary. It might not seem like much, but at the rate it's going, it will be deadly in three years. Sorry for all of the supporters of 2050 out there, but I have a time machine, and I am not afraid to use it. After years of prejudice and controversy, I'm ready to time travel to 2001, the year I've selected. Even though I will probably end up in the crime section of the news, I know that this will prevail and will kill all things mistakenly here on this earth for a better place by the year 2051, which is coming in about ten days. Waiting patiently for the right moment to travel is hard, but time traveling is hard. I have to be precise, and I have to be able to withstand great amounts of pain. Whatever the case may be, besides actually doing it, nothing should get in the way of my time traveling. I thank God for that.

Richard, Jim, and Jen continued to plot to pull off a heist in the middle of the night and take Patrick's time machine to the giant office building. Then they'd pull Patrick from his apartment and send him to court.

"We are under the wing of almost all of the public," Mr. Clark said. "I think we can steal the time machine from him and use it to benefit us instead."

"Agreed," Jen said. "Everyone out there should agree with us; no one can stand Shields."

"I think we should set out," Jim said, his voice stern. "It's now nine o'clock at night; he worked freaking hard on it!"

All three of them laughed.

"Anyhow," Mr. Clark said, "let's go get that time machine."

All three of them slammed closed their briefcases, packed up their other items, and headed out of the basement meeting point and into the hallway.

"I think we should grasp our 'tools,'" Jen said, heading down the hallway. "Can't just barge in like a bunch of idiots."

"We will," Mr. Clark replied, walking by her side." But it's quite alright; he thinks all of society are idiots now."

All three walked quickly down the hallway in silence.

"We should have grappling hooks," Jen said, rushing into the secret department, unbeknownst to anyone else.

"Are you kidding me?" Mr. Clark responded with a sigh. "We don't have time to spare. Just take whatever you can!"

Jen and Jim did so, rushing in and out of the organized storage areas. Soon they exited the area and came back into the hallway, where the bright LED streetlights of downtown shined above the four-hundred-foot–high buildings.

Without a word, all three of them left the emporium-like office building through the revolving doors, went down the silver escalators, and found Mr. Clark's autonomous car.

"Here we are," Mr. Clark said, unlocking the car with his iPhone 36. "Toss the gadgets into the trunk. We have to get that time machine and put it into production!"

Jen and Jim stuck their heads under the sleek roofline of Mr. Clark's car and got into the rear seats as Mr. Clark climbed into the front.

"Push the button," Mr. Clark said to himself. "Here we go."

The autonomous car drove itself out of the parking area and onto the concrete roadway, where the car kept to the speed limit, a slightly sluggish thirty miles per hour.

"I am not very knowledgeable of autonomous cars," Jen said, "but can you pick up the pace slightly? Do you know what kind of situation we are in?"

"Of course I do," Mr. Clark replied. "The vehicle is programmed to travel only at the speed limit, not to go above or below."

"I guess Shields was aggravatingly correct about the autonomous cars," Jim said, crossing his arms and relaxing in the backseat.

"Too bad he won't be around long enough to see it advance," Mr. Clark replied.

The computer atop the dashboard led the car to Patrick's apartment complex, where Patrick was fast asleep. The car made only a subtle sound; the contact of the tire on the pavement was the only noise to be heard, thus making echoes throughout the alley, a ringing in the ears.

"We should arrive right around now," Mr. Clark said, unbuckling his seatbelt. "Thank God."

The car crept silently behind the apartment complex and sat in the puddles left from the night's rain as the computer figured out where the car was and automatically shut it off.

"Excellent," Richard said confidently. "Let's go grab the time machine."

The three got out of the car as quickly and as quietly as they could. The trunk automatically opened, revealing their tools. Jen took the tools, slammed the trunk shut, and caught up to the two men, who already had reached the back of the apartment complex.

"Jen, you have that needle of melatonin, right?" Mr. Clark asked.

"Why would we need that in a situation like this?" Jen asked, pulling the needle from her pocket.

"Put it in Shields," Mr. Clark whispered. "Can't let him know that we're taking his 'priceless' invention."

"Jen, use the grappling hook to climb up the complex and put Shields to sleep," Jim said.

She launched the indestructible grappling hook toward the granite window sill, and it gradually carried her up as her black coat shined in the bright moonlight.

"You and I get the good stuff," Mr. Clark said, smiling. They then ran silently up the rusting stairs and then would hack into the security system of the complex. What they didn't know was that it would unlock Krystal's back entrance as well.

"Type random numbers until the computer says error, then smash it, unlocking the door," Jim explained to Mr. Clark.

"Got it," Mr. Clark replied, doing exactly that. After a few moments, the procedure had worked, almost cartoonishly.

"We're in." He opened the door.

They then rushed in, not being very cautious about the numerous traps and cameras surrounding Patrick's entire apartment.

***

I had been sleeping on the second floor of my apartment, dreaming of how successful my time machine would be and unaware of anything else, but for some reason, I sensed a shadow on top of me. Then I knew *someone* was there. I could feel the presence of a being in my gut. And I could only assume it was Mr. Clark and his gang. There was only one thing to do now—put the gobsmack on them.

As Jen threw the needle down by my hip, I peered at what was happening, making her assume that I was still sleeping. But no, once I'm awake, I stay awake. So I sprang out of bed and swatted the needle from Jen's hands, making it hit the wall, shattering it.

"Holy crap!" Jen shouted, backing up as I picked up the sharp needle from the floor, with my clothes, of course, covered in melatonin fluid.

"There is fluid still inside this needle," I said calmly, pointing it at her. "Would you like to try?"

As I brought the needle closer to her, she sprang out the window, knowing she couldn't do much to fight back. She'd already broken the window when she came in.

They want my time machine, I thought. *They are not going to keep it for long. How did they get here? Good Lord, there are intuitive, aren't they?*

But I had no time to think that out. I wrote on a piece of paper, "They have come for it." Attaching the note to the needle, I threw it out my shattered window and through Krystal's, which was parallel to mine.

When the needle came through her window, Krystal became alert, and was ready to rescue my time machine.

She and I ran through our apartments, as the three had the time machine and were putting it inside Mr. Clark's autonomous hatchback.

Right when Krystal and I stepped outside, we saw the entire contraption inside the car, which Mr. Clark was starting. It automatically drove away from the complex.

"And there they go!" I shouted, looking at the car drive down the eight-lane highway.

"Well, you really have no way to catch them," Krystal said, running up to me. "All autonomous cars are programmed to the same speed limit and the quickest route, so you really don't have a chance."

"Yes, I do," I replied confidently.

She frowned. "What device do you have this time?"

"A have my dad's car. He always has innovative technology through his business corporation. He and I never really got along."

"Hmm ... sad."

"Anyhow, his car is a two-hundred-mile-per-hour beast ... that you actually drive," I explained to Krystal. She seemed delighted to hear that.

"You don't have a garage attached to your complex," Krystal said. "Where the heck would the car be?"

I pressed a button on the other security system, opening up a secret garage. The garage door was covered in white vinyl, just like the surrounding walls, just enough so it wasn't noticeable. It opened up, revealing my dad's thirty-five-year-old car, which he and I had restored.

"Certainly looks fast," Krystal said. "How did you manage to build an entire garage? Such graceful lines, simple lights—simple yet aerodynamic. It looked great. Not a big egg on stilts. Lovely."

"When you are stuck in an apartment complex for more than twenty years, you have a lot of time on your hands. Now that's settled," I said, walking up to the sports sedan, "I need my time machine back."

CHAPTER 8

"We need a plan for all of this," Krystal said. "What should we do? Just drive fast?"

"Not quite what I would have imagined," I replied, heading back into my apartment, with Krystal following. "We need to be secretive."

I unlocked the door, which was still broken and open by the breached security system. Krystal and I then headed inside as I closed the garage door.

"Here is our plan," I said, already generating ideas.

"Which will be ..." she began, sitting on my couch.

"Nothing," I replied, sitting next to her.

She then became slightly perplexed. "So after all this work with the time machine and stuff—"

"No, not exactly," I interrupted. "We just sit back and relax, until they get a false sense of confidence that we are not coming to get the time machine."

"I see," Krystal said. "How long must we wait?"

"At least an hour. Again, we need to keep them convinced."

Krystal and I spent the next hour watching some television.

"I'll check the news," I said, grabbing the remote, "to see if the meteorologist has noticed the rise in temperature lately."

The TV turned on; it was already programmed to the exact news channel.

"It says here that three businesspeople are on a journey to save our world from going backwards," Krystal said. "One man wants the world to stop innovating, which is sickening."

"And that is exactly why I hate today's world," I said. "The news, which is supposed to be neutral somewhat, doesn't even realize the situation we are in."

"No one can comprehend what you have in mind," Krystal replied.

"We can spend time by planning how to reduce population as well," I said.

"That just seems like whole bunch of hate crimes," Krystal replied, concerned.

"What would be a way to kill off a bunch of people more commonly than any cancer?" I asked.

"All right, done and done," Krystal replied, smiling. "We should develop a medicine then."

"Developing one and selling it on the market would take too much valuable time."

"What then?"

"We should insert it into an already over-the-counter medication," I said.

"And just how is that plausible?"

"I have no idea at this moment." I then decided to think of a solution for the temperature issue. "I have something, but it will be up to you only."

"Oh, really?" she asked, seeming more and more perplexed.

"You see, I'll secretly withdraw my opposing invention of a time machine, and you state on my blog that the fans need to do that; to evolve our plan."

"How do you write?" Krystal asked.

"I don't think we have any time to get into the specifics." I got up, opening up the blog on a laptop. "Here you are," I said, setting it on her lap.

"Nice blog," Krystal said, exploring my blog. "Love what you've done with blue background—"

"Oh, shut up," I said, laughing. She smiled. "Now, let's write out this plan." I ran out of the cramped living room, leaving Krystal to herself, just with my blog. "You got this, correct?" I asked as I rushed out the door.

"I'm definitely be more concerned about you, actually," Krystal replied. "You're on the verge of death and everything."

"Very funny," I said, "but now I have no time to waste; just do your thing on my blog."

"All right," Krystal replied calmly. "Go get that invention of an era!"

I said not a word but stepped out door immediately, lurching silently into the cleverly hidden garage, where the sports sedan sat under dim lighting. I got in, not knowing if someone in the distance was watching my every step. I pressed the ignition and set off, feeling good to actually drive, having a sense of control once more. *It may be the last car I'll drive,* I thought. I crept the car through the dark alley, with the LED lights on the front giving it a posed glare. I then drove it off the road, as the V8 engine roared off the line. It felt awesome to be back in a human-powered car once again, instead of the delirious whirr of an electric motor. It was cool for a minute; then it was just "bleh."

My best guess about Jen, Mr. Clark, and Jim was that those three were plotting revenge on me at his grand hall of an office. So I would rush there, which was a thirty-minute drive by autonomous car. *I'll bet I can snip at least two-thirds off of that by driving hard.*

And I did so, rushing through every single stop light, whether green or red. I did not care if cameras were lurking over my shoulder. This was obviously important.

As it turned out, with the difference in the time between piloted machine and man-driven machine, I was right behind Mr. Clark and his bland autonomous car. They were going at a sluggish yet now matching thirty miles per hour. I knew they could spot the LED strips at the front of my car, so before they could spot anything peculiar, I swerved onto a side street to the left.

"Now, I'll sneak up to them by speeding up and getting the cops to come, trapping Mr. Clark inside the cops and me," I plotted to myself, pointing fingers in the air. "Let's do this."

I put the shift paddles in manual mode and took off as the fastest car in 2050. I turned left, turned right, and was then ahead of Mr. Clark and his gang. I expected the cops to approach behind Richard any moment, but before they did, I'd have the chance to reclaim the time machine.

I moved over to the right on the outer lane, which was empty at 10:00 p.m.

***

"Those are interesting taillights on that autonomous car," Jim noticed, pointing ahead. "And how is he moving when there is no traffic?"

"As we all know, it can be only one hell of a threat," Mr. Clark said seriously. "Shields."

***

I sensed they were picking up signals that I was near and on full blast. I decided to slow down, bringing the car right next to theirs. And with Richard on edge, I knew that I needed one thing that was not banned in 2050—guns. I pulled one out and, without looking at what was ahead, pointed it directly at the tire of the autonomous car. Out of the corner of my right eye, I noticed something much worse—Jim had a gun aimed smack-dab at my face.

"We've got you now!" Jim shouted out the window. "Don't move a muscle."

"I have one thing you don't have," I stated confidently. "Control."

I floored the car away from their sluggish alternative. Even though Jim continued to shoot at my rear window, I swerved and then sudden slowed from eighty to twenty-five miles an hour, which the other three didn't expect.

I now ended up behind the gang, and I saw sirens flashing out my rear window. The cops were about to show up and run me down. I had to think fast and shoot up the trunk in order to retrieve the machine.

Since he and I were only battling at thirty miles per hour, the police could catch us quickly—they, at the least, were not autonomous. Stupidly, Mr. Clark decided to drive the autonomous car away, even though he couldn't.

I pulled the gun from the back seat, rolled down the window, and opened fire.

And with an intoxicating boom, the trunk opened straight up. Their car swerved a little. I saw the time machine, stuffed inside the back seat and trunk. But how would I get it out of there?

I would certainly have to shoot the tires; an autonomous car only stops when it needs to. I drove up to the tire once more and shot it right way. Not only would I do that, but I'd blaze fire in every direction, knowing that the bumbling gang was right on their feet.

***

"He literally shot up the tire!" Jim shouted furiously. "What the hell are we going to do to keep the car rolling?"

"Let it roll away into the grass," Mr. Clark replied calmly. "I have a backup plan to stop him."

***

I had a plan as well. If all went well, the time machine would fall out of the rear of Mr. Clark's car to the ground, where I would take it back, once and for all.

The autonomous car started to abruptly screech its three remaining tires to the wheel arch and slide across the rest of the six lanes to the side and into a field that sat underneath bright LED lighting. The car came to a complete stop, surprisingly very steadily, and the abrupt halt caused the time machine to fall out of the back. This time, I was lucky. I stopped my car, left it running, ran out the door, and rushed to recover the machine.

But before I could, the three were already there.

"Hey, do me a favor, would ya?" Mr. Clark said sarcastically, as I recovered the now-priceless invention.

"What now, you joke of a boss?" I remarked confidently.

"Drop the gun," he said; he knew I still had it.

"What was that?"

"Drop the gun."

I pulled it out of my pocket and set it on the ground. What Mr. Clark didn't realize was that I was about to fake a ceasefire.

"You know what's coming to you, right?" Jen asked calmly but assertively, as Jim dug out some handcuffs.

"I would be more concerned about what is coming to *you*."

"What is that supposed to mean?" Mr. Clark asked, somewhat oblivious.

I had the gun on the ground, pointed directly at Mr. Clark's left leg—not his face, his leg.

I stepped on the gun, firing the pistol directly into Richard's leg. The bullet flew fast and, in an instant, was stuck in his leg.

"You idiot!" Mr. Clark shouted in pain.

I carefully put the time machine into the trunk of my car.

"Don't just stand there, you two! Shoot him down!"

The two followers did exactly so, pointing guns at me. Too bad I was already inside, driving away. A screech of tires and the roar of a petrol-powered engine, and I was off.

***

"He got away!" Jim shouted, frustrated. "And man, is that thing fast."

"Screw it," Mr. Clark replied as Jen repaired his injury. "The sure-footed police will catch him."

***

I ultimately passed them on the other side of the highway, leaving them in the dust.

There was now no time to waste; it was either now or never on traveling back to 2001, before someone caught me. I rushed back to my apartment as quickly as I could.

Chapter 9

Sirens whirred, lights flashed, engines roared. It seemed as if I was on a chase for everything, even getting started. If all failed, I would die, with cause of death due to bewildering circumstances of the state in 2050.

Oh glory, what a year.

After all I'd been through, I couldn't give up now. I kept sprinting back to the apartment complex, where Krystal had hopefully completed the assignment I'd given her.

As the cops somehow chased behind me, I pulled into the apartment complex, where the garage was closed. It swooped up with a technological creak, and I drove the sports sedan into the garage, parking it. I then rushed out under the dim lighting and back into my own apartment, daringly leaving the time machine out back.

"Krystal," I said, breathing heavily, "we absolutely have to get to 2001 right now!"

"I know," she stated calmly. "I have successfully updated the post to your blog."

"Thank you so much," I said, begging inside my head for her to shut up. "We have to run now; the cops and Mr. Clark are on my ass."

"What did you do to retrieve the time machine, exactly?"

"Shot Clark."

She gasped and then said, "Well, good for you." She got up from the couch and followed me as I sprinted out the door and back to the car as quickly as I could.

Unfortunately, the police had already surrounded us and the time machine—bats in hand, guns loaded, handcuffs out. It seemed like a smidge of a chance.

"The cops have us surrounded," Krystal exclaimed; then she whispered in my ear. "How are we going to get inside it?"

"You sneak in as I distract them somehow," I whispered. "I am their main target."

"Lady, you're fine," one of the police officers said as she sneaked past them and luckily hid underneath the control area of the machine. "Shields is the main target here."

"Surrender immediately," another said.

I put my hands up, but I then noticed something useful was behind the police officer—a grappling hook. *What dipstick brought that?*

"Tonight, you are going somewhere and staying there for a long time."

"Cuff him."

The police gradually walked up to me, about to cuff me. I was nervous, my shadow crouching on the vinyl wall. No one's eyes were on Krystal; the police thought she was just a simple bystander.

Ah, but no. She was the one support I had left.

She acted casually and kicked the grappling hook between the police officers' legs, handing it, bewilderingly, from those police to me.

Without a word, I grabbed that grappling hook and launched it up to the roof, bringing me up there in a flash. Using my fight or flight instincts, I launched myself downward and inside the group of cops, who were completely shocked. I climbed inside the open-air time machine, where Krystal was still standing, shocked as well.

"You all knew in the beginning that I was a force to be reckoned with," I said confidently. "I was never meant to be tested."

I shut the door, leaving Krystal and me locked inside. A warm feeling then shot inside me, along with a bit of cold shock as well.

"How will we know this worked?" Krystal asked, sweating.

"We don't know," I said. "I never try to make a dramatization. We can only hope."

Palms sweating, heart beating, nerves pumping with blood, I couldn't resist. I slammed the start button, set the date to 2001, and held on tight—Krystal watched, seemingly about to have a stroke. There was little motion inside as the cabin started to sway. The policemen backed up slowly, clearly in fear, as the time machine began to make a generator-whirr noise, a bit like an electric car on overdrive, and made huge amounts of light evaporate like water vapor, dissipating completely.

And that was all I saw.

> Molecules grinding
> in harmony
> in a surrounding
> light, yet splashed
> with darkness;
> then it happened
> breath was lost
> separation of DNA
> yet all still touching
> force not felt, but a presence
> still there
> departure
> words began being simplified

He rode through the fields and valleys
of time and space
nothingness was not
it was always there
technology died
inventions died
the stone age was in
the population was out
what would this do to the planet earth?
he wondered
and what would it do to him?
the planet earth wondered;
only he would know
but not in his present form;
would this fade,
or would it escalate
to a bigger object?

Hearing was regained
molecules were brought back together
force was starting to die down
vision was regained.

***

Patrick finally reopened his eyes in wonder and confusion. Krystal had awakened, surprised, yet disturbed. Where they were or what they would find was somewhat of a mystery right now … but they would certainly be in for a shock.

It was full of sand.

"Krystal," Patrick said, "are you all right?"

She, dizzy on the floor of the machine, did not appear responsive after the time travel. "Yes," she said, holding her head.

"Just slightly woozy after the time travel. Anyhow, where the heck are we after that rush of an experience?"

"The time machine always travels to the most populated area of that certain era. We ought to be in Shanghai, which could be a hot spot for some of the things I want to do to the planet."

"All right. Shall we see what we have to work with on the outside?"

"For sure."

Patrick shut off the time machine with the click of a switch and stepped closer to the door, which he unlocked with another press of a button.

Krystal looked over his shoulder in caution and excitement.

Patrick, who was nervous about what they would find on the outside, nudged the door open. He walked out of the machine and took a deep breath—he would either find loss or discovery.

But he sensed a feeling in his feet before he could think of anything.

"What the heck?" he said, looking down. Surprisingly, sand blew against his legs and past them into the time machine.

The only thing he could do now was look ahead.

"Oh … my … God …" Patrick said, staring ahead into the distance. "What the hell …"

"Seconded," Krystal said, much calmer than Patrick. "It appears to be a vast desert."

Sand hills and dunes went on for miles through the barren desert landscape, where sand particles were swept up and blown in the dry winds, generating a noise that howled like a wolf.

"Something is wrong … deeply wrong …" Patrick said. "I messed up somehow."

"You said it traveled to the most populated area of that area, right?" Krystal asked.

"If you don't insert a location, yes," Patrick replied in agony.

"I'll inspect the time machine." He walked back inside the machine.

"At least the time machine did its job," Krystal said with delight.

"You're right," Patrick replied. "It actually worked. I actually pulled it off." He looked to the right silently, watching the sand dance, with sweat dripping off his nose. "But wait …" He waved his hands and continued to walk back.

"Now wait …" Krystal said, walking inside the time machine. "Why couldn't we just travel into the future if we set the correct date?"

"We can't," Patrick explained, leaning on a certain lever. "Do you know how much energy this takes? One time-travel, forward or back, takes a whole charge. We aren't that advanced yet."

"I see."

"Dang it all," Patrick complained, slamming his hands down in disgust. "Guess where we are."

Krystal had no idea and did not want to answer.

"We're in 401 … BCE," Patrick said, pacing back and forth.

"You set it to *401 BCE*?" Krystal yelled, mad as hell. "That simple of a mistake …"

It was a classic mistake, written all over the books involving any time machine, but it was real this time.

"Well? After all of this, you ought to have a solution!" she shouted.

Patrick replied with a simple no.

"Really?"

"No solution."

"You are kidding."

"Nope. We are stuck here until we can find some source of power … of which there is none, wherever we are." He sat on the floor of the machine, as more sand blew inside, becoming more insistent.

The wind blew in subtle silence as Krystal tried to find a solution for the now-important issue. "After all you have been through ..." Krystal said.

"What?" Patrick asked.

"You can't just give up now. You could change the earth, if all goes as planned. You would be a legend that would get passed on from generation to generation."

"I just thought of something."

"There you go," Krystal said, relieved.

"If I can assemble an outlet and power source from parts of the time machine, yet still get it connected to it ..."

"Yes?"

"This could work."

"And there you go ... problem solved!"

Patrick walked back inside the time machine and attempted to find the power box. "Well, I wouldn't say that exactly," he replied, examining the power box. "I guess since all is fixed right about now, we should figure out where the heck we are."

"Indeed," Krystal replied, confident. "Let's head off then."

Patrick and Krystal headed out of the time machine and into the dense desert, which shone white in the sunlight.

"What about the time machine?" Krystal asked. "Wouldn't some citizen, looming around with a camel, mess with it?"

"Bring it along, please," Patrick replied. "It is quite lightweight, actually. I used aluminum and other materials."

"All right," she said, latching on to the time machine. "You're right, actually."

They trekked on, where a hole in the desert marked a special moment in time—where the time machine had landed, something that would be in the history books. In the surrounding brightness of the sand and sun lay an opposing layer of melancholy, which gave a bit of darkness to the open desert.

The desert really didn't seem to end, as when it met the

horizon, where nothing was then visible to the eye, it still kept on rolling in a swift yet subtle pattern. The experience was funny in that time kept passing, even as they went back.

To find their own path among these lands was extremely stressful for the two. Even more stressful was that where they were … what wandered through their heads with every passing moment … was if they would make it. All would be lost if anything seen would actually be seen. Anything told would actually be heard. A memory would be lost … a passing one for sure. But that created a memory to never forget.

The wind picked up. The sand blew harder. Patrick rose to the peak of a sand dune, which was the absolute cornerstone and provided the best view. As Krystal followed slowly after, struggling to pull the time machine, Patrick found something that was not a sand dune—quite remarkable for the situation they were in—sticking up near the golden-blue horizon.

"Hey … would you look at that …" Patrick pointed. "A ribbon of black into the distance."

"Oh yeah …" Krystal responded with glee. "Could this shed some light on where we are?"

"Well, let's figure it out …most populated city … 401 BC. I believe we are in the ancient city of Meroe."

Krystal could not believe for one second that he had figured it out. "Oh, really?"

"Yes, I do believe so," Patrick said. "If you want real proof, would you like to continue on and find some historical markings?"

"I know what those are there."

"Of course you do."

"But I wouldn't call anything around here historical or ancient … we are in that era of time; get used to it."

"I know that as well … come on."

"You're the one wasting time here." She gave him an encouraging smile.

"Let's get moving, then."

They continued through the slowly winding deserts of Sudan, which did not seem to get any easier to manage but seemed to become a somewhat darker shade of tan. This was for a simple reason; night had fallen in the city of Meroe. A gradual sunset from the west shimmered pink upon the low-lying ground of Egypt. It gradually changed to a blackout, similar to the one Patrick's parents had died in—complete blackness, no light, not even from the city or anything, just reflections of the shimmering moonlight along the ocean, which touched the still-visible horizon.

"Are you still capable of dragging that time machine?" Patrick asked, handing her an extremely bright LED flashlight that he'd brought along.

"Yes, I'm fine," Krystal said. "More important, try not to expose anything advanced or technological around these parts; anything at all like that will startle the crap out of these people."

"I would not complain much," Patrick said, stepping through sand. "You've a got a machine strapped to your back."

Krystal gave him an uncertain disgruntled look.

"I think I see something in the distance," Patrick continued. "Hand me the flashlight, please."

"You're kidding me, right?" Krystal said. "After all that—"

"It is clearly a nonworking object," Patrick said. "It is also clearly stable, an excellent place to build the outlet."

"All right," Krystal replied. "But you realize that you need a conductor."

"The River Nile," Patrick responded. "I sense that we are at low ground … maybe the Nile is right across that wall … shaped like something … familiar."

It turned out that the big burgundy structure was shaped like a passing thought and moment … the last scene of his parents' house, still standing but engulfed in flames. Not only was it a big burden but depression-inducing.

"And there is the Nile," Patrick said, now slightly heavy-hearted.

"All right," Krystal replied, sitting down beside the sparkling purple Nile. "I guess you should start working on the controls and variables now."

Patrick then began doing so, disassembling the main control area, where he would then assemble an outlet to connect to the River Nile, which he would use as an advanced control system to suck up waste and transverse that into energy.

"Get inside the machine," Patrick said, rushing to get it prepared.

"All right. How long might this take?"

"At least two more minutes," Patrick replied, working. "I am an engineering marvel when it comes to this stuff."

Krystal shook her head and waited patiently as the process happened.

"Here we go ..." Patrick confirmed, polishing it off. "Get ready to move over ... I need to rush in as soon as possible."

Patrick cautiously dipped the two wires into the glistening Nile and backed up as energy traveled. He then ran into the time machine as soon as possible, and the energy traveled into the power box and up into the machine, powering it with blue light and a whir of an engineering marvel. He didn't know what he would do next.

Too focused to know, they had to leave the generator, the power source, there-in 401 BCE.

Chapter 10

A blue light appeared out of nowhere. A wraith of vapor, surrounded by theoretical noise. A flash of an object behind a building—a closing entrance to something extraordinary. *What is that?* I wondered. *Is it magical? Is it an illusion? A hallucination? Has our God forsaken us?*

Nothing.

It was strange because it was that exact fact. Also strange was that it was not a killing or a massacre. What I had found was a striking piece of machinery, sitting on the levee of the River Nile, that seemed to be from a time that had not seemed possible.

Under royal-blue moonlight was some sort of cord or wire. Attached to its oddly shaped body were two ends, which looked like they could be brought together with a click. So many questions, starting with where did it come from? Who brought it here? No one has the subtle technology to bring even the slightest amount of *this* to life.

It was the confusion of another time.

I then realized that a bit of good could be made from this thing, surprisingly. Whatever it was, it could help our great city of Meroe be even more advanced, even more profound. This was absolutely groundbreaking for our city, if not the world.

But there was more to be discovered; in the city night, what was the big blue light? That was the much bigger question, as well as where this cord-thing had come from. Something was off with the whole experience. I believe someone delivered it here, if it was not the God above. Whoever it was, it was a mystery for now. This invention would be used for our advantage.

I then picked the foreign object from the river, knowing that this was one of many—at least wherever this came from. I absolutely had to tell the good citizens of Meroe about this extraordinary discovery. I would become the legend of this area. I could become the next warrior. We could all benefit from this.

Get more riches.

Live a better life.

Destroy future civilizations.

Thank you, God above, if you brought us this amazing piece of technology. We will conclude with whatever you desire—more baskets of sage, anything. We pray to you.

Merotic Alphabet to English Language
Written in 43 BCE

Dear successors reading this:

If you are holding this in your hand, we say that humans from a distant time have used, quite simply, much more advanced technology to travel to our time. Not having had a glimpse of them yet, we know a force is out there. Who knows what or who it could be? Do not be afraid to battle them. Do not be afraid to ask them

all the unanswered questions that planet earth
needs to know.

Expect them.
Wait for them.

—unknown

***

Shields's Journal
December 22

Sometimes I feel like I am the only the one who is taking a risk
within his life. This is right now. Sitting in Rome at the moment,
I have a few people under my wings. I have a partner at my side
and will make do with what we have.

In truth, the only reason I am writing this is because this will
be a true artifact later on in life, whether I am living or dead. If
all works as I want it to, this will be a feat that should be passed
along from generation to generation. If I fail, let me explain that
this was all one crazy man's idea in order to kill one society, drop
pollution levels, and make that one half of 2050's society live a
better, more livable life.

God, let me live another day to see the for-once bright future
that I might have caused. Send this to the last person alive on
earth, so he/she may know that I tried. Thank you.

Am I the only one who wants humans to live another day?

Apparently so.

Can't the world just listen once, open up, and give what is
better for some for a simple man like me?

I don't think so.

I have the cover of stealth in my current years, and they will
want me no matter what has been uncovered in the invisible (to

many) black hole of misery, otherwise known as life in 2050. I love planet earth. I just wish I could enjoy it, knowing what might happen in five years. What is that? Who really knows? A basic idea, yes. But certainty? No.

I end this message by praying to you up there.

***

The time machine once again had stopped stirring about. Landing next would be in the most populated area, of course, in the farthest time its battery could reach in the year 360. Patrick and Krystal had ended up in Rome, where they were at their most powerful point in terms of the empire.

"Well, then ..." Patrick said, shutting off the time machine with the on/off button. "Let's see what Rome is like."

"Now, before we do any of that," Krystal said, tugging on his shoulder, "there are a ton of problems that we could run into with our time here."

"I knew you would say something like that. I realize that we should try not to expose ourselves, no matter how much of a footprint we make."

Krystal continued to blatantly think of more precautions.

"Is that all?"

"I guess so," Krystal replied, nervous. "Let's go out and find what we are in for."

Patrick crept up to the steel door of the time machine to see what life-or-death situation would confront him. What appeared was nothing out of the ordinary, unless someone would call Ancient Rome ordinary.

"All right," Patrick whispered, nudging the door fully open and letting himself out.

"That's good, correct?" Krystal asked, glancing outward.

They both saw an era of advancement and technology—numerous roads stretched from each radial view. People strode along each road network, traveling from building to building for which a different custom was proposed.

"I believe we are in the height of the Roman Empire." Patrick studied the scene, analyzing the extremes of the area.

"Okay, great," Krystal replied, seeming reluctant. "Is there a reason why we're in the Roman Empire?"

"Well, for one, the time machine can only travel so far. The only power in this era is the social pyramid."

They both paused for a few moments.

"Speaking of reasons …" Patrick said.

"Okay, I'm out. Either find the Mediterranean or some other power source, or I am out of this whole experiment of an idea."

"No … wait … we can influence or change the earth so much when we are here. Think about it. This is Rome—our one chance to dramatically change 2050."

"I thought you wanted technology and human population to go back and decrease, not revolt into more."

"The human reduction is covered—hopefully—by my fans in counterpart."

"You're about to make me crawl up an aqueduct and hide," Krystal said.

"Please, just listen to me this one time."

"All right, fine."

"Look at where we are at this moment—the Roman Empire, the height of all things beautiful, ranging from clothes, to architecture, to art. This is the era when we put effort into what we created—not some tie and suit, or a line on a square, or a military assault box."

"Okay, I get that you love Roman architecture and stuff."

"No, this idea is much more than that. What I am trying to say is that I want this thoughtfulness and effort of architecture and design that fits everyone."

"But it's considered classic; nobody wants to downgrade."

"But in the end, it's an upgrade to be more beautiful and retain more functionality."

"That could actually be one hell of an idea," Krystal agreed, "but I don't see how it's plausible."

"I promise you this: we will get out of here, doing whatever we can under the cover of darkness, and take their ideas and work with us."

"Let's do exactly that."

Both then hobbled down a cobblestone path, which took a slight thirty-degree incline into numerous rows of pillars and exquisite detailing on each roof. The path then turned to the right, bending at seventy degrees, where the cobblestones gradually continued to get smaller.

"Okay," Krystal said. "Romans are very serious about their military status. You would not be an intruder in this era."

"I explained this to you over and over—"

"Just taking precautions. You never know what could happen to us, such stand-outs."

"All right, fair enough proposal," Patrick replied.

"Maybe we should just exempt out of this whole architecture shake-up and move on like you said."

Both then traveled to the slight south as gray clouds rushed in, taking their eyes off the bright white buildings. Down the hill they traversed. Rome was a city full of activity. Everyone was doing something, either in slavery or a force of power.

"I have another thought," Patrick commented with a slight sense of fear.

"Oh God, no," Krystal replied, agitated.

"Exactly that," Patrick replied. "Try not to say 'God' or

anything mainstream like that. They are very sensitive about their religion and crap."

Krystal gave him a frustrated glare. "Now who's taking precautions, eh?"

Patrick laughed.

Absent-minded about the current situation, both continued to travel the behemoth city of the Roman Empire.

But things remained subtle for only a few moments. Ahead was an issue no one could have imagined; ahead was an idea nobody *wanted* to imagine.

"Wait a second!" Krystal attempted to shout but ended up whispering. "I see a straight line of Roman warriors over in that street."

"What the heck?" Patrick wondered, frantically peering over some rough green bushes.

"Well, did someone see us, or is it a classic military battle?" Krystal wondered, begging for an answer.

"I don't think we have a solution," Patrick answered.

Krystal ended the conversation by abruptly sprinting up the grainy dirt path.

"Well, then," Patrick said with a sigh. He ran up the dirt path as well, scampering like a rat.

One of the warriors shouted, running quickly up the path. A few others decided to follow.

"Are we away from all of 'em yet?" Krystal frantically shouted.

"I am guessing no," Patrick replied, pointing down the hill at the warrior who had shouted.

"What should we do? We can't really time travel out of here at this moment."

"Just run to the time machine," Patrick said. "That's probably what they want."

Both sprinted as fast as they could back to the machine,

which was planted along a steep, rocky cliff that led down to the Mediterranean.

"Just guard it," Patrick shouted as Krystal blocked half of it.

Almost thirty soldiers and warriors of Ancient Rome surrounded the building in front of them. The warriors took a strong stance in their gold and red uniforms, clad in armor. They held swords and daggers. It was as if each warrior was ready for a war or battle.

But they weren't.

One warrior stepped out of the crowd. They saw Patrick and Krystal before them like two prominent statues, although they could move. Patrick felt they recognized him. All eyes were staring right into his soul. They spoke Latin, yet their tone indicated they were desperate to communicate with the two.

"What the hell are they saying?" Patrick whispered to Krystal.

"They are speaking Latin," Krystal explained. "And this is the only time I ever will."

One warrior continued to speak to both of them. The desperation continued.

Krystal replied, attempting to speak fluent Latin. Patrick stood silent in the background.

The warrior continued to speak.

"What are they talking about?" Patrick asked.

"They're saying that they want no trouble," Krystal explained. "This is quite interesting."

Another warrior then proudly spoke. He seemed less desperate than the first one, happier to speak of what they had discovered.

"What was that?" Patrick asked.

"They say ancient legends have told them to expect us to show up here."

"What?" Patrick remarked. "How the hell—"

Another one, dressed oddly, entirely in gold, appeared to be the leader. He spoke, and Krystal listened, as she was the translator for Patrick.

"They also say we first embarked on an ancient city that they have taken over."

"Let's see … ancient city … knew we were …" Patrick attempted to figure everything out. "Dammit."

"What happened?" Krystal asked.

"Someone saw us while we were in Meroe, I'll bet," Patrick figured, somewhat disappointed.

"Really?" Krystal asked with a shocked tone.

"There must have been … Meroe behind that stone building, the most populated city in Kush."

"All right," Krystal replied, sounding worried. "But how can you prove that?"

Another stepped out of the background and came by the two, presenting them with the warriors' certain gift.

That gift was something both Patrick and Krystal had owned, approximately seven hundred years ago.

The warrior walked over to them with caution, handing over the *generator from ancient Meroe.*

"What …" Patrick started, staring into the power generator. "How …"

One warrior replied, and Krystal translated.

"He says they got it from Meroe, where it had been preserved for hundreds of years. It was a gift from the stars, they say."

"I see," Patrick remarked. "This is quite the accomplishment."

Krystal spoke to the warriors with a positive response. The warriors bowed with ease.

"They all love you!" Krystal whispered loudly.

"Excellent," Patrick said. "But I think we need to set off and find our next time-travel destination."

Krystal explained to the warriors that they needed to continue their journey and then waved to the Romans. She and Patrick ran off to the time machine, which was still sitting in the position as they'd left it.

"All right," Krystal said, holding on to the time machine. "I see the Mediterranean down the cliff."

"That's where we're heading," Patrick said happily. "Let's get a move on."

Both held their pieces of machinery carefully as they rushed down the hundred-foot shrubbery-covered cliff.

Krystal then saw millions and millions of people watching and cheering for them, as Patrick stumbled down the sandy ocean floor, plugging in the two wires on the Mediterranean.

"Go. Come on," Krystal begged, as the people also began throwing stuff at them.

"There we are," Patrick said, attaching the generator box to the time machine. "Get in right now."

Patrick and Krystal hopped into the machine frantically. He picked up the generator, wrapping the wires around the exterior. Both held on and shut their eyes as water began to shake, and the mysterious blue light appeared for the third time.

The warrior above shouted with delight.

All cheered with absolute joy as the time machine faded away with almost blinding light in front of them.

They all chanted with pure excitement.

The time machine whisked off into a hole of nothing, right in front of the people—the first to have that experience.

Chapter II

The time machine, along with the power generator, landed safely in a nearby woods, which surrounded a city.

The steel floor hit the ground like a feather, slowly crunching weeds and twigs beneath.

"Okay," Krystal said, feeling agitated and dizzy. "After time traveling consecutively in a round of three and dealing with sand and warriors in my eyes and face, I would like to start and finish whatever plot you had in the beginning."

"I'm guessing you would like to be in 2001, right?" Patrick said.

"Yes, very much," Krystal responded. "Please tell me that we are somewhere near that."

"Sorry, but don't expect anything from 2001. I have sent us to 1901."

Krystal became agitated. "Oh, my God!" Krystal held her head.

"Don't judge my decision yet," Patrick said, attempting to explain himself. "I will justify it later."

"All right, fine."

"Let's just figure out where we landed first."

Both of them stepped out of the time machine hatch, decidedly curious of their surroundings. The woods stood tall and silent, yet the humming of the wind and chirping of the birds were present as well.

"Where do you think we are?" Krystal asked, uncovering a trail underneath twigs and leaves.

"Somewhere in America, I believe," Patrick replied, listening to the rustling of the trees. "I wanted the time machine to end up somewhere in the United States anyhow."

"So your time machine can do that as well, eh?" Krystal said, impressed. "And I see you are foreshadowing as well."

"All right, fine," Patrick said, irritated. "I sent us here because many of our daily problems that still exist in 2050 were derived from America's troubled history."

"You could actually be right about that," Krystal said, pleased. "We could stop a ton of crap that ruins the—this time—the social state of our present world."

"That was specifically my goal," Patrick replied, happy. "Ranging from slavery, to the Great Depression, to just justifying the difference between rich white men and women and blacks."

"Even more specific. Let's just continue onward for now and find out where we are."

They continued through the deep oak woods. Each tree seemed as if it had been planted by humankind and stretched on in rows. It looked as if the oak woods were a painting on a backdrop because a light, sort of lemon-yellow appeared in the back.

That light continued to get brighter ... and also appeared to get darker as they inched closer.

"I think the forest is winding down," Krystal said.

"Perhaps we landed in some sort of city."

"I bet," Krystal replied.

They walked near the end of the oak forest and reached a fence.

"Borderline," Patrick stated, holding onto the fence as Krystal reached it from behind.

The fence was a wrap-around that stretched from end to end. It was made of wood, designed like a typical fence.

"Whoa," Patrick said.

Krystal pulled him down under the fence. "Keep a cover, man," Krystal whispered, looking underneath the fence. "This whole thing could be just like Rome all over again. They may be expecting us to turn up somewhere."

"Probably," Patrick replied straight away.

"So that's all you are going to say about that, huh?" Krystal remarked, shocked.

"Okay, hold on; let me elaborate," Patrick replied. "It is probably a stretched-out myth that nobody believes."

"Well, don't make them think it's true just yet," Krystal said.

Patrick smirked at her. "Let me get a closer look at our surroundings. Patrick inched his head across the side of the fence, as if he was entering a school as a child for the first time.

The city was full of action cars, such as Fords and Studebakers, that roamed the asphalt-paved streets. Methane lights lit the gray street, which offset the darkness of everything, including the brownstones and other buildings, which were considered tall back in 1901.

"I really can't say which town—or perhaps city," Patrick said with slight disappointment.

"Maybe we should find some shelter," Krystal suggested. "It seems quite cold out … plus it's December 23 after all."

"Let's go," Patrick said, collecting himself. "Let's cross that street as quickly as we can, without anyone seeing us."

Both ran to the left to the crosswalk and across the old paved street as fast as they could, under the dim lighting.

Night had descended, and all suddenly became silent throughout the area. No activity. No people were found on the streets. No cars either. It was just the two of them, looking for shelter like a poor man—desperate.

"What should we do?" Krystal asked. "Should we find an abandoned brownstone? A shop?"

"Exactly what I was thinking," Patrick replied. "Find some building without any signs of activity."

Both ran down the cobblestone walkway in different directions, looking inside each brownstone or home for signs it was empty.

"Found one?" Patrick asked.

"Maybe," Krystal answered.

"Well, it has to be for certain."

She peered inside the classic brownstone but still was not certain. "I'm no good with architecture. You take a look."

Patrick walked up and peered into the brownstone, which had no livable amenities whatsoever. There were only a few dust clouds in the corners and spiderwebs attached to the remaining wooden floor planks and the wooden walls. "Looks pretty much deserted to me," Patrick said with confidence.

They entered the building, trying to be as quiet as possible.

"I seriously doubt we should be doing any of this," Krystal said.

"I'm sure we'll be fine," Patrick said, attempting to be happy. "Maybe we should traverse to the second floor for added security." He climbed up the wooden walls and through a hole in the floor, only letting a few creaks out.

Krystal was still worried. "Are you sure?" she asked. "The floor could collapse and give us away."

"Just be careful," Patrick whispered. "You know what else will give us away? Your hemming and hawing."

Krystal looked at him, disgruntled. "If you must," Krystal said.

Patrick reached down to grab her hand and pulled her up to the second floor.

They didn't make any noise, but some wooden planks fell from the second floor, crashing onto the broken ones on the ground floor.

"Shoot!" Krystal said, attempting to hide. "That might have given us away."

"Oh, no!" Patrick whispered. "Just hide under the windows or something."

Both crawled under the three slightly damaged windows on the second floor, attempting to hide.

"All right," Krystal said, breathing hard. "How are we going to warn the public about the segregation war and the Great Depression when we have to hide?"

"I'll just write a bunch of descriptive notes and send them to the public somehow," Patrick said. "While I'm doing that, you watch out the window for any intruders."

"Got it," Krystal conceded. She then did so, examining each view like a radar gun.

Patrick wrote quickly on a paper, making his way through the Great Depression. "Have to sound convincing and descriptive," Patrick said, still writing. "They have to believe a supposed myth, coming from a myth's mouth. Patrick continued to write on the small piece of paper, almost completely filling it up. "Any signs of danger?"

"Nope, not yet." Krystal continued to keep a close eye on the outside.

"Finished on the Great Depression part," Patrick said happily. "I decided to only explain the Great Depression, actually. Why don't you take a look?"

Krystal got the paper from Patrick and began reading.

Dear all good citizens reading this message,

Remember the myth about the man and the woman time traveling from place to place, bringing some sort of outrageous technology to wherever they showed up? Well, we are here, and we have written this letter to let you know we are here. All the technology that you have currently—a slice of it came from us.

But we have no more technology to bring to you, unfortunately. We have a few, much more important warnings to address to you.

Krystal stopped reading for a second.

"Why did you stop?" Patrick asked.

"I don't know," she answered, confused. "Just forget about it for now." She kept on reading.

In 1929, twenty-eight years from now, America, your country, will induce a Dow Jones economic slump due to a loss of confidence in the warfare marketing. Your country will be affected, but so will Europe, Canada, Turkey, and others. Whoever is reading this, please attempt to stop that from happening. Millions of Americans will be much better off if that incident is prevented by you, the reader. Thanks for believing in us, and thanks for trying to do whatever possible to make our country better."

"Should I list our names, or keep us anonymous?" Patrick asked.

"Keep us secret. They could eventually figure out our plot—to get rid of all of this."

Patrick then wrote *anonymous* at the bottom of the letter. He folded it up and put it in the right pocket of his blue jeans.

"Wait …" Krystal shook her head vigorously. "The window!" She continued to look out frantically once again, and this time, she found something. Not just something—*someone*. "Oh … crap!" Krystal shouted, trying to calm herself. "Someone appears to be lurking about in the streets. He also appears to have some sort of gun."

"Well, don't just stand there. Get down on the ground!" Patrick whispered, trying not to scream. "Just get down and don't say anything or move anything."

Both ducked down, as if a tornado was about to rip the big brownstone right off its underpinnings. They could no longer see the man's activity.

"I have always been looking for you two," the man shouted, holding his gun by his left side. "Your myth doesn't lie, but that doesn't mean you don't."

The man appeared to be dressed casually—red tie, white shirt unbuttoned at the collar, and gray overalls. He also wore a black beret and appeared to have not shaved in quite a while. He seemed to be in his mid-twenties.

Patrick decided to get a glimpse of the man by peering out the middle window.

"He looks quite a bit like Richard!" Patrick said.

"Don't speak!" Krystal whispered abruptly. Both quieted down.

"I heard you guys," the man said with a rigid voice. He then entered the old decommissioned brownstone, pointing his gun out in all directions.

They heard him and continued to take cover.

Then, straight afterward, the man seemed to be trying to climb up the broken staircase to confront the two. Both Patrick and Krystal were sweating like pigs.

Instead, the man walked abruptly out of the brownstone.

Krystal and Patrick saw him walk across the street out the window, amazed and relieved.

"Okay, Krystal," Patrick said, no longer ducking. "We're safe now."

"Awesome," Krystal replied, getting up.

Both watched the mysterious man enter the woods nearby, where the time machine sat.

"Patrick …" Krystal pointed directly out the window. "That guy is heading into the woods."

"So what?" Patrick asked. "That guy is pretty much a dolt."

"No, not really," Krystal insisted. "He's heading straight to the time machine!"

Patrick looked closely outside and saw the machine, which was protruding from the trees, and started shaking. "Crap, he's got the time machine in his hands!" Patrick shouted. He jumped out of the window like a crazed criminal, glass flying in all directions.

Krystal rushed down the broken stairs to the ground level.

Both ran as fast as they could across the old street, leaped across the giant wooden fence once again, and found the same path as they'd taken previously.

"Run, man!" Patrick shouted, as both picked up the pace.

Down the path and through the deep, thick branches they pushed their way, slowing down as they made their way to the time machine once again.

"Be silent," Patrick said, ending up tiptoeing through the woods. "You don't want him to notice us."

"I already have," the man shouted, pointing a gun directly into Patrick's face.

"Drop the gun," Patrick said.

"Are you kidding me?" the man asked with a slight British accent. "I have finally caught you two, and I know you are doing more than influencing technology. You want to do something else with it."

"No, you don't!" Krystal shouted, already inside the time machine.

"How the hell did she get in there?" the man snarled, scratching his head like a dolt.

Patrick was about to climb in as quickly as he could, when he suddenly realized he'd forgotten something.

"Krystal," Patrick whispered. "I forgot about the letter!"

She said nothing but gave him a thumbs-up.

Patrick ran off as fast as he could with the message, back in the other direction.

"Get back here!" the man shouted, about to run after him.

Luckily, Krystal was there to distract him. "Hold up, you!" Krystal shouted, stepping out of the time machine and confronting the man. She held out a huge LED lantern that had thirty light-emitting diodes, enough to blind a man. She abruptly shined it directly in the man's face. "Give us a name!" Krystal shouted confidently, yet underneath she was nervous. "We have more power than you think."

"All right, fine," the man said with irritation, trying not to look directly into the LED light. "Calhoun Clark."

Krystal was pleasantly surprised. "That's all I needed to hear," Krystal said with a smirk. She took the LED lantern, swung it, and hit Clark directly on his cheekbone, practically knocking him out. He took a tumble to the ground.

Krystal then threw the lantern into the time machine and waited patiently for Patrick to return. When he did, he was out of breath.

"Letter taped … on telephone pole …" Patrick mumbled, light-headed.

"Good enough," Krystal said pleasantly. "Back to more important matters—I am entirely sick of time traveling, and I think we should just get to 2001 and stay there."

"I get it," Patrick said, recovering his breath. "Let's head on out before anyone sees us."

Patrick disconnected the power generator and brought it inside the time machine. Krystal shut the hatch tight.

"Are you well enough to time travel again?" Patrick asked, about to press the start button.

"I am more worried about you," Krystal said. "Let's get on with it."

Patrick pressed the big red button and clutched the handlebar at the top.

The time machine started to whir once again and eventually disappeared from the oak woods like a flash of lightning.

CHAPTER 12

December 24, 1901
New York City

New York Times, news section

The rumors of two mystical persons, who have been portrayed as "undeniable gifts to the earth" since the Mesopotamian era, are believed to be one man and one woman who travel throughout time in a device known as a time machine, which is portrayed in the H. G. Wells novel.

On the more important side of the situation, though, legends have been supposedly uncovered inside a wood on the northside of Central Park, along Fifth Avenue.

The sighting was at around 12:30 a.m., December 24, in an abandoned brownstone. A man, identified as Calhoun Clark, believes that these two are doing more than influencing resources; they are on the run—at least they are, according to Calhoun.

"I remember absolutely nothing about their appearance," Calhoun stated in an interview. "All I know is that I was tracking them down and attempted to confront them and find out what this was actually all about."

The man remembers basically nothing from the experience,

due to the fact that he was attacked by what he believes was the female of the two.

"I managed to slip a note inside the time machine," Calhoun said abruptly. "Ever since I knew about the myth, I always thought they were up to something more, but of course I don't want to be a convicted criminal."

The two are rumored to be traveling to a time in the future, so the note he sent in the time machine could have something to do with that. Calhoun refused to share it with us.

Continued on pages 4A–4b.

December 24, 2050

The Northwestern Mutual Commons office in the city of Milwaukee was chiming with activity and noise, which was unlike most days, especially Christmas Eve, when usually there was either no activity or there was the classic standby—a Christmas party.

Today, though, it was not very pleasant. It wasn't ever very pleasant at an office building, but today was much more serious.

One thing was on the mind of those in the office—finding what was behind Patrick Shields's plan.

Jen and Jim, who were still distressed by the whole idea of him being out there, headed to that singular office building. The sun was just rising that morning, and the gray, still flat, grassy turf inlays were yet to be covered in any decent amount of snow, even on December 24.

"Enough with this absolute disgrace to planet earth," Jim said, pushing himself through the glass doors.

"First," Jen interrupted, "he absolutely bashes the planet and our entire lifestyle, and then he tries to kill us all?"

"He thinks he has power, spewing as he goes further," Jim said.

"But hopefully he will either come to his demise or his senses."

"Doubt it."

Both ran into the lift, which could take them to the op in no less than thirty seconds.

"Ever notice something ... strange happening ... changing?" Jim asked.

"Like what?"

"I have seen the world dramatically change overnight," Jim said. "It's like the entire city of Milwaukee morphed overnight."

Jen chimed in, now stirring with ideas. "I think this elevator got faster as well."

"Oh, please," Jim said.

"No, it's like you said. It's the little improvements that shape this earth. I think the world is actually morphing in our hands."

Both ran out of the elevator and continued at a fast walking pace out the glass sliding doors.

"It's obviously Shields," Jim said brimming with confidence. "He's really the only person who could possibly alter our world."

They took a sharp turn left, passing the levels of glass windows that overlooked the cityscape. They turned down that same gloom-surrounded white hallway, which looked like a never-ending path and had outlets from which they could never escape.

"Let's find out what's on Mr. Clark's mind for work today," Jim said, raising an eyebrow in disgust.

Both headed inside Mr. Clark's office, looking as presentable as possible.

"Hello, good people," Richard said, wheeling up in his silver and navy-blue leather-seated wheelchair. "Really decent persons." Clark was extremely agitated because of Patrick's having shot him in the leg, which explained the wheelchair. "I am absolutely enraged by Shields's plan," Richard fumed as his colleagues set down their numerous briefcases. "Come talk with me at the end table." He scratched his leg beneath his white cast, and all three situated themselves at the end table at the northernmost point of the office building.

"I'm going to address some sort of plan to find Shields," Richard explained as they huddled around the glass table. "But for now, there are more imposing things literally popping up in our faces."

"Is it the new technology that's unexplainably developing throughout the city?" Jen asked.

"I would say more like the entire earth," Jim replied.

"Anyhow, this must have something to do with Shields and his plot for his path of destruction," Mr. Clark explained. "It seems to be revolting—whatever his plan is, it certainly … well, it's not really working."

"Right," Jen remarked. "And it is actually quite impeccable. He's bringing more stuff to our liking."

"I would thank him," Richard said, "but that would be odd."

"I'll have the FBI put a ton of major cities on lockdown once he returns."

"He's … well, not much more than a white terrorist," Jen said.

"Enough with the major upgrades," Mr. Clark said. "Rumors say he has done more than that."

"Like what?" Jen asked.

"I'm not entirely sure," Mr. Clark said. "But,he supposedly has it on his blog."

"Well, bring it up then," Jen said.

Mr. Clark unlocked his one briefcase and pulled out an ordinary laptop. "I will have to hack into his account. I obviously don't know his password. You know how easy it is to hack into crap these days." Mr. Clark easily did so, getting onto Patrick's personal website in no less than thirty seconds. "Here we are," Mr. Clark seemed unimpressed.

"Wow," Jim said. "He has a pretty decent website, considering he barely has a computer."

Mr. Clark then clicked on the newest post, titled "Important Message," which was posted under Patrick's account on December 19:

> Dear all friends of Patrick Shields,
>
> You have heard about his plan to destroy most of our civilizations' technology, correct? Well, Patrick wants to do more than that, actually, and he needs your help. You might agree that there are too many people, and that may also be the primary source of pollution. All he is saying is that he wants you to literally kill those mass amounts, those clusters of humans, to slow down population, slow down pollution, and make the rest of our generation better. It's a huge favor, and hopefully, you won't be considered any sort of criminal because maybe this thing will work. Choose whatever city, whatever country—and don't get caught for sure. Thanks a bunch, if you are willing to do so, guys and gals.
>
> —Anonymous

"Well, then," Mr. Clark announced, going back to the home screen, "he seems to have an assistant as well, from various other things."

"I believe the assistant was a woman," Jen said, looking again at the post from December 19. "That's all I remember, though."

"Could she possibly be dumb enough to join with Shields?" Mr. Clark asked. "Too bad for her."

"I think we have to head out and alert the city and the whole earth about this 'terror' threat," Jim said, beginning to rush.

"The post also stated that they will launch specifically at midnight," Mr. Clark said, looking at the computer. "We only have sixteen hours to do this, at the least."

"Were almost to the brink of extinction," Jen began to shout. "This is a life-or-death situation. Let's leak this first."

"Right," Mr. Clark agreed. "But how?"

"I say we leak this on some websites of big news stations," Jen suggested.

"That could work," Mr. Clark remarked. 'Sounds simpler than it is."

"Which news station is most watched currently?" Jim wondered.

"Doesn't matter, hopefully," Jen replied, as the boss got to work. "It will spread, as usual."

Mr. Clark pulled up CNN's email address as a start. "All right," he said, entering it in the now highly developed email address. "Let's see what's convincing enough to enter to CNN."

Clark began writing as Jim and Jen collected themselves and walked around the gigantic room, away from Mr. Clark.

"This man is absolutely insane," Jen whispered.

"We figured that out in the beginning," Jim replied, slightly irritated.

"No, he was just a crazy, somewhat-suicidal hippie about a week ago," Jen explained. "And now he just slips away from law enforcement? For God's sake … what is this earth coming to?"

"He's beginning to sound … correct about our planet," Jim said, slapping his hand over his mouth.

Mr. Clark, thankfully, had not heard or noticed, due to being busy typing.

"Oh, my God, that was way too close," Jim whispered.

"I still think Patrick has gone way too far with all of this," Jen said. "But until now, I never really knew he had an actual reason for it."

"Put crazy aside," Jim said, refocusing. "This country bomb threat is nothing but absolutely incredible."

"That was my one point, if you happened to miss that," Jen said.

"His plan is about to be a bit of a dud pretty soon."

Mr. Clark was just about finished with the quite stretched-out email, which took up around a page or so on the format. "I guess this could be the rough draft," Mr. Clark said, showing the laptop screen to Jen and Jim.

"That's quite impressive, considering your rate of productivity," Jim sniped.

Jen began reading, as Jim followed.

Dear personnel at CNN News:

This is an important message from a man you probably have never heard of—but that is beside the point I am trying to justify.

Ever heard of Patrick Shields? That one guy on earth who is against all forms of anything?

Sounds like child's play, but the guy is real. He has his own beliefs in his own class. He was considered the lunatic of Milwaukee once. Well, in hindsight, he is.

But now, unfortunately, he has escaped his primitive grounds and has fled to a different time in the only possibly way—a time machine. Technology is progressing rapidly, by the minute, which you have probably noticed. That is because of Shields and his incomprehensible plan; both are failing, predictably.

One out of two of his plans are kaput, at least.

Patrick's other plan is to strike to kill—yes, literally kill a group of humans across the country. It sounds absolutely obvious and unreasonable to do so, but he actually did. No fairy tale of any sort. If it sounds that illogical, check out his blog.

Anyhow, this will kill approximately two billion people, which is around 15 percent of the planet. This would be the first human mass extinction since the Black Death of the twelfth century, if placed in other countries as well. This was done, surprisingly, by the twenty-five in fifteen billion people who are his fans, yesterday and probably today.

It is absolutely crazy. I have no idea about how Milwaukee managed to let him and his little friends escape and do this. That is why you are reading this.

Please share this with the country and the world—every single country and news station— if you will, urgently. This is like a 9/11 threat to every single damn city in the world. The nation's supposed survival is in your hands, CNN. Thanks for your help.

Sincerely,
Richard Clark, Northwestern Mutual Commons manager, Milwaukee, WI

"Pretty convincing," Jim said as he finished reading the email. "I think CNN will buy it, and hopefully won't think it's one of their weekly hacks."

"Probably," Jen said. "Now send it immediately. Who knows

how long—or short—a time it will be before each and every last bomb explodes?"

"Got it," Mr. Clark said. Richard then casually dragged his finger to the send icon, and instantaneously and abruptly, the entire screen blacked out right in front of his eyes, with a bit of a white flash in between.

"What the hell just happened?" Richard cried, holding his arms out in absolute shock. "What fucking *just happened?*"

"The internet must have blacked out, of course," Jen said, attempting to calm Richard down. "But why would it happen so abruptly?"

"Before he has a meltdown, let's see if another laptop is doing this," Jim suggested, running along the long glass table to find his tablet at the other end. Jen followed.

Out of breath, he turned on his tablet—and nothing happened. He continuously pressed it again and again; still nothing happened.

Jen and Jim stood there in shock.

CHAPTER 13

The time machine landed abruptly, seemingly much faster, much more responsive, and much smoother, much like an automatic versus a manual transmission. That was because power was speeding up, as Patrick and Krystal had finally landed in 2001—the exact year Patrick and then Krystal had desired.

But they had yet to find that out.

"Are you at all dizzy yet?" Patrick asked, strangely unharmed after the third time travel in just two days.

"No, not really," Krystal replied, appearing slightly weakened. "At least not yet."

"More important, I have sent us to 2001, finally," Patrick continued. "We should arrive in Shanghai, the most populous city in 2001, I believe."

"You told me that before," Krystal reminded him, beginning to sound slightly pissed. "How are you sure, anyhow?"

"Look at the control center," Patrick said, reaching his arms out in that direction.

Krystal looked squeamishly at the control area, where the year 2001 was surrounded by blinking lights and radar controls. "Yep, you're right. Now, let's get a move on."

Patrick had no reply. Even more nervously than ever, he

glanced out the door of the time machine. At first glance, they had appeared to be in Shanghai, mercifully.

"Holy crap," Patrick said, looking upward. "God above."

Krystal didn't hesitate to look, of course, and was just as shocked as Patrick had been. "Look at that," Krystal said, her eyes as wide as saucers. "Imagine what Shanghai looks like in 2050."

Shanghai was full of common activity, much like any other city, except there was more. It was packed tighter than a drum, with people scampering about, getting from place to place on red and green bicycles, or doing the same in maroon taxis. Looking more closely, though, they could see pollution in the very dense air, as smoke from buses to cars to other vehicles was making it rain chemicals. The buildings stood tall and blended in because each was equally as defyingly tall as the next.

Down the street, Shields and Krystal walked, and the buildings gave way to the one ten-lane highway.

"Well, where do we go now?" Krystal asked.

Patrick knew he couldn't give a simple answer. His ideas had turned into mere foibles, for Patrick couldn't afford another mistake, especially being closer to the present.

Much closer.

"I ... don't know," Patrick replied with uncertainty.

Krystal wasn't fond of this. His being confident in his decisions would permanently alter history. "Look on the brighter side of things," Krystal suggested. "Through all the bullshit, we have made it through 401 BCE, the Roman Empire, and now we're back finally in the twenty-first century. We have to change something—well, you do. I'm not responsible for whatever it turns out to be."

Patrick felt bitter remorse. He wanted to finally get it right and alter history for the better, but he simply couldn't stand to flashback and envision the supposed damage he had made.

"Technology had once reached the proximity of other

high-tech cities here in Shanghai," Patrick noted, reaffirming the significance. "This is where I could make do, simply with what they have. No verbal reassurance needed."

Krystal was reluctant to agree with his statement. The cord appeared short in her eyes, with the longevity dwindling. "All I know now is that there isn't much time. In retrospect, we're only forty-nine years away from the present!" Krystal pleaded. "Something has to be done now."

Patrick took a moment to himself to consider his thoughts. He knew—he absolutely knew—that he had no room for any extra incentive. He had to conceive his plan now and forever. Krystal, with her patience dwindling by the second, held on to the reins to gain traction in such a sordid situation.

"Anything?" she asked.

"We have to track down a company's source and destroy whatever they're creating," Patrick said, looking up at the glass sky of Shanghai.

"We what?" Krystal asked, confused.

"Do you know how influential large factories were in this time?" Patrick asked. "If we could somehow implode one of them, then others would take note of unsafe production, resulting in less tech under the influence."

Krystal attempted to make sense of this idea. She couldn't but went with it anyway. "I guess that could work. It's just the fact that it's *somewhat* illegal. How are we going to make this endeavor seem innocent?"

Patrick had become stumped yet again. As confident as he might have seemed, his doubt had remained locked away, ready to open at any moment if the key was anywhere in sight. "We only have one option, and that is to try," Patrick replied, a little shaken. "That's what we have been doing this whole time. If we stay persistent, an outcome is bound to happen."

"That's literally the only thing we have been doing this entire time!" Krystal accused him. "Nothing—at least nothing that we know of—has changed yet, besides all the trying. What makes it different this time?"

Patrick shot a quick response. "It's easier now. We're so much closer to the actual present, it should be simpler to create a solution now; would you not agree?"

Asked with such vehemence, Krystal didn't have a word in reply.

"We found electricity in BCE, for Christ's sake. I think we might just have a chance at pulling this off."

Krystal, with reluctance, cautiously nodded.

"Let's set out."

And so they did. Whether innocuously or blatantly, Patrick and Krystal departed from the grassy plain where their time machine rested. Feeling weaker, they decided not to bring the machine with them this time. It was a risk both were willing to take, for not a scratch was on it.

They walked down a winding, slightly graded road, eastward, descending to a valley, with nature surrounding them, yet urban sprawl prevalent. Shanghai was fully visible on the horizon, with lights flickering, sounds buzzing, and people living. It seemed quite appropriate for the turn of the century, with the digital age encroaching ever so slowly. But alas, it was still quite prevalent, as bright digital screens could grab the attention of virtually anyone—the attention of something, furthermore. Something concealed as well.

Under brighter lights as the night approached, Krystal anticipated that Patrick had a certain direction in mind and knew where he was going. Wanting more knowledge, Krystal raised more questions.

"Patrick, do you have a clue—any sort—of where this factory or the conglomeration of them are?" Krystal asked with tension.

She tugged at Patrick's shoulder; he was a pace or two ahead of her, leading the way to something.

"I would say a little bit," Patrick replied, lacking inspiration. "It's probably located more toward the coast of the Pacific."

A little bit? Krystal thought. *I'm a 'little bit' pissed.* "So is this all just a huge assumption?" she asked, raising her voice. "How long until it comes within our vision?"

"Night is near, okay?" Patrick reassured her impatiently. "The darkness is our virtual cover. Yes, doors are locked, but it gives us something to open it with."

As they argued on how to get there, they logically drew near. Downtown was increasingly prevalent, as buildings grew taller, and the impatience of marketers got smaller.

With every step they took, a feeling of anticipation grew that, for once, these two could get something done and make the change that Patrick had always wanted. He knew, in the past, that he did indeed change something. He had no clue what, but it was there. Right in the back of his mind. Krystal's, too. He just used that to add fuel to the fire, for he was up in flames at this point.

Downtown was lit up. While the dawn had approached early, but the labor of many Chinese men and women remained bright as day.

The area along the coastline reeked with the smell of grain, rice, and the transition of goods, and this smell, as endearing as it seemed, was nothing but a good sign for the two. It showed that they were nearing the outlets of mass production, on the point of what Patrick was looking for.

"Are you absolutely sure this is right?" Krystal was still doubtful, as anyone would be.

"They aren't erecting a factory inland; they're putting it where its products can get shipped as fast as possible to America."

"Who's *they*?"

"Who made your phone?"

Moonlight had spread over the barren black ocean, and white ripples shone through the endless bottom, resembling morning waves of a better time.

Industry was booming, with constant activity going for twenty-four hours every day, hoping to justify the economy of China and provide enough money for dinner for the average worker.

Krystal had an eye for tech, as she had proved to Patrick beforehand. It made her wonder what they were going to disconnect. "What factory are we diving on into?" Krystal asked. "What kind—"

"Something that affects the future greatly," Patrick replied. "You'll see."

Krystal paused a moment and then said, "I'd have a better chance of getting struck by lightning than getting a straight answer from you."

An answer wasn't exactly straight, for it was shaped more like a fruit. Within a short distance, the tall building present in Shanghai's long and streaky skyline had spread out and then faded into much smaller buildings. It was as if they had tipped over, for they were long, flat, and everywhere. Yet they lacked the lighting of the skyscrapers, for these buildings produced glass; they didn't wear it. Much like those who made the clothes worn in America, they made it; they didn't wear it.

Patrick could see his supposed destination along the horizon. Within a box of black darkness, a penetrating white light had shone into their eyes. Within the tech production company, an apple adorned the west side of the building, and it was pretty clear to both of them what the company was.

"So you want to get rid of Apple?" Krystal asked.

"It's basically the first source of what everyone is in the present," Patrick explained. "Lazy. Disconnected from the real world. Get it? Disconnected?"

He smirked, but she frowned.

"I might need chopsticks to get hold of that one," she replied, instantly regretting it.

Under a dim neon streetlight, the Apple logo was within their grasp. Patrick continued down the slim, asphalt-paved alleyway, down a small valley, getting closer to the industrialized shoreline. Krystal followed in his footsteps, whether willingly or not.

He had a job to do. And his name wasn't Steve.

Through bends and turns within small streets and even smaller alleys, they used the beaming light of the company's logo to illuminate their way to where it all began.

Everything else had already happened; the right thing might as well happen right now.

Patrick and Krystal were nearing the entrance of the plant, wherever it might be. The plant was two blocks away, to their delight.

They knew approximately where they were, but they didn't have a clue as to where the industrial entrance was.

"Do you think there are just doors, or would there be large ports that trucks and ships can fit into?" Patrick asked.

"And how would I ever know this?" Krystal asked. "I'm not here, knowing the complete design of an Apple plant in Shanghai."

"Who else am I supposed to ask?" Patrick retorted. "I've always thought you were smart as well."

She raised an eyebrow in return.

"You're the only one who has ever had the patience to believe my theory," he said. "I trust you. I need just a little support."

Krystal, with some doubt lingering, grew a bit of a smile. "I always saw your point in the end," she replied. "I always agreed with what you thought. I've just never thought it would end up like this."

Patrick considered what she'd said, and although he wanted to remain confident, he agreed. "Neither did I," Patrick said, a little heavy-hearted. "I simply wanted to end up here in the first place. But thank whoever you please because now we are. We can put all of what happened behind us. We should—no, we *have* to—get this right."

Krystal was hesitant to give him a chance, but she would concede because she might as well; there was no way of getting out of here without the expense of his time machine.

"Let's get on and find this entrance," Krystal said, to Patrick's delight.

He gave a slight smile.

Running to assess cover from any lingering workers, both preferred to show up at the west wall of the plant, sooner rather than later. Lights faded; noises did too. The point seemed meaningless, and they turned toward the location of the entrance.

Patrick peeked around the northwest corner; Krystal followed. The west side was all vinyl but no doors in sight. Once they turned the corner, though, they saw all the entrances, with ports to the sea right next to them. Light glimmered in mosaic pieces across the entire body of murky water, but an even brighter sight is what both of them were looking for.

"Here they are!" Patrick beamed with encouragement. "This is it!"

"Ugh, finally." Krystal put her head down in tiredness.

One piece of the puzzle was complete. The next one had a bit more complicated shape.

"Well, there's one step," Krystal said, with her doubt starting to profusely bleed once again. "How do we exactly open it?"

Patrick drew a blank. He got to the place where he wanted to be, but he just needed to know how to get in.

"Well, shit … we have to break in. These doors are as tight as a drum, and it says it's only accessible to those who work there."

The sign was white and had big red text in Chinese on the front, with fine print in English reading, "Only workers permitted."

Regardless of what the sign said, it was closed.

"I'm gonna take a closer look. Watch for anyone who might show up," Patrick instructed Krystal.

She was bored with the instructions, but kept her head up and her eyes peeled—contrary to Patrick, whose eyes were laser-focused on the entrance to the factory. He analyzed every nook and cranny, looking for where it opened, how it opened, and if it seemingly could be opened at all.

"I can't confirm much," Patrick said, somewhat resentful. Krystal's head turned in his direction, her arms crossed. "But what I do know is that it isn't a digital screen or code at all."

In retrospect, it looked like an average security door of the early twenty-first century. A knob with a lock. Just a regular key lock.

"I found the supposed lock it has," Patrick continued.

Krystal's focus on him increased. "Okay, what is it?" she asked.

"It's merely a key that's necessary," Patrick explained. "Nothing like today's or the present kind of locks. No code or screen about it."

"Is that not to be expected?" she asked. "We've gone back forty-nine years. Things were a lot different then."

"Well, no shit," Patrick replied arrogantly. "It's just I don't have a key on me. I haven't had a key in my pocket for over twenty years."

Krystal knew she didn't have one but checked her pockets anyway. "Neither do I. Not a single one."

The lock seemed foreign and didn't resemble the shape of any American keyhole, at least when meticulously analyzed.

"Is there anything to pick the lock with?" Krystal asked.

Patrick looked around on the ground for anything that even slightly resembled the shape of the keyhole. There wasn't much that seemed useful; the asphalt was entirely clean. Not a single speck of dust rose into the air when Patrick felt the ground with his bare hands.

"Nothing," Patrick told Krystal. "There isn't much here. The ground is clear."

"That's somewhat unusual," Krystal said. "China is notorious for bad working conditions, but I've never seen anything so refined."

"Well, it's Apple," Patrick explained. "But yes, it's odd at the very least." He kept examining the lock and then studied the mechanics of the large door; he analyzed the hinges for a minute or so.

He was silent for longer than Krystal would have liked, so she finally asked, "Well, uh … when or if we get in, what will we do, exactly?"

Patrick paused and turned toward her. "We have to shut down and break production. If we do that, they'll think it's a digital fault—that's what they use to produce the phones and tablets. If we shut that down, they'll have to rethink how they manufacture."

Krystal raised an eyebrow. "So we just go in there and destroy the output—or what makes the output?"

"Both couldn't hurt; we're here, and we have to do whatever it takes. I'd prefer to destroy the output, but we need to do absolutely everything."

Krystal nodded in agreement. She remained in her lookout position, and Patrick kept trying to unhinge the larger door. Krystal, though, was bored as the late night got later, and the bright white moon got brighter. It appeared that not a single worker was out, and not a single noise was heard. She didn't see anything but an empty, lifeless port filled with ships and forklifts.

She was about to drift off to sleep when a loud slam sounded near her. Her head instantly perked up. "Did you unhinge the door? Did you?" she instantly asked Patrick.

"What?" Patrick asked, seeming confused. "No, I'm still trying to rip the hinges apart."

"Didn't you hear that loud slam?"

"Nope, I'm focused down here. If you heard something, keep on the lookout."

Krystal rolled her eyes, crossed her arms again, and remained on lookout but was a little shaken. She didn't hear another sound for a few moments, but then ... it sounded like footsteps.

She was now visibly nervous. Sweat beaded along her hairline and trickled down her face, resembling tears. She turned to Patrick, wondering if she should say something but didn't. She looked to the right and the barren Pacific but saw nothing. She looked forward toward the port but again saw nothing.

Then she looked down the west side. In the shadows under a dim, neon-orange streetlight stood a man. She heard the footsteps again as the shadow moved closer and seemed to get larger by the second.

"Patrick!" Krystal hissed.

Still on his knees, he turned instantly toward her. "What is it?" he asked, annoyed with the interruption.

"Look down the west wall, would ya?" she said nervously.

Patrick let go of the hinge and looked slowly to the right. What he saw was paralyzingly frightening.

The man had shut a door that was the primary entrance to the plant and now stood next to Patrick, looming over him. He appeared to be Chinese, and on his uniform was a Chinese badge. He was a security officer. "Hands in the air!" he shouted, much to their surprise that he spoke English. "Both of you! Immediately!"

Patrick and Krystal instantly knew what they were in for. They both nervously stood up with their arms above their heads and looked the officer in the eyes. He studied the pair.

Patrick glanced at Krystal, but she didn't look back.

The lower hinge of the door broke apart. Screws tumbled to the ground.

Yet their smiles had long faded.

CHAPTER 14

Milwaukee
December 24, 2050

The light was concentrated. The day was cold—all of Milwaukee was cold.

Everyone thought Christmas was white, but the white light had vanished.

On the thirty-second floor of the Northwestern Mutual Commons office tower, the rooms remained lit. Several other floors below had gone completely black, but this room still had its horizontal LED lighting fixtures as bright as ever; they hung by thin strings along the angled roof.

Even though the floor appeared full of life, the meeting room—with panoramic views of downtown—was empty. The sky was dark. The glass seemed invisible and leaked the gray into the room, providing a strong contrast to the white vinyl walls.

Behind closed yet unlocked doors, Richard Clark was in a shallow state; his chin rested on his chest, and his hands were clasped in his lap. He sat at a table, where all seats were empty except for his. Nothing was on the table, except for Richard's laptop.

Which was blank.

"How …" Richard held his head in fear. "How … in the name of God … did this happen?" He was in complete shock and didn't know what to think of the circumstance. Jim and Jen had left the building, fearing more failures that were bound to happen.

In retrospect, Richard realized he should have doubted what those two thought was happening—was indeed happening. He wouldn't believe it. He couldn't, not after what he had been through and at the expense of what he thought was true.

"I've never had a problem with this, ever," he reassured himself.

Richard, being the promoter of modern technology he was, wouldn't go against what the digital premise had read. The idea that Patrick might be right was in the back of his mind, encroaching on him ever so slowly, like a virus waiting to pounce.

He desperately attempted to revive his tablet. He knew some tricks, but none could compare to Patrick's ingenuity.

Constantly tapping it wasn't going to do much. He knew it wouldn't go back on. He had lost hope in that aspect.

But he still had hope that it was just him.

"All right … this has to be me. This only has to be my laptop. It has to."

Richard had his case now, but he didn't really have anything to back it up with. He rose from his chair for the first time in nearly an hour. His shirt and the seat were soaked with sweat as his nervousness bled from his body.

He thought he had enough energy already, but he decided he would head down to the coffee shop on the ground floor. He creaked open the thin, one-pane glass door, leaving his laptop in the room. He knew no one would be in there to take it.

He headed to the lonely elevator, which was to the left of the room. The scanner used his fingerprint to send the elevator to the floor, and the doors—thankfully—opened. He stepped in, more cautious than on a normal workday, and the doors shut tight.

He stared at the flashing lights in the slight gaps above the doors as the elevator passed each floor. These gaps of light seemed longer than usual, but that was only because some floors were completely dark.

Richard noticed, but he wouldn't say a word about it. Still, it was disheartening to see, at the very least.

A moment later he reached the ground floor and stepped out. He turned to the left toward the coffee bar, which was deserted. All the flavors were presented on the wall, and the cups were stacked two feet high next to the dishwasher.

He climbed over the countertop—the bar's door was locked—and proceeded to make himself a cup of coffee. He was exhausted, but he was really drinking coffee for the betterment of humankind. He slid his cup under the espresso machine, praying to someone above that it would indeed make some coffee.

Within seconds, it did. Like any other Tuesday.

"So that works," he said aloud. He took a sip and instantly set it down. "But what about the rest of the technology?"

He knew damn well that the lights inside were merely turned off. It was Christmas Eve, after all, and everyone was at home.

With this in mind, he couldn't tell if the lights were turned off or if they had broken and were shut off permanently.

Richard would have to find out in a different way.

"I have to know if this has happened to anyone else!"

He picked up his cup of joe, finished it in one gulp, smashed the glass down, and burst out of the coffee bar and out the front door of the commons of the tower. He had to get a glimpse of what was happening outside the building.

And he got a really good one.

The gray sky had grown darker. The waters of Lake Michigan were even darker than previously, yet light of the buildings still remained.

Richard looked around for anyone or anything that could

give a better sense of detail. He knew he should go west, near the business center of downtown, following along Wisconsin Avenue.

But he was instantly stopped in his tracks.

Up above and all around, lights started flickering. Flashing lights penetrated through fog, like laser beams in a concert. Richard's eyes grew wide open at the sight, and his jaw dropped to the concrete sidewalk.

Lights were flashing at a higher rate than ever before. Nothing had ever compared to what Richard was seeing. It was a mesmerizing metamorphosis of color and a kaleidoscope of different shades and shapes. It was never to great or too little but was quite consistent in the inconsistency of what was changing.

Then the dagger came and stabbed right through the heart of Milwaukee.

The entire fuse of the Northwestern Mutual Commons building crashed.

It was now as dark as the sky.

Richard's eyes sunk into the back of his head. His heart sank to the back of his chest. It was no longer just his laptop now, for sure.

He heard Jim and Jen. He knew one possibility of what was behind all of this. He didn't want to believe it, but he knew that it could be.

He didn't want to believe it.

So he didn't.

He put the building's shutdown out of his mind and charged forward down Wisconsin. Along the street, all the lights that had been turned on earlier in the day were still on—all but one atop the Gas Light building, which hadn't turned on in fifteen years.

It seemed that only the Northwestern Mutual Commons building's fuse had burned out, but that notion also seemed odd.

He was eventually in line with Jefferson Street, three blocks away from the dark tower. He had a feeling that something could go wrong at a flip of a switch—or at least the flip of a fuse.

With this worry holding him back, he still ran forward in desperation. He wanted some help for whatever the situation was, but he couldn't find any. Everyone was cooped up inside for the holidays. He was at a loss for words at the sight and was losing his mind.

And the light of day was lost. An explosion of flickering lights and buzzing and flashing cast an explosion of confusion and nervousness within the street and within Richard. The colors turned on and off, changing their appearance by the second. Nothing looked the same then, and nothing would ever be the same either.

As the flashes got faster, and as Richard got increasingly tense, he again stopped in his tracks. The flashes went to a climax, and then suddenly, all went black. Every single light flashed for the last time. A collective loud whir took place as the fuses in all of downtown broke and shut off, spiraling down into a quieter, lower-pitched noise. The whirring stopped. It was silent once again. The lights had gone off. It was nearly as dark as night.

And chaos was about to ensue.

Suddenly, a mass number of doors on every single building along the street collectively opened. Richard simply stood in shock as a bystander. With a burst of speed, groups of people shot out of the buildings as fast as Richard had ever seen, and the flood of these people transformed the avenue into the Wisconsin River.

These people were visibly afraid and shaken. They were running around, confused, looking for someone or something to shed light on this.

Richard blended in with the crowd, in plain sight now—or chaotic sight, being the notorious character he was. He knew that something was going terribly wrong, but it wasn't at full effect yet.

Out in the distance in Westown, the majority of lights remained on. Richard knew in an instant he had to get there.

He began running, pushing and shoving his desperate way through the deep, loud, confused crowd. He wanted to get to Milwaukee's sports arena, where there was a large TV screen. He knew that rather than displaying a Manchester game across the globe, it would be displaying news of a supposed technical widespread crash.

He had no time for a free kick.

He continued following along Wisconsin Avenue into the valley of the Milwaukee River, and he ran right into Westown. Some people stood in confusion, but it was a lot less prevalent than East Town. Perhaps the majority wondered what in the hell was going on in East Town. Everything seemed fine across the river.

Until the entire Hilton Tower went black.

Richard made a right at Plankinton, giving him nearly direct access to Third Street, where the larger-than-life TV was located. He ran through the vast canyon of cream brick, concrete, and former industry and quickly got to where he wanted to be.

As he did, though, more and more people came out of every building and filled the streets to the brim. He still wasn't near East Town but was getting closer by the second.

With this in mind, he kept pushing his way across Pere Marquette, through a soggy-grass field of a former park, and he soon found himself along the crowded sidewalk of Third.

Some people were standing still; some were running for their lives. Richard didn't care to pick who was who; he kept running toward the screen, accessed by an alleyway, which used to be a walk-in bar.

He was now in front of the alleyway and was going to run straight into it. As soon as he fully saw the alleyway, he also saw the area was full of people. The entire length and width of the alleyway was jam-packed and blocked with people, running rampant for an answer.

He knew the exact kind of answer he would get. All of these people surrounded that same TV screen. It was showing the news of the dilemma. This many never turned up for any sporting event.

He pushed his way through the crowd, not caring whether he was being rude. There were more pressing matters than good manners on the table.

As he got closer to the TV, he could see reporters speaking urgently on the situation. His feelings had changed quickly, and he thought he knew what had really happened. Or did he?

The reporters got consistently louder. Richard thought about remaining where he was, but he couldn't quite make out what the reporters were saying, so he kept inching closer.

He saw Jim and Jen in the near distance. They had left the Mutual building and had the same idea as Richard. They were nearly in front of the TV screen.

"It's almost like they were expecting it," Richard said to himself. "But how?"

He made his way through most of the crowd, eventually, and soon he could hear precisely what the reporter was saying.

He caught the end of the sentence—"for the lives of others"—and then the reporter said, "There is no exact time, but this international broadcast could cut out at any moment. Thank you for your time. Once again, as previously stated, across the entire nation and within the entire world, major blackouts are occurring, left and right. We do not know what the source is, but we do know that the world's cloud infrastructure might be crumbling."

As the reporters scrambled for more information, the crowd turned to themselves, gasping. Everyone had their own theories on the cause, but not one was in verbal agreement with another.

"Yes, indeed, it appears our previous thoughts were correct," one reporter continued. "All of the digital virtual industry and casual everyday life is based and centered on each other. As we know, the technology feeds off each other, and power is regenerated and stored for other uses. Based off that notion, if one sector or fuse fails, others will. If power can't be generated for something, it will shut off; in the end, that will cause others to shut off."

Richard dropped his jaw once again.

He knew that this was how the system worked, and he would never cheat that system, but he didn't know that it could possibly break. It had never, ever done this. Not once. It was more efficient than ever.

He was in paralyzing shock.

"Many fuses across the United States have failed already on a dark Christmas Eve, which has only gotten darker by the second. It seems that no one knows how to get back this power. It has come to a full demise. The digital system that our world revolves around is falling apart. It's collapsing. Spinning on its axis. Dwindling into nothing. We can't rest upon our laurels. The earth is dying. Our very lifestyle is collapsing, creating the collapse of us as a human race. Do not look back. Do not attempt to restore power in any way. Gather whatever physical resources you can—food, water, shelter, the basic necessities. Do whatever you can to weather this digital storm, for this storm has no end in sight. I repeat, do not—"

Black. The TV cut out. The power was lacerated from the source. And the verbal noises and sounds of the large group watching were cut from their mouths.

And chaos, of course, would ensue.

People began screaming and running in all sorts of directions, going back for their resources. Richard remained still, though completely surrendered in shock.

His eyes were wide. His mouth was open; he didn't want to shut it.

He then saw Jim and Jen, who were together. They weren't

running like the rest but walking down the wide block where parties had been held. He had no clue what they were doing or thinking. He had no clue what he was doing or thinking either, as continuous screaming and footsteps rang in his ears.

He had lost this battle. It wasn't his fault. It wasn't his cause. But he had lost.

Hope still remained, even with all the trouble, hope to uncover who was behind all of this.

An empty chair was to his left, and he took a seat in it. He would use this chair to sit down and think, however that might be, under a steel roof, with lights faded into their strings and beer pushed back into the rack. He would sit and nervously think of different possibilities, mumble to himself, and jumble up different things.

He couldn't bear to see the harsh reality ahead. But the least he could do was be somewhat of a hero and say what caused this ... disaster.

Nothing was as prevalent to Richard's eyes as the dark sky. His focus had shifted away from the consequences to a more upfront situation.

What in the hell ... he thought, looking down at the patterned concrete floor. Perhaps the dislocated, randomly shaped pieces that made up the ground surrounding him would give him an answer.

As screams continued, he felt deserted in the bar plaza. He remained alone with his thoughts. Life had lost its liveliness. The streets had lost their cars. The buildings had lost their lights. People surrounded Richard, yet the mood cast by others made him feel alone, isolated in thought.

He had come up with nothing—for now. What lay ahead, ironically, held him back. He couldn't think of why because he wanted to know what.

What happens next?

What happened next would be even worse than he could imagine, he assumed. He did not want to think about it—but he had to. He had to think of a rational idea—grinding his teeth, fists clenched, palms sweating—and so he did.

And he grinned slightly at the thought. "It isn't me. It's not any of us. We're all innocent. Who is not here right now?" He looked over his shoulder at all of the people running in fear. He thought who actually wasn't here right now.

One name did occur. One notorious, bewildering, bitter-tasting name.

Patrick Shields.

"Shields? Could this be his fault?" He wondered some more, in an attempt to gather reasons why. He didn't have many when the name first occurred, but he did have an everlasting hatred of his opinion and whoever he gained support from.

He could use that alone, but he chose not to, as that reasoning had gotten him nowhere over the past few weeks. Using the same reasoning would drive him down a further hole, for most people thought Patrick's time-travel attempts were a joke.

But it would soon turn out to be no laughing matter.

Richard Clark now had his reason. His fists clenched once again, and his veins pulsated with furious blood. He was eager to tell people what he had in mind, but his reason drove him mad with what he thought Patrick had caused.

He then saw Jim and Jen in the distance.

He absolutely had to tell them about this.

They were down the block at the intersection of Fourth and State Streets. He shot out of his chair and ran faster than he had in a long time.

Jim and Jen were walking slower than before, merely taking in all of what had horrifically changed.

Richard only ran faster at the sight, fearing they would turn a corner. He didn't know where they were going. "Jim! Jen!"

he called out loudly, hoping his voice would reach over the screaming crowds. "I know what happened! I know who caused this! I know!"

Jim's head turned around in confusion.

"You will not believe it!"

CHAPTER 15

"I saw something," a news reporter said. "I stand behind this glorified contraption, shining like the bright sun above."

The reporters were Chinese, like all in the Shanghai area, but these two, in particular, spoke their best in English.

"Now, nothing is known for sure, but it appears to be the notorious time machine told of in old legends and folklore. It appears that all the tales are true and that the two owners of this machine have traveled back from a certain year and landed here, in 2001. I can't prove this makes any sense, but I sure hope it does to all those watching. We don't know where the two time-travelers are right now, but some say what is going on is no joke. For the people who don't know what happened, I'll recap. Two people snuck into Shanghai's Apple plant and stole some information. We don't have any reports on what they stole, but we do know that whoever it was will be thrown into jail, if they aren't already in a cell somewhere. We have no faces or fingerprints, but we will find some kind of DNA at the entrance of the building.

"Not only will these two be interrogated, but they will also be locked up for an unknown period. They could be doing damage, or perhaps they could be doing good. Although nothing is known, all are innocent until proven guilty, as they say. Like this silver machine behind me, and the entire skyline of Shanghai out even further, I can only speak for what I know—and I don't know much. One thing I do know, however, is that there will be plenty of information soon coming our way. From the ice-cold weather, to the blazing sun, this is Zhang Kun, and I'm out."

"Thank you, Zhang. Like he said, we don't know much, but we will present to you everything we do. As of now, a night and dawn after they arrived, we know that they have come here for a reason. As stated before, they supposedly invaded the local Apple product manufacturing plant. Why they traveled back in time to go there is beyond my belief and most likely beyond our comprehension. They are obviously from the future, as the man and woman are wearing clothes completely at odds with our attire for today, and the machine is too modern for anything engineered today.

"It's only a matter of time before we know what their cause is. It's not so much fear, as of yet, but it's the feeling of anticipation. What could they be doing here? Is there something they're looking for? Something they're trying to create? Destroy? It's of our duty to find out for all the innocent people of Shanghai and the rest of China. We may all be innocent, but we aren't free of danger. I just have a feeling that these two time-travelers might be up to no good—"

Black. The TV cut out. The power was cut from the source.

Except it wasn't from a fuse; it was from a remote.

In Patrick's hand.

"Oh, you have to be kidding," he said, disgusted, throwing the remote on the prison cell floor.

Krystal looked on from behind, sitting on the prison bed. She rolled her eyes in remorse at the sight of it. "I'm not one to put fault on anyone," she said, "but this is, I'm certain, your fault."

"Well ..." Patrick thought of a reply. "You're probably right."

Light shone through the cell door to the right of Patrick, and a lot more light shone through the small window behind Krystal and the prison bed. The bright blue sky penetrated through the clouds and reflected the disappointment of the two time-travelers. They were shaken to the point of exhaustion.

Patrick and Krystal figured this might happen. But even though it did, they were still angered by it—especially Krystal, who was getting a tad sick of the whole deal.

"We really are in jail," she said, as reality pulled the life out of her. "We fucked up *again*. Or should I say, you did."

"How am I supposed to judge whether or not we're gonna get caught?" Patrick argued. "I was only trying to get the door open, and *you* were supposed to remain on lookout."

Krystal rolled her eyes at the response. "I damn well did," she snarled. "And you know what happened? Someone came out of the real entrance. How the hell was I supposed to prevent that from happening?"

"You could have at least warned me sooner."

"Uh, all right, you were too focused on unhinging a cargo port door. I told you as soon as I saw it."

"Speak up."

Krystal had no response except to slam her head into the musty prison-bed pillow and lie down facing the concrete wall, away from Shields.

"I'm done with that particular door," Patrick continued. "We have to focus on this one." He pointed at the prison door, looking at Krystal. She didn't have a rebuttal. He remained silent for a few moments. Krystal was not about to support him in this new case, and he was not going to pressure her to do so. This gave him time to think. Reset his goals. Reset his mind.

He wasn't sure what good it would do.

As Krystal lay on the bed, perched against the wall, Patrick sat in a wooden chair. He was thinking about how to break out of jail. What tool should he use, what technique, what design? It wasn't like the old door on the Apple plant.

But then, as those thoughts came along, others did as well.

He wanted to get out—but at what cost?

He held his head in bewilderment and fear. He wondered about the consequences of this time-traveling experience. He'd only had one goal, and that had been to end up in 2001. They ended up in 401 BCE and had to expose themselves while trying to reach power to get anywhere closer to this year.

Eventually, he had done it.

And now they were locked up.

Constant changes and interruptions penetrated their minds, especially Patrick's. He was beginning to think that his plan was somehow foiled and that his ideas were unraveling at the seams. He didn't want to find out the changes that occurred in the present, but he sort of had to know.

He felt like they couldn't be that bad, if there were any at all. He hadn't even accomplished what he had wanted to do in 2001. He wanted to change the course of history, and by those means, he wanted to slow down all of technology. He wanted to make the world more stable, fearing a crash.

He was afraid nothing had changed.

Nothing at all.

He hated the world of the present. The world of 2050. But he really did want to go back because he didn't know for sure what had changed. He honestly had no clue if it was his fault—or what was his fault. He wanted to break out of jail a lot less after these thoughts penetrated his mind, his will. What if he could just stay here and live out the rest of his life in 2001 in another country?

He relinquished that idea, due to his own existence back in Milwaukee. He was born in 2003. Thoughts of that nature, reaching to that end of the spectrum, were far too much for Shields to comprehend now. He didn't want to look back, but he didn't want to head forward either.

He had to speak his thoughts aloud.

"I don't think ..." Patrick began. "I don't think anything

has actually changed." He wasn't mumbling to himself. He was looking for a response from Krystal, who was ignoring him at every breath. "We went way back in time … but just to get out. I wanted to push technology back to this year, 2001, but to no avail. I honestly don't think anything will be different when we go back."

A pause penetrated the prison walls. Krystal moved just a bit. She then fully turned around and opened her eyes. "You really think nothing changed?" she asked, tired. "You really think we two, from forty-nine years in the future, have not influenced change at all?"

Patrick examined his morals. "Well, I don't know. I just don't. We haven't accomplished any of the ideas we set out to make true. We haven't pushed back development at all, it seems."

Krystal raised an eyebrow at the statement, much to Patrick's surprise. "I was plenty pissed off earlier," Krystal said with slightly more enthusiasm, "but it was only because we ended up trapped once again." A pause. Patrick kept listening. "But we damn well changed history."

Patrick was internally delighted to hear her statement but didn't smile. Doubt was external. "How, exactly?" he asked.

Krystal tried to think of exactly how they had. She knew they had, just not what, specifically. "We went back in time. Remember everyone who noticed us previously. They were afraid, wouldn't you say?"

Patrick called up his memory. "Well, in further retrospect, yes," Patrick quietly agreed. "But I would say they are more afraid of us, our clothing, our appearance."

"You have to remember that shiny time machine that was with us the whole time. Yes, their eyes were on us, but they stayed on the machine."

Patrick collected a response. "What change is going to happen from them simply seeing it?"

"Well, they're afraid. They're scared. They don't want to know what happens in the future, and they don't want to see it turn out like that."

"Your point being?"

"We have made change. These people don't want this kind of highly technological future, now that it has been shown to them. They want to slow down. They want to remain the same and adapt slower."

Patrick raised an eyebrow. "Do you really think it worked?"

"Indeed. I believe you have changed history."

Patrick smiled, but his lips instantly tightened as he asked, in doubt, "How can we know any of this for sure?"

"I'm not usually the one coming up with theories or ideas," Krystal said. "But you have come up with plenty. You weren't necessarily wrong with any of them."

Patrick now raised both eyebrows. Hope had been injected into his blood, if not previously removed at all. He wished and waited for more time to generate a response, but the lottery had happened two days ago. "Maybe you're right. Just maybe we did something."

"Not only something but something incredible."

Patrick cracked a genuine smile for the first time in a long time. He wanted to hold it back in fear of further consequences, but he didn't. He felt he knew what he had done. Doubt persisted because he only felt it. He knew nothing for sure.

"Well, we can only do one thing for sure," Patrick concluded. He grabbed the bars of the jail cell. "We gotta break the hell out of here."

Krystal was somewhat livid that he wanted to finally go back and witness the change he had made possible. Then again, she remembered they had to open a damn door again.

Doors hadn't led to the right room in the past. He had his keys, but they didn't unlock any doors he could see.

In retrospect, he had been through tougher times. He had solved the tougher problems.

Like getting power for his machine, when all power was gone. In 401 BCE.

"You've basically accomplished the impossible," Krystal reassured Patrick. "If you could do that, we can get out of a jail cell, at the very least."

Patrick took to his own thoughts once again and asked himself if all was really true and if he could get out of this cell—his cell that was locked for infinity.

Or was it?

"Well, I might have an idea or two," Patrick said. "But after all of the times you have disagreed with me, why are you encouraging me?"

Krystal looked down to gather a response. "It's frustrating how many setbacks there have been, but we have made it and prevailed in the end—so far."

Patrick smiled.

"Plus, there really wasn't anyone else to help you."

Patrick felt much-needed inspiration for the first time in a long time. He now wanted to get out and see all of the supposed things he had accomplished. He pushed through all the trouble and against thoughts of what could go wrong, and he got up. He shuffled his tired yet motivated body and toward the prison cell door, where he began to crack down the code to set him and Krystal free.

The door's mechanics differed from those of the Apple plant. The hinges were longer and swung open and closed horizontally. There were thirteen bars lined three inches apart, just enough room to sneak a hand through but nothing else.

He had the mind and power within to get this door unlocked, but he didn't know exactly how. With the modern technology of

2050, he could easily slice the bars right through and push his way out. But this was 2001.

Plus, he couldn't make much noise. Security guards stood at every corner on every level.

There was a drought of ideas in his already deserted mind. He couldn't find any key that might unlock it, and when he got thrown into the cell with Krystal, everything moved too fast to notice how the door locked in permanent place.

He peered over to the left. Krystal waited in the back. He soon found the convoluted, double-jointed lock in the middle of the concrete wall. It wasn't like any other lock he had imagined. There was no simple digital read-out, and it wasn't like any bicycle lock. It was complicated, like five different keys stitched together to form one bigger lock. And the key for it couldn't be bought or molded anywhere.

This key was in the security officer's pocket—Officer Zhang Wei—but he had to get out to retrieve it.

Patrick pondered for a bit, and Krystal waited a tad longer. He was looking for a way to just get it unlocked. He had absolutely nothing to use as a tool. Patrick once again hit a lull in terms of gaining traction on a slippery surface. He was zoning out, staring out at the bars of empty prison cells, looking for answer, yet the text in bright red above every cell was in Chinese.

"Do you know of anything we have around here," Patrick asked Krystal, not looking in her direction, "that could have a chance of unlocking this door?"

Krystal looked around, as if trying to pull an answer out of the air. She couldn't get one.

"Come on—the sky isn't falling!" Patrick exclaimed. *Yet.*

He continued developing something on his own. He analyzed every corner possible, every single centimeter, as he was just so desperate to find something to get them out.

In previous times, he would have been out of hope, but he felt more motivated than ever because of Krystal's help and what was at stake in the future.

He remembered once again that he got power into his machine from a river in 401 BCE.

He thought he could manage.

Thoughts were attempting to find him. Patrick kept desperately looking for anything to break the code that would let him and Krystal out—the code that would let both of them know what their actions had led to and what their future held. The future of the present.

He leaned against the cell bars and looked under the bed for anything that could break the cell open. He found nothing, but then the solution came right to him.

The bar broke under his weight. As he fell, he stretched out his arm to brace himself. He was a little surprised but then smiled. He went over to the lock, swung his left arm, gaining a little momentum, and hit the expensive-looking lock. It broke with an instant strike of Patrick's hand, and the door creaked open, sliding toward the right.

Patrick was delighted by how weak the lock was. It was Chinese, after all.

"Krystal," Patrick said with a grin, "let's get the hell out of Shanghai." He slowly slid the door open further, just enough wide to allow Krystal and him to pass through, and they slowly tiptoed out of the cell to the surprise of other inmates. As they did, they began to devise a second plan—a plan to get back to the time machine.

Chapter 16

Within a deserted plain and a deserted street filled with old trash and old belongings, Richard ran toward the only light that remained within the entire city of Milwaukee.

Jim and Jen were walking down Fourth Street, emotionless. Richard had no idea what they were gunning for. All he heard were the vociferous screams of those paralyzed with fear.

Richard had fear too. So did Jim and Jen. Yet all three were silent. All three were worried, yet none of them called for help.

Richard also was a little frustrated. "You guys!" he called as he caught up to the bewildered Jim and Jen, who turned around in surprise.

"Oh," Jen said, somewhat shocked to see him. "You've finally come back to us."

"How was it to stay in the tower?" Jim sniped. "Heard it was the first building to shut off."

Richard rolled his eyes, as he'd been the head of that business on the lakefront, but he had a lot more pressing matters to address now. "Whatever—that doesn't matter," Richard said. "I have a feeling what caused all of this disaster."

The sky still was dark gray, and there was no activity to be found above—no birds, no planes. Only the calls of those on the ground were heard.

And the supposed desire of Jim and Jen lingered as well.

"You, out of everyone, think you know what happened?" Jim asked.

"We'll listen," Jen said, "for now. Be quick; time is dwindling, obviously."

Richard collected a final idea to propose in the midst of all the silent chaos. Jim and Jen looked on, even as they looked ahead into the distant permanent darkness.

"Patrick Shields. It's his fault," Clark said.

"Oh, dear God, of course it is," Jen replied within a moment, her eyes widening.

Jim, sitting silent and bewildered, finally said, "I don't think one single person could cause this magnitude of damage to seemingly all of society."

Richard considered that thought but then persisted. "I can't believe I'm saying this—or that I'd ever say it—but do you know how much power he had? With the machine and shit?"

"I guess," Jen concluded, "though I refuse to believe he caused this. Maybe—dare I say—he was right?"

"Richard, Richard," Jim said. "Go on."

Richard took a deep breath and continued forward—or somewhere. "Okay, he literally had to use his time machine to get back in time, right?"

Jim and Jen agreed.

"Well, his idea was to slow down technology, or destroy technology, or whatever bullshit he came up with. He didn't do that. He never did that, thank God."

"So?" Jim asked.

"What he did was completely the opposite. It seems that he actually pushed technology faster. Normally, I'd be delighted to hear those words. But no, he pushed the future so damn hard that the fuses and servers and clouds of the digital spectrum couldn't take it."

Jim and Jen stared at Richard; they were all eyes and ears but had no words.

"I remember him saying that he was afraid of a major crash," Jim said.

"That was his biggest fear," Richard agreed. "The fear of falling apart. The fear of the death of digital life—of society itself. Except in the end, he is the one who caused it."

Jen's jaw dropped. Jim's arms relaxed. Richard crossed his; he knew he was on to something.

"I think you might damn well be right," Jen said. "It sounds possible. Very possible. We just don't know for sure."

"We may never know," Jim came in. "We may never—"

"But we do know for sure," Richard interrupted. "At least I think so. In the end, who could dream this up? Who could possibly want to do this to us? To prove a point in such a diabolical way? To end society as we know it? To rid us of all the resources we had?"

Jim looked at Richard. "It could only be that son of a bastard, the one who wanted to rid us of all that we had going for us."

"And he did," Richard said.

The screams had faded ever so slightly as the crowds shifted to the south. Richard, Jim, and Jen also had moved farther down Fourth, whether intentional or not.

The first feeling—of the loss of hope for society in general—had sunk in, even if it had only existed for an hour. But this newfound feeling was more profound than the first. It was strange. And it was very, very angering.

The anger was that the man who wanted the end of it all had gotten his very wish. Regardless of whether it was how he'd exactly wanted it, he got it. And it was to the suffering and apparent eventual death of all those left behind.

Or forward.

Although nothing was proven, Jim, Jen, and Richard knew

damn well they had busted their britches enough, and there was nothing they could do to save this situation. Being digital, no pieces could be picked up and pressed together again. The damage and process of damage formed was finished.

And society was as well.

Richard joined Jim and Jen as they slowly walked forward into the former Fourth Street, a current black hole depicting what had just happened. It didn't matter if it was a simple mental image or a picturesque illusion resembling something dark; it was real.

Reality had crushed every soul who had lived or who began to stop living below the sky. Richard now knew the complete cause of it. He'd thought of it, yes, but now he knew for sure. He knew no one else would have done this. He knew no one else could.

He knew now.

But like forty-nine years ago, at what cost?

If life was but a dream, then those dreams talked of nothing. The hope was gone. The dreams were shot. The cord was cut.

And Richard was angry.

"Thanks for the tip, Richard," Jim said with a touch of sarcasm. "I guess it's good to know what caused this devastation."

"But at what cost?" Jen asked. "What point is there in knowing who caused the situation if there's no solution in sight?"

Richard contemplated her words.

"It may be better to not worry about who caused this in the end. We can't stress—there's no reason for the stress," Jim suggested.

Richard thought about it for a minute. Yes, he had concluded who was behind it all, but why, exactly?

"You know him, being his confident little self," Richard said. "He probably thinks what he did was right. He most likely thinks all the tech is gone."

"Well, it is," Jen said.

"But not like this. Not like his own little heaven he dreamed of. This is what he feared."

"Then are we not to agree that he was right?" Jim asked, squinting at the thought. "He had a feeling this was bound to happen. He wasn't exactly wrong."

"You think this is the time to agree with that devilish fraud?" Jen asked, with anger rising like steam off a lake.

"It doesn't matter whether this was going to happen or not," Richard said firmly, yet sadly. "He may come back to see his 'amazing' results."

"What?" Jim and Jen said in unison.

"He may drag his ass back to the present. Did you think he would just migrate back to 2002 or whatever and stay there?"

"Well, it's come to my attention that he hates the present," Jim said.

"Don't ask me about the decisions he makes. I will never have an answer." Richard held his head in agony.

Jim wondered what would happen next. So did the other two. They decided to head back to the commons.

A pit of darkness covering the block of Fourth got darker as they headed farther south. To the right, the convention center was as empty as a city block in Detroit. To the left, the former Wisconsin Hotel had one light remaining, lighting an alleyway to the north of it, just enough to show the old cobblestone walkway and the protruding darkness ahead.

Soon enough, even after gazing at all the life and the vibe that was lost and forgotten in downtown, the three—the only three who remained outside—turned the corner.

As soon as they reached Wisconsin Avenue, they saw it was just a shell of its former 'Grand Avenue' name. The white masonry buildings had turned a pitched black. The gray street was darker than ever. Any cars left were only parked.

A corpse of a dead street was all that remained.

The shell's skin was peeling off the exterior. All had looked the same, yet everything was drastically changing. Life was nothing but a dream at this point, but the people who were hiding talked of nothing, it seemed.

The air had a crisp, sharp punch and wit to it, and the thoughts of its mind blew in and out of broken windows. The punch had faded into and out of the waters of the river and the lake. It was dense, confined, and innocuous, yet Richard, Jim, and Jen all knew that it was evil. It was blowing in doubt and concealing the signs of hope that had any chance of coming forward.

In a daze, within a shadow, within a look, they slowly moved forward. Soon, they were crossing a dated, rickety lift bridge that used to carry daily traffic over the Milwaukee River.

The water was a misty greenish-gray. The water stood still. It wouldn't move for a single damn second.

Yet without these movements, it would conduct an evil choir that played its never-ending music directly into the ears of all those who could still hear.

Whether wanting to or not, Richard had bought tickets to the front row. He didn't think the Trans-Siberian Orchestra was coming this December anyway.

"Are we heading back to the Northwestern Mutual Commons Tower?" Jen asked, breaking the silence.

"Yes, indeed," Jim answered. "As to why, I don't know."

"We're making a decision," Richard said, giving way to the former question. "The last business decision we will make. Possibly ever."

They walked past deserted Water Street, a paused city hall clock, a silent city hall bell. Soon after, at the top of the hill where they saw the lakeshore once again, they found a lonely bench in the midst of the commons gardens.

All of the benches were empty. A simple Starbucks cup remained on one, perched sideways.

Richard, Jim, and Jen reached the bench. They sat and rested

there, as well as laying out some ideas. As to what, they had yet
to find out.

"What is the purpose of knowing that he did this?" Jim asked.

"He is coming back," Richard insisted.

"We need to serve him justice."

Richard took a seat on the bench, made of elder wood and
finished in metal. Jim and Jen took the two remaining spaces.

The silent prosecution began.

"All right," Richard said, "what Patrick Shields did to our
earth, in simple terms, is completely unprecedented. It is simply
notorious."

"We know that," Jim said.

"I'm simply emphasizing the danger of the situation," Richard
explained. "We can't go on and simply die of no food, water, or
viable resources, without our last deed being to serve justice."

"We have to, and I agree," Jen chimed in. "This is—most
likely—the very end. We can't go out and not let him know that
this diabolic action has a godforsaken consequence."

Jen nodded. Richard did as well. The second level was reached.
What remained was the justice itself.

"This is *and always will be* the worst crime in all of modern
history," Jim said. "What should we do?"

"I don't know what will happen to him," Richard replied. "But
whatever it may be, it most likely should result in his death."

Jen had an idea—or more of a criticism. "Thing is, whoever
resides here now eventually will pass away. It would be redundant
to kill him off like that. Something else may need to—"

"Another thing is," Richard interrupted, "is that he can't go
out like the rest of us. He has to go out with a bang. He must die
with fierce pain, as terrible as it sounds."

"Look in the mirror, in the other direction," Jim suggested.
"Everything he has done is leading to the complete, irreversible
collapse of society as we know it. Look around. Look how damn

dark and black it is. Everywhere. None of this would have happened, regardless if he was correct about the imminence of this or not, but we can't go out without his ass being served what it needs."

Richard agreed. Jen did as well.

They began to contemplate a plan again.

Looking around and observing every corner of downtown, they realized the actual significance of the change that had happened within hours was extremely drastic. There was no light on any street or within any building.

And there was no light within anyone's soul.

All that light that once was there had since dissipated, faded into nothing. The light that remained had shut itself off, waiting the inevitable death, before the gravity of the situation sucked it out of the hearts of every living human left on the planet.

All of Wisconsin Avenue was dark. All of Prospect Avenue was dark. All of the tower was dark.

All of Milwaukee was dark.

The year 2050 was dark.

But wasn't it always?

Not to Richard. Not to Jim or Jen. Not to most of society.

But hell yes for Patrick.

All that Patrick had foreseen for ten years into the future had happened. The complete death of society. The complete collapse of Earth. It was there. In its absolute darkest yet purest form.

The game had failed. The game they were all forced to play.

Perhaps they could play it right next time.

Richard didn't want any notes to hit him, but the line, "Look how damn dark it is" really resonated with him.

A link was forming. Just a simple link.

"The darkness reminds me of something." Richard broke the silence. "My dad Calhoun would always say it was dark in that courthouse. Always doing business pleas and logistics in that courthouse."

"This whole thing has reminded you of the county courthouse?" Jim asked, confused.

"Well, yes," Richard replied. "I'm getting to something."

Jim waited, and Jen lifted her head to direct her eyes to Richard.

"Inside that courthouse, he told me about a room," Richard continued. "A room locked off from everyone, even the jury or judge."

"Okay, and …?" Jen asked impatiently.

"Jesus, let me think for a damn second." Richard held his head in his hands. He was searching for the lost memory with his eyes shut. "Inside that room … what was guarded off, I think, was an electric chair."

Jim's eyes opened wide. Jen's eyes squinted at the thought.

"It was only used when the very worst crimes were committed. They were so damn horrible that only death was a serviceable punishment and that it was only imminent for the criminals themselves." Richard then gained the slightest bit of confidence. His eyes gleamed; his voice lowered. "Just like the crime Patrick Shields committed."

Jen's eyes grew wide, as Jim's remained opened. Eyebrows were raised; jaws dropped.

They might now know what justice must be served.

"If I do indeed remember this correctly," Richard said to be sure, "then I think it would be best to serve justice with that damn electric chair."

"This honestly may be the best idea," Jen agreed. "He can't go on and die like the rest of us, like we said before. He needs to go out with a shock."

"Good one," Jim added. "I also agree. There's really not much else left that we can manage."

"The world is most likely coming to an end," Richard said. "This is the last bit of satisfaction we can pull out of this misery. And it's knowing that we did the right thing, finally. After all this prolonged time."

The solution was settled, and the prosecution had ended.

All that remained was to wait for Patrick Shields.

"Hey, Jim, Jen," Richard called. "Do one last favor for me."

"And what would that be?" Jen inquired.

"Head to that military base along Sixth and Brown," Richard commanded. "We may need some stuff from that outlet. Stuff that actually works."

It came to their attention that independent servers would be ideal for the technology of the present, but as nothing can get out black holes, there was absolutely no looking back at this point.

Jim and Jen collected themselves and whatever belongings remained with them.

They proceeded down the gray sidewalk that twisted and wound through dead plants and trees, and they made their way to the dark black canyon formally known as Wisconsin Avenue.

The sky had closed in upon the city and everyone's mind. The sky had grown darker, much like everyone's mind. Everyone was hiding in the closeness, yet all remained in isolation. The scene was dark. It was a whirlwind of mesmerizing power of evil, and the heretics of hope had crashed through and ended the potential that remained inside their hearts and beyond their minds. Nothing had remained the same. Everything was different, and it was all for the worse at the expense of the death of all who still wished to live.

One thing had remained constant, though, through all the trouble.

Richard sat on that bench outside his dead commons and the Mutual Commons Tower. He was alone, staring into the black sky; whatever lay ahead in his shortened life looked exactly like that.

He was silent; the frustration had settled in entirely. He might be out of hope, but he was hoping for just one more thing—and one more unusual thing at that.

"Dear God, whatever may happen," Richard said, looking above, "let that man, Patrick Shields, come back to the present."

And chaos would ensue.

Silent chaos.

CHAPTER 17

The rising sun exposed all things visible throughout Shanghai. It reflected from building to building, street to street, in bright pink and orange. Activity throughout downtown had reached its pinnacle for morning hours already, and this meant a tight escape for Patrick—security for the jail cell was also at its peak.

Three Chinese policemen, dressed in olive green, rushed right behind.

"Find a vehicle, bicycle, anything at all!" Patrick shouted, as Krystal ran in front.

Nothing of this silent escape for Patrick and Krystal had gone right. After all, the time machine was directed toward the left.

"In front of the cell is a parking lot full of cars," Krystal said, pointing to the right.

Both turned to the right, hoping to dodge the three policemen. But of course, neither group would stop running.

"I believe I see a McLaren right over there," Patrick said nervously. "I've heard McLarens have manual driving modes. An autonomous car would be useless right now." Both swept through a puddle, around broken concrete, and past a maroon dumpster, where the yellow McLaren sat around the corner in a damaged parking lot. It stood out as more general vehicles surrounded it.

They ran to the supercar without saying anything, slid up the scissor door, and scrambled inside.

The cabin instantly spelled "speed" in Patrick's eyes. They shut the doors loudly, and Patrick pressed the ignition. A loud rumble suddenly burst out of the rear end and even more so behind Patrick's and Krystal's heads.

Patrick then put the supercar in reverse, then neutral, and backed out of the parking lot. Much more aggressively, he threw it into first and accelerated out of the lot with a snarl from the engine. Only a slip of a wheel spin was let out the rear.

The Chinese police had only managed to reach the lot. "They're gone," Zhang Wei said, a bit shocked, pointing to the multilane highway that ran slightly uphill to the east. "But hopefully not for long."

Next to him, another replied in a stern tone, "Hopefully, he'll have no chance with a bit of backup."

Meanwhile, Patrick and Krystal were rushing down the ten-lane highway, moving so fast it seemed like the city's skyscrapers were multiplying, following the same road in a straight line.

"We left the time machine at the city custody, which …" Patrick continued shifting a gear, but suddenly, he couldn't finish his sentence.

"Which … what?" Krystal asked.

Patrick paused for a moment, as the roaring V12 engine shook the bucket seats. "I don't remember where the custody area is."

"Are you kidding me?" she asked, getting angry. "After all of the time travel, the escaping from prison, and avoiding every single godforsaken witness we've stumbled across, it greatly worries me that you don't know where the silly custody area is."

"We got carried in a blacked-out, windowless prison transport truck. If I could have seen out, I would remember where it is, obviously."

Patrick then noticed he was approaching a red stoplight to the west, which was both a mountain of a problem and a mountain of red in his eyes.

In the end, Patrick decided to simply stop at the red light, where traffic was closing into a dense, compact zone of noise and exhaust fumes.

Neither of them spoke a word; both just sat inside the cabin in silence. The atmosphere was dark and tense, especially when screeching sirens came from behind.

Luckily, the light with cross traffic wasn't a long one. A green light in Patrick's face spelled the green light to escape. The supercar screeched out on the street past numerous bicycles and other cars. With a throw of two gears and a gas pedal skimming the concrete, that supercar was gone and was out of sight, out of mind to the other drivers.

Krystal, with a movement of 0.5 g-forces churning within her chest, decided to glance out the tight rear window to see if there were any signs of police creeping up out back.

"It appears that another red light has stopped the police vehicles—"

Before she could finish, three police vehicles turned right to them, and one other—a prison truck—drove straight. That prison truck turned its sirens off.

"We better hurry up and find the contraption," Krystal said, a little more calmly than before. "The police aren't off our back just yet."

Patrick thought about that for a moment as he put the car into top gear.

"It's a time machine," Patrick replied in a stern yet calm voice. "It should easily stand out."

Down the winding road they went, as it continued to gain more car lanes, more bicycle lanes, more concrete to traverse atop. A spider web of buildings and streets that included loops and turns and splattered white paint were conjoined by one screaming supercar on a distant chase to the other side of the city. The other side of jail. The other side of survival.

Patrick decided to point the sharp car's nose to the west, as he had spotted the sun going down when arrested. He hoped the time machine would show along the side of the major highway they were traveling on.

"No signs of any police on the back stretch," Krystal said, looking at the ten empty lanes.

"The time machine should be on a grassy hill," Patrick explained, considerably slowing down and starting to look around. "I'm getting more of a presence of where it was. I don't think it was in the custody at all."

Normally, this field would hide nothing, with its golden-brown wildflowers, grass stalks, and abundant insects. A casual field—no harm, no foul. The bare eye wouldn't see a time machine inside it, but maybe someone would. Patrick would.

"Oh, thank God," Patrick said, breathing heavily. "There it is!"

"Great," Krystal replied, out of breath as well. Patrick threw the vehicle into neutral, and coasted to the other side of the road, where he parked it.

They slid up the scissor doors and ran across the four lanes and three white stripes, leaving the doors open.

Across the highway, the machine was in a respectable condition; the existing dents and scratches were the only damage. The contraption was surrounded by more stalks of grass and purple flowers and sat atop a slightly sloped hill, which led from the city to the Pacific.

"I absolutely cannot believe it is still here!" Patrick shouted, holding his hands out in shock. "It's still here!"

Patrick traced circles around the device, as Krystal determined that the police weren't out of sight just yet. She suddenly heard sirens, coming from down and up the road. The time between plausible time travel and an arrest was inching closer and closer.

"I hear police sirens, Patrick!" Krystal said. "We'd better head on back pretty soon—"

"Where's the generator?" Patrick interrupted.

"What?"

"Where's the generator?"

"I don't know!" she shouted back.

"Well, great. There's is no longer anything to power this now."

Sirens began to get even closer, so near, in fact, that for Krystal, survival became second nature.

"It's in that one office building."

"The office building?" Patrick repeated.

"The one we set foot into before we were arrested."

"You sure?"

"Positive."

"Let's go back," he said, now increasingly determined.

They ran across the field and road, where they'd left the time machine.

"Do we want to leave the machine here?" she asked, so scared that she ended up calm.

"Yes, we do," Patrick insisted, throwing himself into the golden-yellow McLaren. "They will be so distracted by our running that if they see it at all, they will leave it."

Krystal then jumped to the other side, and both shut the scissor doors. Patrick turned the car on.

The power steering tugged the car out of the field, reversed it, and then pointed it back toward Shanghai.

As one squad car suddenly came storming over the treeless crest, the McLaren, at a much slower speed, was still steadily getting its nose forward. That steadiness was broken when the squad car hit the McLaren in the rear end, shattering a taillight. The cop inside was much too distracted to even see the machine out of the corner of his eye.

Patrick was much too distracted as well. He didn't have to spy out his rearview mirror; he already picked up the signal. With a squad car trailing right behind, he punched the gas to the ground with all of the might left inside his weary body, kicking up dirt and dust, kicking up the RPMs to the limit.

The sky then turned to pink as the skyline went from gray to black and white. Patrick, the squad car, and eventually three police vehicles followed down the hill and deep down on a river of pavement into Shanghai.

One more vehicle had yet to reach the crest—the blacked-out, stealthy prison transport truck, with its numerous badges either blacked out or covered up.

Once it reached that crest, the truck traveled considerably slower than the rest of the police vehicles. By those means, the driver could see the time machine and possibly give a crap about it.

Consequently, the man driving it did see it. He slowed the truck down and parked it on the side of the road, opposite to Patrick's. He then turned it off.

At first glance, he had already lost all words and was in a complete state of shock. He opened the truck door and then wandered out aimlessly, with wide eyes and a gaping maw, like a child in a cornfield. But a destination was just ahead. And it stood before him like an abandoned home on Halloween evening. The glaring sun produced a shadow on the opposite side from where he was looking—a tall, lengthy shadow, which highlighted it even more so.

He eventually stood by it, the dazing and confusing machine.

And dazed and confused he was.

Sometimes, in a feeling of shock, words simply don't cut it. All this humble Chinese man could let out was a simple *wow*, for the sake of it.

The man then continued to silently wander about, solemnly taking in that he was touching—a time machine—like an ancient explorer finding his new settlement. He was the explorer.

The time machine felt both smooth and rough in some areas, at least on the exterior, almost a perforated aluminum. There were no windows, just a simple door on the other side, leading to the inside of this machine.

The man curiously and, eventually, carefully set foot into the time machine. It was one small step from out to in, but one giant leap for the man's mind. He couldn't bear to comprehend that he was inside something from the science fiction bookshelf.

On the inside, the shock only got more intense. There were no signs of convoluted buttons; he saw only a few. His reaction almost exactly duplicated Krystal's, but it being 2001 influenced his reaction more.

Instead of buttons were two square feet of glass and wires— simply put, a touchscreen. The man, who was already stressed and excited, decided not to mess with any of the controls. He assumed he wouldn't be able to figure it out anyway.

Suddenly, he heard a crunch on the floor. At first he thought he'd crushed the floorboards and was hesitant to look down. He was relieved to find no damage to it, but, interestingly, a small white paper with ink blots was attached to his shoe. He peeled it off and saw that it was a letter written in English cursive. Consequently, the Chinese man was unable to sort it out. Oddly enough, he could understand English, but he couldn't speak or read it.

He didn't know what to do with the letter. If it was anything important, he would have to translate it. The only people he knew who could speak English were the criminals he was chasing.

This led to second thoughts. Gigantic second thoughts.

Nevertheless, he remained undecided. So he crumpled up the note and stuck it in his black dress pants pocket. After doing so, he abruptly decided that his experience with the time machine wasn't getting him anywhere.

I have two criminals to find, he thought. *But those two couldn't necessarily be criminals.*

In the end, he walked back to the police prison-transport truck, jumped in, shut the door, and turned on the ignition. While doing so, he examined his thoughts, one specifically and maybe a few others. What if those two weren't criminals? What if they were just misunderstood heroes? If not, what if *he* could become the hero?

But he didn't want to overthink it, so he kept driving.

Chapter 18

The chase ran on, now deep within Shanghai. Lights abound giving each building a big bow of its own, implying it was as great as the next biggest. It created a bubble of light, more so a shield, that rivaled the stars in the night sky. Then again, it was shunned by constant stop-and-go traffic on the wide, long spider web of highways. And then soon, that was shunned by four sets of sirens. And a V12 within a supercar.

A convoluted three-loop ring designed for traffic flow was empty at 10:00 p.m., Christmas Eve. But one car made equally as much noise as any congestion would. One car came soaring around it soon enough.

The McLaren, which Patrick decided not to slow down for the gigantic spring-shaped circle of concrete meshed with steel. Even though he was already ahead far enough of the four police vehicles, he insisted to take the mess of a highway flat out.

Krystal felt a stream of nauseating nervousness travel up her spine, as a slight slope for the loop pushed the car up forty degrees suddenly. Patrick also felt the same trickle within his body, but he overcame it with the perturbing goal in mind—find that generator.

The ramp induced a general increase in elevation for the road, with three white lanes open. He would use all three. The supercar reached the triple-decker left turn, braking as hard as it could down to eighty miles per hour, where its handling limits would be tested.

The three-hundred–wide profile tires could barely handle the excessive speed and pulled to the opposite direction, tugging the steering wheel into an oversteer. Nor could the white-purple HID Xenon headlights, which moved and turned about so quickly that Patrick and Krystal could barely see the walls of it—the borders of life and death. Both could only pray not to crash.

With Patrick turning to the left harder than he desired, he kept the accelerator floored to balance out the effect. With hope being the only underpinning—and possibly the only underpinning to the Backwards Era project literally around the corner—Patrick bravely shifted down two more gears to second and stayed at seventy for the rest of the corner.

Then, five-hundred–plus torque shot the supercar out of the ring, almost like a bow and arrow, in which the supercar was drop dead that.

With a shout and a scream, the supercar ran across the decorative red bridge, but it was all under control, so it seemed like a walk in the park for the car. That bridge shot across the Huangpu River, which gleamed with ripples of black mixed with white from the moon. It made a revolving calm scene with a quite hectic one. The supercar was now on the other side of Shanghai, where the skyscrapers dissipated slightly but not enough to not call it downtown. That one office building in the search was smuggled in there somewhere—the needle in the haystack.

The bridge came to an end, as Patrick saw the convoluted loop was just starting for the police. A behemoth of a red eye then came before Patrick and proclaimed the car should stop. It loomed over them like a big red sore, putting pressure on his already boiling-over mind.

He dismissed it.

Shooting by at more than 130 miles per hour, the red eye went away instantly. His speed increased, as the elevation was flat, and the cops were nowhere in sight. The journey became almost boring.

But that idea was shut down as a screaming siren scorched the valleys of Shanghai. Patrick was suddenly scared to death once again. He then became desperate.

"Do you have any idea what that building looked like?" Patrick asked. "I have an uneasy feeling that there are now more police cars than we thought."

"It was curved at the bottom and sort of traveled up around the corner," Krystal said, describing the building over the hum of the V12 engine. "With all of the pressure of getting out of jail, I completely forgot the rest."

Patrick took it as no joke and squinted hard at each building. They were covered in the black night sky with only a glint of a reflection off the glass as they passed. In Shanghai at night, all of the buildings fit the same description.

"The hell …" Patrick said, shifting his eyes back to the road. "They all look the same."

"You know I can't help that," Krystal replied quietly.

"I will try to spot the generator," Patrick suggested. "You look out along the road for me."

"Fair enough," she agreed.

Patrick scouted the surrounding area, staring into each building. He slowed down considerably, taking churning levels of gravitational force into his mid-body. The McLaren was now coasting at a steady forty miles per hour, which seemed like almost nothing after the nauseating sprint they had just made. Krystal couldn't find anything ahead. It was all steel and pavement in a big black hole.

"Keep looking," Krystal shouted, looking directly at him.

"Wait! I see something very peculiar inside that building! It appears to be shaped like a generator!"

"Are you sure?" Krystal replied. "If it's anything, it will probably be an air conditioner." Patrick considered that for a moment and replied.

"I am not taking any chances."

He slowed the car down to a crawl. The shadowed object was to the right. Patrick pulled into the right lane and then into the dimly lit alleyway in between.

The dark hole of an alley was almost completely black, the only light being the light coming out of the back of it. Who knew what this alley secretly hid? Perhaps another police car?

The object suddenly flashed its halogens, which absolutely scared the crap out of both, as they sat right before it. Then, the lights were turned off. The right door opened up, revealing a taller shadow than the ones already around it. That shadow then moved closer and then suddenly turned to the left, approaching Patrick's side of the car, slowly but surely.

Without speaking, he indicated Patrick should open his scissor door.

Patrick knew he should, but he wanted to escape. He would have instantly reversed and found another hiding spot or an alley of some sort nearby. But he couldn't, as a police-vehicle–shaped shadow was closing off the alley from the street.

Patrick had a burst of shock explode within his stomach—a negative feeling. What would he do now?

The policeman knocked on the front window—hard.

Patrick had no certainty of anything. Would he escape and grab that generator? Or would he finally accept his fate and end this masterful journey abruptly?

"Come on!" Krystal nervously shouted. "Again, after all of this … there must be a solution hidden in there somewhere. God forbid none!"

That's when Patrick snapped. He suddenly threw the HIDs on, put the gears into drive, and literally smashed into the front of the police car before him. The man backed up in deliberate shock, illuminating his body.

Then he smashed the gas pedal into the floor—hard. The tires in the rear started to spin, all the way to maximum RPMs once again, even exceeding that. Gravel and dirt were thrown into the side of the police car. Glowing red lights and smoke from the quad exhaust tips created an intimidating scene for the man waiting inside.

Patrick was trying something that scared and confused Krystal; he pushed the front car out of the way with the might of a McLaren supercar. Krystal at first thought it was impossible—a car pushing another three thousand pounds of steel.

But when you have 640 horsepower on tap, and the man forgot to pull up the hand brake inside the police vehicle, Patrick could surprisingly manage.

The car was forcefully pushed outward to the other side of the alley and slid out into the neighboring street with ease. This meant Patrick could guide the McLaren into another entrance into the office building.

Flooring the car once again, he led it to an entrance ramp on the other face of the building, where a door seemed like a gateway to freedom for them. It was, really. He looked at the men behind them, chasing them, running.

Patrick stopped the car and left the engine running. They both swooped up the doors, burst out, and ran to the glass door, where they planned to escape inside the office building. Unfortunately, the door was locked.

Patrick looked back as the two policemen who were sprinting hard in their direction.

"Damn, they're close!" Patrick exclaimed, desperate. "Unscrew the door—do something!"

Krystal had no screwdriver on hand, and she couldn't really

kick down the locked door. But one element focused on form over function—glass.

The McLaren had picked up rocks from the damaged asphalt when it had spun its wheels. Consequently, loose rocks lay all over the area. Patrick thought fast, snatched a rock from the ground, and threw it at the window.

He cringed at the result, but he had to look, knowing they had around ten seconds left to get that generator. Luckily, a crack appeared in the center of the glass door. That would be just enough for Patrick to break into the building.

With a big *boom* and cracks of shattering glass, Patrick and Krystal bolted into the building, leading bits of glass into the building. They slipped across the tile with uncertainty of where that generator was located.

Patrick regained his breath and stopped running. Looking forward into the dark area, a shadow sat with an object hidden underneath. He approached very slowly but was champing at the bit to find out. That shadow and object got bigger until he finally saw that it had two wires; it was cylinder shaped, had gauges on it, and was finished in aluminum. To the untrained eye, it looked like a vacuum cleaner. But Patrick knew it was the generator.

"Oh, thank God!" Patrick shouted, out of breath. "It's here!"

At that moment, Krystal pointed out two men in the back of the building.

"You," a police officer said; he was holding a long gun in his hand. "The run is over."

The other officer then pulled out the same machinery. Patrick and Krystal consequently surrendered immediately. As they did, a big black truck came zipping by, with a big black flash in the background.

"You're kidding me," Krystal said, looking directly at Patrick. "This is it, eh?"

Patrick didn't respond.

"We are surrounded by two policemen, about to shoot; there is no outlet out of here, and there is no one to rescue us," Krystal complained.

Patrick still didn't say anything. He let go of the generator, setting it down. He didn't know what to do. He'd used the last bit of ideas he had. He didn't know what to do because he thought there wasn't anything to do. He thought it was time to face the music and consider his plan kaput.

The big police truck then came flying through the alley and stopped hard, spitting brake dust in all directions. The short Chinese man came out of the truck and headed directly to the crime scene in a fast-paced matter. Patrick thought this was where he would end up in a matter of seconds.

He didn't think hard enough.

The man shouted something in Chinese as he held onto the window, out of breath.

"What's he saying?" Krystal asked.

"He is shouting *stop* for some reason," replied Zhang, a little unsure. "Why would he say something like that?"

That man, named Bo, couldn't understand what he was saying, so he took a pencil from his pocket, as well as the note he'd found. He scribbled a message on the back of it and gave it to Patrick.

"It says that we are not criminals," Patrick said, handing it to Krystal.

"They aren't?" Zhang Wei asked. "How would anyone, especially you, know that?"

Bo snatched the piece of paper and wrote on it some more.

"We are supposed to be arresting these people," Zhang Wei said.

Bo finished writing and handed the note to Krystal.

"It says, 'I saw the machine,'" Patrick read over Krystal's shoulder. "It appears that these spirits are more ingenious than we think."

"I think he's starting to get it," Krystal said. "That is absolutely correct. We are not criminals."

"But what about all the things that made us think you were doing wrong?" Zhang asked.

"I'll give him the gist of it," Patrick whispered to Krystal. He walked up to Zhang. "Sometimes you need to destroy a little to gain a little. If you lived in 2050, you would understand."

"So you are coming from forty-nine years from now, eh?"

Patrick noted that this police officer was strangely taking this procedure calmer than he thought he would. "Yes. You see, all this upcoming technology has bubbled up way too much, and by 2060, it just might be the death of us. The people there think I am crazy. They think my plans are ludicrous. But they were brought up in a bad state, surrounded by all of what is known to be prosperous. Simply put, I was brought up differently."

"But dude, the machine—that this is absolutely astounding! The technology is incredible. Why don't you appreciate it?"

"Trust me; if you lived in 2050, you would understand. Maybe it's the people. But it's not figuring out why it's happening; it's figuring out how to stop it."

"What do you want me to do?"

Patrick shrugged and stuffed his hands in his pockets. "Let us go."

"What?" Krystal whispered, standing next to him.

"So we can let your children live."

"Are you honestly serious about the death of us and how ridiculous it will be?"

"Completely."

"Yes," Krystal said, backing up Patrick.

"If you are so confident—"

Krystal and Patrick rejoiced, hugging each other with absolute glee.

"But wait," Zhang continued. "Since you are here, when will it become so 'horrible'?"

"Oh, in like five years or so. You two better believe me."

Krystal and Patrick then collected themselves and walked back to the McLaren. Krystal got in, but Patrick only opened his door.

"And you two—you tell everyone you possibly can," he said.

"Would they not get upset at our opinions?" Zhang asked.

"Who gives a damn? I have been through more bullshit than you two will ever experience. Look, just tell everyone you can. People will listen. Then tell the country, then the entire planet. And in 2050, everything will be like it is right now in 2001—absolutely perfect. Just the right amount of technology and people."

Without a word from Zhang, Patrick picked up the generator, shut the door, lit the ignition, and then drove his way out of the alley. He floored the supercar away from the two Chinese men.

"What did that note say you were writing on?" Zhang Wei asked.

"Yes," Bo replied, translating the English. "It said something about killing the two people we just saw."

"Do you think it's okay that I put that note in their car?"

"Yes."

Zhang walked out of the building and back to the squad car. "I honestly don't know what to do with this time machine sighting. Do we believe the crazy guy, or take it for more info?" He looked aimlessly up at the sky as Bo walked up to him. "Eh, well, it's 2001," Zhang said. "We won't be living in 2050 anyhow. I'd love to experience that power now. Tell me everything you know about that time machine. What did it look like?"

CHAPTER 19

Patrick and Krystal drove out of Shanghai, leaving themselves alone within the city. An eerie feeling wrapped the borders of the downtown area. Every big gray building stood shining needles, pointing directly at the stars above.

But that situation was not important to either of them; after ancient Meroe, Rome, 1901 in New York, and running away from armies of police in China, they could finally get back to the year in question and see their results.

"I honestly can't believe it," Patrick said to Krystal, entering the bridge over the Huangpu River once again. "We made it through everything. And since we didn't do much, the two Chinese men can take of fixing the future."

"Are you really that sure about that?" Krystal asked. "They seemed to be in their mid-forties. They likely will be dead in 2050. They want to invest while they can—like you said, money over empathy."

After listening to Krystal, a more negative thought was unblocked, and before being consumed by a swirl of positive thinking, Patrick once again began to rethink his plan.

"Nobody is really that trustworthy, are they?" Patrick kept driving, as Krystal just watched the road. The city's skyline simply kept going, since Patrick decided to not break the speed limit again. "I have been through a lot in these past two days. It seems everyone wants to squeeze out their last bit of doubt they can on to me."

"Again, what do you expect?" Krystal asked. "What you want to do could kill off all the tech they know and love. It may be what you want but not what society wants."

"Maybe I am too smart for this society."

Krystal couldn't reply. Soon enough, they were out of downtown, as less and less building density gave way to a growing country and rolling, grassy hills. The time machine, they hoped, would be ahead on the shining brow of the prairie.

"You see, this plan has two paths. Both look the same at first. You don't know which one you are going down. But one has the man and the woman getting everything wrong, with an uncertain consequence. The other has the man and the woman getting everything right, with an uncertain consequence. The only way to find out which path you are going on is to see the solution at the end of it."

"Okay, now you sound very uncertain about what we did this week. You sounded so confident before. If you hate 2050 so much, why won't you stay here, where you just said everything was perfect?"

"Three reasons. I will still be alive forty-nine years from now and won't be able to help then. I don't want to run into myself when I am born in 2003. And I am not a selfish person. At least, I don't think so. I want everyone to see the light."

"A loophole, but I just keep questioning you because I am so afraid. You know, this is just one great big idea that I really don't understand, but I want to fix it."

"Let me get back to 2050—and you will see the other side. People will be screaming and shouting at me; they will be looking."

In the next ten minutes, the last bits of Shanghai were drained out behind Patrick and Krystal. The rolling hills and prairies then consumed the landscape entirely. The lonely machine should show up somewhere. Maybe. Hopefully.

Then, a big even-blacker-than-the-night shadow was in the distance. It was a fuzzy rectangular prism in the distance, but it got more streamlined as they got closer to it. Patrick and Krystal instantly knew it was the one and only time machine.

"And … there it is!" Patrick said, pointing it out. He pulled over the yellow McLaren to the side of the street, with minimal damage to the body. They swung up the doors for the last time and got out. Patrick swooped up the generator and ran across the road.

"Okay," Patrick said, relieved. "Let's get out of here." He ran into the machine, and Krystal followed shortly after.

"I am completely exhausted," Krystal said as Patrick set up the machine and generator. "I am probably incapable of time traveling right now."

"Honestly, I am too," Patrick replied. "But I am not going to wait another day and let another set of policemen find me."

The wires were in place. The generator was stable. The machine was then charged instantly to the point of enough power to get ahead forty-nine years. This guy and this gal and this machine were ready to finally see what they'd come up with.

Suddenly, Patrick hesitated before pressing the start button. With all of his confidence bubbling up, he completely stopped— and this was not to Krystal's liking.

"Um … what are you doing?" Krystal asked, beginning to get angry. "You have to see what you have done. You can't do this again."

Patrick didn't respond at first. Then he said, "What if the result is horrible? What if I caused more damage than society already had?"

"It's a time machine," Krystal replied. "You invented one. Amazing. More important, you had the courage to stand up against these people your entire life. What you have already done is good enough. Changing planet earth is another."

Patrick thought for a moment. He wanted to go back—very, extremely badly. He knew that what he had wanted to happen might have just done so. But this was without having light shed on the possibility of the very opposite—the opposite that he was paralyzed in fear about and always would be, until he finally knew for sure.

He decided to not have a choice.

"Fine, we'll go back."

Patrick unplugged the generator from the machine and brought it inside. Krystal walked in right after him.

She smiled at Patrick as he collected himself again.

He stood there in silence for a few seconds. Then he shrugged. Then he slammed that red start button.

> The man never said to mess with society
> The man also never said to not take a risk
> This man was just a lowly worker
> He was just sitting in a box
> Taped shut
> With no light let in
> He had his own imaginary world in there
> Enclosed from society
> But who could hide such a wonderful thing?
> He built an invention
> A machine out of Doctor Who
> Who was that doctor?
> Society asked
> The man who wanted to destroy it
> He went back in time, back in evolution
> To create a different evolution
> It was the ultimate game of Sudoku

He knew he was playing right
His solution could be wrong
And that last number would be filled in now

The last rumble played its tune. Patrick and Krystal could then see again. They could hear again. The last bit of shock had exited their bodies through the arms and legs. They were finally back in Milwaukee. In 2050.

***

"Oh, thank God it's over," I mumbled, holding my tired head. But I was in the year in question again. Christmas Day. Nighttime. One 2, one 5, and two zeros.

"Are we back?" Krystal asked, confused as well.

We stood up eventually, shaking the last bit of grief and intensity out of ourselves.

"Ready?" she asked, raising an eyebrow.

I looked at her, not with a confident silence but more a depressed silence.

I shrugged. "Sure."

I took two steps to the left. A window was carved into the side. It was for lightweight purposes at first, but now was something revealing to me.

I opened my eyes.

"What do you see?" Krystal asked. "Is it what you hoped? Is it more than what you hoped?"

I had a delayed reaction.

"Wow," I said quietly, without making direct eye contact with Krystal. "That is really all I want to say at the moment."

Outside, nothing much was there to be seen; for one, it was dark. But looking closer, I could find slightly more. I saw no street lights or lights from buildings along the Milwaukee skyline. I was then concerned. The only light was from an eerie glow of a fire in the distance and the moon in the northwestern corner, which poured its white light out of its shell like a waterfall that pours its water down to the ground.

I was shocked.

"What's out there?" Krystal asked, jumping to the window. She then peered out the window, taking in all of the visual information. "Oh, wow. There are no street lights on!"

"Let's go find out what the hell is going on," I said, running out of the machine with the swing of the door. Krystal followed, like the sidekick she was.

We stepped onto ground near Sixth and Brown, behind the apartment that I was stopped in on the twentieth of December.

No traffic was on any road, and there was no noise, except a slight tapping from behind. A ghost town. A ghost city. Krystal and I stood there like two new visitors to an extraterrestrial planet.

"There is no activity at all—"

Before I could finish, I was suddenly thrown to the concrete ground, face first, with a smash. Then, my vision turned black. I could easily assume I was then unconscious. I didn't know who knocked me out. I didn't know if Krystal was knocked out. And I didn't know where I was going. But I was soon to find out.

God Almighty, something is wrong.

December 25, 2050
3:00 a.m.

My vision regained. My hearing regained. I had no idea how long I was out cold. Thankfully, Krystal was by my side, and she had already gained consciousness.

"Where the heck are we?" I asked, shaking my head.

Then I heard a smug voice whisper, "You are on the top floor of the Northwestern Mutual Commons building. And now, you will face the … well, let's say *consequences* of your actions."

That voice sounded familiar. A deep sort of voice that liked to speak in interesting ways.

I eventually figured out who that guy in the shadows was. He often spoke in metaphors and riddles. And only he would hate my outlook on the world so much as to interrogate me like this.

Lo and behold, it was Richard Clark.

No room light was turned on, and no flashlight was flashed. A laptop with a diagram was not shown to me. Somehow, Clark lit a candle, and the flame gave away a previous time.

God, I was impressed. A candle! What fun. Did I really downgrade society all the way to the point of a candle again?

Clark then said, "You really have done it … this time." Richard directed the candle to the middle of the table. "How did you?"

"Are you that upset about all of the improvements I made?" I asked with a smirk.

"I think something's wrong here," Krystal whispered to me, leaning over.

"Is that the sickest thought you can come up with?" Clark shouted.

"Yeah, you're mad about the changes, clearly," I said, sort of looking indirectly at him.

Clark paced like an enraged animal, ready to fly out of the cage. He then tried to speak again, clamping his two hands on the desk. "Allow me to explain things a little bit," Richard said in an eerie tone. "With your … *changes*, you expect all the laptops and smart devices to be gone, right?"

Because he phrased it like that, I assumed it meant the laptops weren't gone.

"Why is it still here then?" He then shoved the laptop underneath the candle, where the fire and my face reflected off the screen.

Man, the irony.

"And … guess what? It does *not* turn on." He constantly clicked the power button to turn it on, but no result showed up. Things then started to go downhill for me. "The lights don't turn on. No lights turn on at all in the city! Also, not one autonomous car works. None of our sinks work. None of our electronics, tablets, appliances, or anything works. *Nothing works!*"

And a shock of turns and nauseating swerves hit me in the face with a loud pow. And in the stomach. An elevator of a chill, blended with heat at each tip, entered and exited the building of my body instantly.

"Oh, and along the way, your little virus code got leaked! And your friends were sent to literally blow up cities in China and the US!"

I had a bit of explaining to do. "How would the government-protected virus get leaked if I canceled that entire idea?" I asked.

"Because when technology was sped up by your fumbling plan, hacking was even easier, and we didn't have the time to advance to protect it, thus letting your little buddies get their hands on it, assuming *you* wanted them to."

I thought my plan would have worked. And I didn't want to make that virus. That was a backup plan. I didn't think to time travel while they were doing that. "And why did those bombs never explode? It would have been reported on … the … news." And now I realized that I was losing more traction every time I tried to gain it.

"We flew to each city, and got it on the news on time to the earth. You are officially convicted of mass murder and homicide."

Feeling a sudden rush of depression and failure, I realized that I shouldn't say anything more.

"Oh … Lord, my God!" Richard shouted. "I can't believe you at all!"

"What are you going to do with the time machine?" I asked quietly. "What are you going to do with me, more importantly?"

Clark, Jen, and Jim collaborated on the punishment for me. As I waited, I looked at Krystal for a split second. She had no response other than to look down at the ground in anger, arms crossed. It basically read, *you arse.*

"For you, dude?" Richard asked, looking back at me. "Oh. Nothing. He-he. You see, we won't lock you in a jail cell or give you the death penalty, like we wanted to. We will leave you here, in the dysfunctional world you hoped for. It's already your jail cell."

"Fine. I'll take it," I said, crossing my arms in confidence.

Krystal and Jim raised an eyebrow at that response. That got me thinking.

Jim stepped in. "About your time machine ... we decided to simply take it away from you."

There went my thinking.

Jen also stepped in. "You can't power it anyway. You took away the electricity! How ironic!"

I then got even more saddened at what had just slapped me in the face. Would this interrogation end here?

"I guess this conversation ... will end here!" Clark concluded, tapping his hands on the table. "Now, I think we will interrogate Krystal next. Patrick, get out of here. Get your sorry ass out of here. I can't believe what you have done to planet earth. We can't even access water or produce food. No more—the electronics are gone! This is, simply put, the first human mass extinction. No resources are accessible due to your time-traveling mishaps. I can't even put it into words. I don't want to. Leave. Die. Do something that cannot affect the innocent lives of the fifteen billion people who are about to pass on this earth."

I guessed that was the signal to leave. I crawled out of the swinging chair and had to walk to the staircase. This building was one of the last to have a staircase in Milwaukee; staircases officially became displaced from all new buildings constructed after 2039.

Ten minutes later, I found myself at the bottom of the Northwestern Mutual Commons building, staring at it in the gasping wind. No lights shone from it. It stood like a giant about to fall. All I could see was a slight sprinkle of light from the top floor—that candle.

***

"Was any of this your idea?" Jim asked Krystal, who was still stuck on the top floor.

"No—I repeat, no—none of this was my idea. I was totally convinced over to his side because he made a time machine. *A time machine*," Krystal shouted back at them. "Such a thing with such a great amount of impossibility achieved quickly in two days. I completely figured that his plan would have worked because if he made *that*, anything could have worked beyond that point."

Richard thought about that for a moment with his gang. A result came shortly after.

"Sounds reasonable," Clark said. "Were you confident the entire journey?"

Krystal instantly responded, "If I was confident the whole time, I would have already been in a state as bad as Patrick's. Of course I wasn't."

"Do you think he'll continue to try to do something? He can't, really, due to no electronics."

"No," she said, glancing out the window, where she saw the gloomy shadow on the ground bottom, which was Patrick.

"I think that's what we all need," Clark said patiently. "You may leave."

Krystal lifted herself out of the chair and began to walk down the steps of the skyscraper.

***

I could only wait patiently for her to return. Would she stick with me? That was the only question I could ask at this point. And the only answer I could assume was a simple no.

Soon, I found her walking through the first floor. She had a grim expression plastered on her face, and her fists were locked.

Then, I faced my ultimate consequence—guilt.

"You, oh God!" Krystal said, pushing the sliding doors open as hard as she could. "I don't really know what to say. Your entire plan failed. You failed. We failed. We failed the entire earth. I can't believe it. Now, every human is going to die due to a lack of water and food!" A tear fell silently from her eye. Would it be bad to say that I wanted to do the same thing?

"I don't know what to say either," I said, depressed. "It all came up to par, spinning around the hole, ready to go in—and just when my confidence was at the rev limiter, the ball spun out and left a hole empty."

"You have to be absolutely ashamed of yourself, or there is something totally wrong with you!" she cried, pointing.

I did not want to respond.

"There are people dying, about to die, ready to die. You have just committed Earth's biggest attack in its entire history. I am sorry, but I can't do anything with you anymore. All of these people died for no reason at all; they didn't have to. They didn't want to. But you are forcing them to and basically cry away the lifestyle."

I sat on the ground, holding my head. My heart sank into my gut, which seemed nonexistent.

"I honestly hope this is the last time I see you. And I honestly hope this is the last time any person like you will exist. Ever. In the new world, when people are revived and start this cycle over again, I hope this species will have evolved and learned how to deal with things they don't like."

I didn't plan to say anything, but the last bit of my anger pushed it out of me. "So you're saying you're on Richard's side now, eh?" I asked quietly.

"Are you *kidding*?" Krystal shouted violently. "Oh lord, no. They … they … I don't know what. Sorry. I can't fix everything."

She then began to walk away down Wisconsin Avenue, which seemed like a black hole of spirals and confinements of guilt and death. Just pure black. Shadows upon shadows. Buildings covering those shadows. Even worse with water blocking your vision.

"Ha-ha, very funny," Krystal said sarcastically. "I am not on their side at all. I'm just not on your side either." She continued walking, leaving me alone with a large moon shining over a large lake. What a sight. I could see it more clearly without stupid streetlights.

As the moon shone on the tallest building, I couldn't help but think, *where did I go wrong?*

I guessed I was the record for many things, after all of this— things such as biggest criminal, most-hated person. *What a feeling.*

It seemed that my plan didn't work at all. It caused all technology to fail, not just the useless stuff, even when I tried to stop it earlier. I wonder how it happened? I would be the only one to know, since I had been the only one there. I felt like a wall had been built in front of me, with no damn way to get through. I'd caused what would be the death of all humans in the coming month. I caused the death of my confidence. Her confidence. If my family were here … Would I have changed my strategy with some levity?

Who the hell knows? I thought. *I don't want to justify it anymore. I only want to say that this has been the ultimate unorthodox paradox.*

CHAPTER 20

I came out of the apartment at Lafayette Park Towers on the north side. I was hungry, distressed, and worried. No sleep. And then, I would just become more of what made the world the profound misery that it is.

It was 7:30 on Christmas morning. No Santa today because today, Monday, would typically be packed.

Not today, I assumed. No way.

Nothing functioned inside. No birds chirped from the top of the apartment. The bed still worked. Somehow. No bugs or diseases in it. My apartment was as tight as a drum. It was crazy.

Yeah, I would think that first, but things can always be raised up. Raise that bar a little. When you pull that curtain open …

Did so.

Sun glared into the window from the east. No snow blanketed the ground. The turf was still brown; the rain had washed the green dye away, all the way into nothingness. The sun glared over the concrete of Prospect Avenue, with its beating rays casting a spell on the cold, barren surface.

Barren? City? Two words that never had been thrown together by humans. But if you'd seen what I had seen, through the two eyes on your face that give the light, you would change opinions.

It was Christmas. Usually no activity on this day, but today …

today ... there was *no* activity. At all. Each door was shut; no moving cars were seen for miles and miles down the path of Prospect. The earth, on Christmas Day—the most joyous day— just shut its doors. And the guy who could see it all knew it was purely his fault. My fault. Would it not make me sad to see what I had done? To get to that other side of the calendar and see what had distorted us. Would I be not willing to kill my own, my only soul, to relieve myself from the circumstances? To believe that this world would end in a little more than a week? To make a time machine, all for nothing? To make such an extravagant plan—so crazy—that it failed? Did I believe this? Did I believe what I was seeing? Did I really believe what had happened to me this entire month? The entire previous decade? *My entire life?* Did I really believe that I'd done any of this?

No.

No, I really didn't. See the light. Ha. Who was seeing anything? I had only been the bystander.

So many questions were asked. So many never really needed to be. This whole project was just one big fat question nobody ever asked. I really hadn't thought that it would work. All the aspiring love and logic, that your friends and your inventions and every little detail warped into something magical, created that confidence. Then you finally saw what came from that magic. You had a dead 50/50—good or bad. Slim pickin's for the good. Yeah, it turned out bad. And the bubble of confidence popped right in front of your face. That felt really nice.

This entire project was one giant game of Sudoku. I got everything right, at least to myself, and then I was on the last number, and nothing worked. Nothing worked.

It's been said to never give up at anything. It's different when everyone wants you to. And I said that it wasn't figuring out why it happened; it was figuring out how to fix it. Well, when you couldn't fix it, you had all the time in the world to figure it out.

Figuring out what to do now was the only thing that I could do, really. I would die of starvation and dehydration in two weeks, suffering for the last one. I could only recount memories and such before I died. And the worst thing about it was that nobody would be here to remember this. Nobody to pass it on.

I always thought I could see the sunlight through my window. I just closed the curtain on that.

What was I supposed to do now?

Couldn't do much when I was waiting to die. For the planet to die. You know?

Maybe I could just say some goodbyes to the people who cared. Those buddies. Ah, they were long gone. Jailed up somewhere in China. I was nearly there. Ha, those Chinese men let me go.

Wait—those Chinese men let me go! They trusted me! Can't believe it. They believed my plans and believed the future. Wow. More guilt. With such, advanced technology, how could the people not prevent a worldwide electronic blackout? It beat me to the point where I needed a beating in the head.

Maybe I could take one last drive. I loved those when I was young. Escape my issues one last time. Cruising the countryside, not worrying about any sort of technology. Those were the days.

My car was on the bottom floor, still inside that same garage, hopefully. Now, the only way to get there was thirty floors of stairs.

Tumbling tumultuously down those stairs I went, slackening by the minute to get down there. I probably could have screamed loudly in the stairwell or cursed all day long. But that wouldn't get me anywhere.

Soon enough, I found myself standing on the ground near the vinyl wall, which still shined in the bright sunshine. Nobody else was out. It was extremely quiet. Unusually quiet. So quiet I heard noises I'd never hear before. A deafening silence.

Later, feeling the vinyl wall, I found the spaces in between the garage door and the surrounding walls. It was still decent-looking. Few stains showed themselves on the wall. The asphalt was still freshly paved. Everything that wasn't electronic still worked. *Shocking.*

I had to pull up the garage door manually to see the car. I did so with the grip of my human hand and using some muscle. In fifteen seconds, that heavy wire-packed garage door was forcefully opened.

Lights didn't work on the inside. Of course they didn't. What still worked, fortunately, were human senses.

I felt for that car, groping for it in the darkness of the garage. Waiting patiently for a response to the touch.

Then I felt an object. Made of aluminum and steel. Felt like a car. Felt like a windshield. Felt like something I knew was mine.

My car was still here. My Cadillac CTS V.

I didn't know why I was so happy about it; it didn't do me too well. But it meant I could escape my bubbling fears that were about to boil over onto the ground one last damn time.

Found the door handle. It was thankfully unlocked. Swung it open. Sat inside.

Well, I was here. What else could I do now? Make it start?

Found the keys in the door pocket. Clenched them with hope. Turned those keys once.

It started.

That V8 engine rumbled loudly in the garage, creating a boxed-in feel of noise and exhaust fumes. I couldn't believe it. The car started. With good ol' gas and a honking V8. Some engineering, old style, still worked after this calamity. *Amazing.*

Something so old still worked? With no technology? With no electricity? It was the only thing that was still running because it wasn't electronic.

Gas worked. Oil worked. This calamity killed everything electronic.

This made me realize something big.

This worldwide hack wasn't my fault.

I really didn't do any of this.

I stepped out of the car, turned it off, shut the door. I had to confront my thoughts for a minute.

I had been the bystander this whole time. My plan didn't work. It influenced technology to a greater level. This made everything even more intertwined in 2050. This caused the worldwide hack. Society did it. Not me.

With my plan, I'd wanted to take technology down to the right amount, to the point where it wasn't annoying, too ridiculous, too dangerous. But somehow, I'd made it even worse. To the point where society made it dangerous in the present time. Society killed itself. I just sort of made them do it.

I got society to see the light. I wanted everyone to see the better side of things. Not the worst. But dumb humans needed to see it to believe it. I got them to see what too much technology did to you by showing what would happen in ten years! Now everybody knew what would have happened.

Once, in middle school, somebody called out, "Imagine what would happen if the internet entirely wiped out." And everybody discussed. What pissed me off the most in the 2010s was everybody thought it would happen, but nobody did anything to prevent it.

Well, it was fun. I figured out what happened to the planet while I was gone, realizing that in the end, it wasn't my fault. Did it make me feel any better? Maybe a little. But not enough to regain confidence. I could regain my confidence if I had the ability to fix it—to try again, now that everybody had seen the light. Everybody knew that it happened, but nobody knew that it was justified, that I did it for a reason. That sort of set me off to the point where I still couldn't make a solution. With the time machine and my car—the only two things that still work now—I could use try to create a solution. I overheard Richard and Jim talking about throwing it into a capsule that ran by itself—in which it still worked. I still couldn't get into it. That meant no time machine.

Which meant no solution.

I couldn't do much else now. I had no machine to go back again and possibly fix it. If I even had the chance, those three wouldn't let me do anything. *I bet they are up on their feet right at this moment,* I thought, *waiting for me to come out and look for the time machine. And they will do whatever possible to see me fall.*

That was all Clark wanted. That was all what the entire earth wanted. I had caused this extinction. At least in their heads. I had no way to explain myself now. No computer. No database. No way to pass info around. And even if I could do *that,* they wouldn't want me to. They wouldn't listen. They'd had enough of me. I had an extra barrier to crash through—my reputation.

I guess I should get on with my last drive, I thought.

But I knew I shouldn't.

I shouldn't because this was the one noise that would be extroverted out to Richard. He would try to find me, so I officially decided to close the drive down.

Now I couldn't do anything—and I really couldn't do anything. I had run out of options.

It was time to close up shop.

And maybe do some thinking.

***

8:30 a.m.

I manually shut the garage door again and fled up the stairwell and back to the same apartment, where I would think in the deepest of depths. Where I would figure out what to do to fix this behemoth of terror. More important, where I would figure out if I should do anything.

Back at the apartment, I went inside and shut the door tight. The other people who lived here should not know what I was doing. Yes, everyone who used to live here still did. Just very quietly. Starving. Dehydrated. Soon to die.

If I could try again, this would not be happening to anyone. Did this inspire me?

A little.

I had three barriers: overcoming my guilt, coming up with a solution, and getting the time machine back. This was like getting through rehab without taking any drugs.

As I lay on the bed, I thought, *I really didn't cause this. I just sort of ordered it. Everything nonelectronic works—my Caddy.*

Electronics that weren't intertwined with the rest, that worked independently, still worked. So why couldn't we just use our instincts and hunt for food? Get some water? Make our own medicine?

I assumed it was because we had been connected for so long that our instincts succumbed to those electronics. It became our instincts. We forgot how to fend for ourselves without it. That was sad, but it made me laugh just a little.

But I couldn't explain myself to the earth.

That broke the guilt barrier just slightly. A crack. Just enough to push my way through it and conquer the next wall.

Now, how in God's name could I actually stop all of this? If I hadn't been so upset, a suggestion would have been to go back in time again, and fix everything. Now that I knew what to really expect, I would kill more technology, like I tried to do in China. But it was so hard to hack in any time before 2010.

But wait—I had no tech from 2050 now. *Ironic.*

I didn't know what to do. If I got the machine back and went to 2001 or something, I would have all the time in the world to think of something, anything.

That's it, I thought. I've got a solution. A feasible solution.

After so much depression and interrogation, I really did have part of a solution, after all this doubt and testimony.

But there was only a small chance that I could pull it off.

It was indescribable how angry these people were with me. Forward to Clark. Forward to Krystal. They all wanted to kill me before they died. Because that was the last smile they would ever create. When they saw me, the last bit of animal inside them would be drained and twisted out of their bodies and confined onto mine. It was that serious.

Most men would say that their lives were complete if they'd traveled back to 1901, 2001, 401 BCE, and 360. When they built a time machine. When they knew that they were ahead of the rest of the planet. When they were in a car chase. When they worked in a skyscraper. The little details.

Mine wasn't.

I'd rather die trying to save the planet and be that unknown hero than to be that guy who made everyone feel so bad in the aftermath. Than to starve to death. Or succumb to my guilt. That wasn't what the hero did.

The hero doesn't hide in the face of adversity. The hero *overcomes it.* The hero rises up to a challenge, and strikes without hesitation. I haven't backed away my whole life; I simply cannot do it now.

I have a low possibility of succeeding. If I wanted society to live, I had to decide now. There was no more time. This was possibly the end of time. *Pressure there for sure.*

I suddenly remembered that if I happened to go all the way back to Meroe once again, I would have to build a better generator to get back to 2050. Of course I wanted to get back to see my results. Now I realized I needed an even bigger generator.

Christ.

I really needed to stop crunching my gears. The planet's population was not going to live much longer. And I only had that much time to create an even more powerful generator. I couldn't wait another week for a decision.

I must decide now, I thought. *It's as simple as that. I have less than five days until the world vanishes. Must do something to help myself right now.*

I'd need to think about that too.

December 25, 2050

My last journal entry since Meroe. And possibly my last one for good. You never know. This one will be written for the records, whether for a new reborn generation of planet earth or a piece of history for the future, something to recreate the emotional state I was in at the time. Whichever one comes first. The fact is I failed. Then realized I only sort of made society flunk out of reality school. Then I got a solution—try again, now that I know what the hell time travel feels like. Feels like a burden. A burden with magical fairy dust sprinkled within and without that gives you the greatest feeling ever. After all of this bull, I face myself in the mirror of burdens and proximity of life within itself and say, "What do I do now?"

I have two very simple choices—escape all my fears and die, or try to save the others. This choice, preferably the second one, would be very legendary if proven to be feasible.

Why is it so hard to come up with such a simple solution? Because of the guilt that has wrapped its wings around me. Hard to think of one. Hard to try to do one. But I gave myself a little confidence backup, and now everything just might play at my pace for once.

Two choices. One man. Right now.

***

9:10 a.m.
Concluded.
Ready.
Here I go.
It's time to close up shop.
And start a better shop.

***

9:25 a.m.
Northwestern Mutual and Commons Tower

Three people—two men and one woman—still lay on the breakable ground that had three layers—anger, fear, and depression.

What rectitude did this ground have?

Clark sat within the wilting garden at ground level of the nearby skyscraper. He was simply thinking—thinking like Patrick a little. Depressed. Enraged. Afraid.

The sun still glittered its shining rays over the mosaic pieces of water that built up Lake Michigan. Shifting, rising, falling. It didn't make Richard feel any better. When imagined in that way, it made him think of society's downfall.

Jim was wandering aimlessly through the garden, around fifty paces to the west of Clark. And around fifty paces to the northeast was that sucker of an invention known as a time machine.

Richard looked at it from the corner of his eye, thinking deeply of what that had influenced this past week. As he did, Jim came about to his side.

"Hey," Jim said quietly. Clark looked up at him for a split second, nodded his head, and continued to look down and fidget with his fingers.

"I have collected some water out of the Milwaukee River to drink," Jim said, handing over a green-tinged dirty bottle to his boss. "It's basically our last resort."

"Thanks for trying, man," Richard replied, only slightly happy. "This will make me sick and die even sooner." He tipped the bottle of muddy water over as Jim frowned. Both previous workers to the tower that stood behind them thought to themselves for a moment.

"Let me show you something," Jim said, sitting on the curb next to his previous boss.

Richard hesitated to look.

"It's a note," Jim said, handing it to Mr. Clark. "I found it inside the time machine. It appears to be very beat up and old."

Richard read with grief. Soon, near the end, he raised an eyebrow. "Oh, wow," Richard said, setting it down for a moment. "It says that those two should have been killed! That doesn't surprise me at all. It also says that the guy who wrote it was Calhoun something." Jim shrugged as Richard looked at him. "I had a great-grandfather named Calhoun."

Jim got up and picked up the bottle. "Want to keep that note?" Jim asked.

Clark thought to himself. "Yeah. Yeah, I will," he replied shortly after. "It might come in handy sometime." He crumpled up the letter, put it into his jeans pocket, and left the scene instantly. Jim followed shortly after.

CHAPTER 21

December 26, 2050
3:00 a.m.

I have officially five days before the human
population starts to die. I have no energy as well.

There is no food or clean water. No cooling
within a grocery store to protect food. No
cleansing of water. No clean water is produced.
I am about to collapse. I need high amounts of
protein to time travel in order to sustain strength.
I know how painful time travel has been with
loads of energy. So ...

My schedule is tight. Extremely tight. Five
days before people start to vanish. I am running
out of protein and energy by the second, and my
health is degrading along the way. Do I use more
energy to build the generator quicker, or take it
slow?

I will go with quick in a life-or-death situation.

I slammed the journal closed, got off the bed, and threw the
journal on the floor. It was time to save the planet.

I opened the wooden closet door, which was basically a door that opened up opportunity, and slammed it against the wall, which was basically the drum roll.

Inside was a 3D printer, stacks of aluminum, computer chips scattered about, and electronics and wires interconnecting them all in a mess. This new generator would be even bigger than before—more electronics stuffed into it. The machine could only handle around five hundred pounds. The structure was a featherweight, so it had the ability to switch direction through two linear paths during time travel.

So this generator would have to be compact, yet under three hundred pounds.

This was hard.

I shifted the parts out of the closet, rolling them out as fast as I could, using the least amount of energy as possible. I threw out all of the remaining parts in the closet; I obviously wanted to make the most use of what I could.

I had the parts. I had the knowledge. And I had just enough time.

Here's to all the people who did something amazing in their lives, I thought.

I was building a generator for a time machine, for God's sake.

***

1:15 p.m.

The city was dead. The hearts and minds of Richard and the others were dead. Turned off. Nobody wanted to think. There was no time to think it through. All they could say to themselves was simply, "Well, it's been fun."

But something was still there. A time machine. It had a full charge from the generator and was begging to be used. Besides Patrick, nobody had the will to use it.

Richard Clark still had the climax of activity jumbling through his head. Then again, any thought could triumph over another.

He was still sitting in front of his former workplace. The only thing he could look at was the lake ahead, still somehow shimmering in the dim sunlight. He still couldn't speak; he hesitated to do anything. Jim was still nearby, finding objects that could do little to sustain life. But he knew it wouldn't help; he was just lumbering about. Jim knew he wanted to die doing something productive rather than just sit.

Clark didn't know what to do.

Over time and thought, Jim eventually decided to confront him again. He slowly, shyly, crept up to him. He thought it probably wouldn't do much. Of course it wouldn't do anything. But he had to say something to him that might have some importance.

"You …" Jim started, looking down at the man. "Want do you want?"

Richard was instantly confused by the question. "What do you mean?" he asked with a pinch of anger.

Jim crossed his arms. "You seem more upset than anyone else I know, if that's possible."

Clark shook his head.

"Would it matter if I stopped?"

"I'm just saying—might there be anything that would push your anger out?"

Richard thought about it for a moment. He still knew that whatever he wanted wouldn't fix much. But then again, it might fix something.

Jim sat beside him gingerly, wanting him to come out with a response.

"I … I … I guess I am just tired of being fooled by that failure. He got away; he wanted to change the perfect planet for good, and then, he just completely abominated it. It's hard to comprehend. I just wish he was gone."

Jim smiled at Richard. "There you go." He patted him on the back and stood up again.

Richard originally had wanted to give Patrick the death penalty. But after what Jim just said, and after all that Patrick had done, he just wanted him dead. In front of his own eyes. Blood and gore gushing out, a pleasant vibe for him.

He knew what he wanted now.

Jim started to walk away again, trying to get more supplies for an inanimate cause. Clark stopped him before he could.

"I would like to kill Patrick." Richard stood up with confidence. Jim looked at him with very little shock and only smiled at him. "I really would," Richard said, holding his hands out.

"May I offer a suggestion?" Jim asked with a grin.

"No, I already know," Richard replied. "I already know how I am going to do it—with that time machine."

Jim was clearly shocked and gaped at Richard. "Um … what do you mean?" Jim asked, clearly perplexed. "You realize he is a mile north of us."

"No, killing him in person would be inconvenient," Clark responded. "You see, if I kill him *back in time*, then nobody would know I'd done it!"

Jim knew Richard was calorie-deficient after no water or food. His brain could barely process thoughts. And clearly, Jim's own brain couldn't either.

"I see what you're trying to get at…" Jim nodded, appearing a tad confused.

"I think it just might work," Richard mumbled with glee. "The time machine is right there. Should I go now? I wonder."

Jim shook his head. He still didn't know what to entirely think of this plan. Then again, like his former colleague had said,

"*Would it really matter if I* ..." He simply put his head down and sat on the step.

Richard said, "I would like to go back and kill the living hell out of the man."

Nothing really mattered anymore. No decision mattered. Jim simply decided to let Clark go ahead. "I'm not the boss," Jim said with a shrug, lifting his head up. "No rules are important anymore." He paused for a moment to comprehend what he was saying. "Go ahead. Kill the man, one way or another. Nothing really matters anymore. My opinion doesn't matter. If it helps you ..."

Clark was joyous with Jim's response. He smiled broadly and said, "Me? It won't just help me. It will help all of us. Maybe before we die a horrible death, we can smile or even laugh for one last time." He raised his eyebrows, turned his head, and began walking toward the machine. He was surprised by how easy this was. Each step took his comprehension further from reality.

Soon enough, it was right in front of him. It seemed like it was glowing ominously.

"Yes!" Richard shouted happily, holding his head. "Finally!" He ran inside the dazzling piece of machinery but then stopped and called out, "Hey, Jim!"

Jim didn't want to respond, but he said quietly, "What?"

"If I don't make it ..." Richard took a step forward. "Tell the living I just tried."

Silence invaded the quiet scenario.

"Sure thing, man," Jim said, being a fantastic sidekick.

Clark simply nodded pleasantly. He shut the door on the time machine.

Jim watched with sadness.

Clark then frantically figured out how to time travel. There were buttons and contraptions he had not seen for a while—some, in fact, he had never seen before—and he couldn't figure out a thing for a minute.

He did enjoy the process of doing it, though.

"Man ..." Richard said with joy. "Wow! This thing is just amazing! So complicated. Such a marvel. How does this thing work? How does it still work?"

Then Richard realized he liked something Patrick Shields had engineered and designed.

Man, the irony, he thought.

"God ... this stuff exceeds anything I have ever imagined!" Clark shouted his lungs out. "And it was all made by the man who didn't want this to ever happen!" He hesitated and didn't speak another word until he said, "I am spewing out love of this time machine, and basically falling into Patrick's power! It's ... it's like he wants me to just break out of the cage! The cage of ... confusion."

He lay on the brushed floor of the machine, trying to contain himself to a smaller flame. He breathed heavily and thought deeply.

This is exactly why I want the man dead, he thought.

Then that cage flew apart. He stood up once again and looked at the navigation pad. Scrolling and pushing his way through it like a hacker, he eventually found a big red button.

"This must mean start," Clark said with confidence. "I have one of these in my autonomous car."

He had to select his date before he could take the trip, though.

"All right ..." Richard said, cracking his knuckles. "How old is that man? Forty-seven?"

He thought for a moment in excitement—and a little bit of terror as well. But he continued on bravely anyway.

"All right ... December ... first. 2005. A little before he was born. Also, better add that location. Milwaukee ... Wouldn't want to end up in Shanghai or something."

Then, he hit the start button with the palm of his hand, a major milestone for the businessman. But he didn't know what time travel took, physically at least.

The recess happened all over again for a third human being, being whisked away into another level of life. The blue light swirled. The water vapor dropped.

Jim couldn't help but look. Eventually, it became too bright, to the point of being blinding. Jim stepped back. The blue light exploded, surrounding the object. Then, the light began to disappear.

The time machine was no longer there.

Jim was in shock.

Excruciating pain exploded during this time travel. So painful Clark couldn't feel anything. He was entirely numb for a few seconds.

A pinnacle of light opened up in his vision. He then saw part of the navigator. He was relieved. Eventually, the pain stopped, and the machine came to rest on some grass.

His regained his vision and hearing. His mind turned back on. Richard currently lay on his back, holding his head. It wasn't enough to block his joy, though.

"Oh … wow. That was simply amazing," Richard said, opening his eyes wide. "Am I in 2005?"

He slowly got up, sore from the roller-coaster ride through time. Richard peered out the small window of the time machine.

He found nothing from 2050. Classic cars rolled down the streets, with humans driving them. Only old buildings stood on every block. A man was reading a book on a bus stop bench. A gust of exhaust came from a bus approaching the bus stop.

Clark gasped, taking his hands off the window. "I don't remember this stuff. Where are people with iPhones?" He knew he couldn't obsess over the past. He had more important things to do. "Right," he said to himself, turning around. "Where's Patrick's house?"

He cracked the portal open and stepped out. He found himself in an alley, north of a busy street. It resembled Patrick's parents' neighborhood. The area had numerous white and blue duplexes, all nearly identical. He soon realized the time machine stood out like a sore thumb. *How am I going to hide the time machine?* he wondered.

He spied a garage door that was slightly open to his left. Cobwebs seemed to connect it to the surrounding white wooden walls. One of the three windows in the door was shattered. It looked to be in a much more deteriorated condition than the surrounding houses.

"Hmm … anything in there?"

He walked across cracked concrete, where weeds poked their heads out, to the old garage. It looked worse as he got closer, but his outlook got better.

"Looks abandoned."

He then leaned over and stuck his fingers under the door. Richard lifted it up as the door creaked and groaned. Inside the garage he found only overgrown weeds and a tiny tinted window that filtered light onto a spot on the ground. "Yes!" Clark said, rejoicing. He could park the time machine there.

He ran back to the machine and carried it into the old garage. Soon enough, with some rough pushing along the concrete, he'd hidden it in plain sight.

Richard slammed the garage door closed and then began to put his plan into action.

"I have to find his house."

He ran to the south, following the alley's direction. The alley ended at Main Street. Richard was shocked by how outdated everything looked.

"Good lord," Richard said, looking around. "How did people

live in 2005?" He saw another man, reading a newspaper at a bus stop, and that gave him an idea. "Maybe I could entirely prevent this incident for these people and not let this happen again."

Richard sprinted across the street to get a closer look at the man. The man didn't seem to care that a stranger breathed heavily above him.

"Hey," Richard began, holding his hands out, "you have to listen to me."

The man lowered his newspaper and looked at Richard in a silent but dastardly way. Then he turned the page of his paper and continued reading.

"I'm from the future!" Richard cried, trying to get the man's attention.

The man lowered his paper again. "No, you're not."

Clark rolled his eyes. "I am from the year 2050. And let me tell you, it sucks *ass*. A man just destroyed all the technology in that year and created a worldwide hack! And I am trying to kill the man who did it all. In case that doesn't happen, you have to build up the tech as much as you can to prevent another hack. Understood?"

As Clark breathed heavily, the man seemed to be thinking about what he'd heard. His response, though, was to shrug and go back to his newspaper.

"I am running out of time! I need to kill the man." Clark turned and ran across the street as fast as he could.

"Try to ease up on the drinking next time!" the man yelled after him.

Clark didn't hear. He ran until he came to an intersection and looked for the street signs. He saw green signs that indicated direction and the names of the streets, spelled out in white lettering. The north-south street was North Thirty-Eighth Street, and the east-west street was West Wisconsin Avenue. He then remembered that Patrick's home had been on Thirty-Eighth Street.

"One step closer," he said happily, looking north. "Getting there."

He ran up the sidewalk, following Thirty-Eighth Street, as fast as he could, passing all of the duplexes in a flash.

A woman stepped out of her duplex to get the mail. She noticed him sprinting along the sidewalk, and she shouted at the top her lungs. "Hey, you!"

Clark stopped in his tracks.

"What you doing?" she asked.

Richard bent over, leaning on his knees to catch him breath. "Oh, you know, just my … afternoon jog."

The woman nodded and continued to get her mail. "Weirdo," she muttered.

Clark again ran toward Patrick's house, trying to remember what the house looked like. He thought it was blue and in almost poverty-like condition. Once he saw it again, he was sure he'd recognize it.

Most of the houses were white or tan. They all had the same type of roof and windows. The houses did what people wanted them to do—provide shelter.

Then Richard saw the house. It was white but had a blue stripe and a light-blue second floor. The roof and door were black.

A memory was unlocked. It was Patrick's house.

"Is this what I've been looking for this entire time?" Richard asked himself. He stepped back into the street for a better view, and that view confirmed it. "Yes!" he shouted.

Now, he had to generate a plan. How would he kill a two-year-old in broad daylight and escape without a trace in almost a bad neighborhood?

"All right—think," he told himself. Clark positioned himself in an almost unnoticeable way. He sat between Patrick's house and the neighboring house, crouching down so Patrick's parents couldn't see him. But Richard's mind was stuck. He had to return in time before the entire earth disappeared into a lost memory.

"Oh God," he groaned. "I can't think of anything!"

He was losing his grip on his mind and his physical energy by the second. That was really the only thing on his mind, unfortunately. He then heard a scream from inside Patrick's house. This made him refocus once again.

"Whoa … what was that?" He stood up and cautiously stuck his left ear against the old window. Inside was a clear view of the living room.

"I can't believe it …" a woman's voice said. "I can't believe he is dead."

With Patrick on his mind, this made Clark think deep. "Who, dammit, *who*?" he shouted, slamming his fist against the window. A bang echoed through the house and through the front yard. Birds flew out of the nearby oak tree. Richard saw the woman— he supposed it was Patrick's mom—through the window, and instantly he hid again.

He clutched his head in anger and confusion. He decided this wouldn't answer the question. He got up and raced to the front door of Patrick's house. He shoved it open and raced through the foyer and into the kitchen. Patrick's mom and dad stood in front of him. Both stared at him in absolute shock.

"Who are you? Why are you in our house?" Mr. Shields cried, his eyes bright with fear.

In the light from the dim chandelier, Richard's eyes glowed with anger and stress, a combination that created an elixir to solve the mystery. *I'll do that right now*, he thought.

"Who … who … who is dead?" Richard asked, holding his hands out desperately.

Patrick's parents appeared to be very depressed. They wore tattered clothes, and tears streamed from their eyes.

Mr. Shields whimpered, "Patrick. Our son ... he just ... disappeared from our arms two weeks ago. We have no idea what happened. One day he was sleeping in the crib; next day, he was gone. No evidence. No sign. I ... I don't want to talk about it." He got out of his chair and left the room. It was clear that he was extremely upset.

"Patrick Shields ... is ... dead?" Richard asked.

"Yes," Mrs. Shields said heavily, wiping away her tears.

A gun was fired through the window. A bomb exploded. Glass shattered. Clark's head was in a state of incomprehensible disbelief. *Patrick is dead. Sounds ... great.*

That was his goal. But *he* didn't do it.

"Who are you?" the mom asked, sobbing loudly.

"Um ... I ... have to leave. Pretend I was never here. Don't say anything!" Richard begged, slowly backing away from Mrs. Shields. He turned around, ran out the door, and sprinted down the street.

Richard turned the corner, nearly slipping on the beat-up sidewalk. He ran between two other houses and eventually found the old garage where he'd stored the time machine.

He bent over, moved his fingers under the old garage door, and lifted it with all of his might. The time machine was still there, just as he'd left it.

Before he could jump in, that same curious woman from earlier stepped out the back door of her house to throw away some trash.

The time machine was pretty noticeable.

"You again?" the woman said angrily. "You crazy man! And ... what the hell is that thing in my garage?"

Richard knew he was in trouble now. He ignored the woman and swung open the aluminum door of the time machine, breaking part of the garage wall as he did. He got in, and just before the woman barged in, he shut and locked the door.

Now he was safe from any interruption. The only problem was that he was inside a garage. *Is it safe to start to time travel from here?* he wondered. *I guess I won't know until I try.* With that, Richard turned around and hit the red start button. Once again, he didn't know what to expect.

From her porch, the woman saw blue light glowing on the roof and walls of the garage. She backed up cautiously. Richard clung on tightly inside. Within three seconds, the time machine exploded with light and was gone.

CHAPTER 22

2:00 p.m.

Everybody thinks a lot of things. Everybody has freedom of rights and their own opinions. Some opinions, however, are uneducated.

Everybody thinks I'm a criminal, lurking at an outpost and chipping away at every nook and cranny, every flaw on the earth. I have always had a reason for that, and now, after killing the planet, I have a reason more than ever before. No one has seen me at midnight. At the pinnacle of time when everything can snap, I will do so. As time progresses, I will become more progressive. I will change from a lunatic to a scientist in a flash. It's the crazy people here that change the world. I can run from place to place when nobody wants to admit they saw it. Nobody wants to realize I am here.

I promise to go from a criminal to a savior of the earth. Watch me unravel into something more radical and unbelievable than ever before.

I make a great deal out of all this jazz. And you know why. It's time to be cohesive. I am down to the point of no return. A wall follows you as you run down the path of life. Soon, you are trapped in front of one, with one in the back. Just push your way through.

The world right now is in an incomprehensible state of helplessness and fearfulness. They have nothing to survive. A bleak canvas. Not to die in twenty days but in twenty hours, maybe. But this is so interesting to watch. Everything looked bleak for me when I returned, but now it isn't. It was the planet itself. They chose not to make the right decision and pull the plug when needed. No, I am not saying this is the end, but it's the very last door. If I can't pull something off today, the world will disappear. It could be a new side of earth. I have completed my more powerful, advanced, amazing generator, and it's ready to be hooked up to the time machine.

It was a small bright spot in my dark room. It was large and cylindrical, like the old one, but much heavier. But with more weight comes more electrics. And with more electrics comes more and more power. I could go anywhere and return with charge left.

Now I just needed that machine. Was I smart to leave it out there in the open? Most likely not. But most likely, it was out of charge anyway.

I shoved everything back into the closet and grabbed the new generator.

I felt confident yet solemn—I didn't know why, though. My confidence fell up and down and was shaken and stirred for a week. I didn't feel too confident with my confidence, but I always try to stay hopeful. Optimism has been shown to bring positive results.

I eventually reached the end of the staircase and made my way out of the short apartment tower. Outside was still a barren landscape. I was the only one out there, making my way back to the office building. I chose not to use my car so I wouldn't give myself away.

***

3:00 p.m.
Office building

The time machine made a loud return right outside the building in the exact spot where it was before. Rocks lifted from the asphalt and were blown away from the landing spot, and trees swayed in the final gust of fiery wind it generated.

Jim barely noticed; he still was sitting where he had been. Clark flung the door up angrily and ran toward Jim, leaving the door wide open. Breathing heavily, Clark stood next to him, and Jim turned his head to look at Richard.

"How did it go?" Jim asked, looking away from him.

"He's already dead!" Richard exclaimed. "The man is already dead!"

"Who's dead … already?" Jim asked cautiously.

"*Patrick!*" he shouted, even more loudly than before. "He was dead when I got there!"

"What year did you travel to?" Jim asked, wondering if he should even question Clark.

"Just after he was born—2005," Richard replied, still unable to calm down. "I rushed into his house—his parents were there but not him! They said he'd just disappeared, and they assumed he was dead."

Jim stood up, feeling revitalized, knowing that he should help Richard. "Isn't that a good thing?" he asked. "If he's already dead back then, it's only logical that he'd be nonexistent now."

"You're right," Richard replied, letting a little bit of anger slide off his shoulders. "Maybe he's dead now. And we might have gotten the last thing we wanted!"

"There you go," Jim said, somewhat glad. "Patrick Shields is gone. It's what we wanted. We got it, thanks to you."

"Not really," Richard disagreed. "But still …"

Richard and Jim thought to themselves that even though the guy who pulled the plug was dead, they still couldn't save the world. But these thoughts got them thinking, opening up doors that had been locked inside their heads for a time.

"Wait, Richard," Jim said. "If Shields was dead in 2005, why wasn't he dead a few weeks ago?"

Richard collapsed at the thought. "Are you kidding me?" Richard said with increasing agitation. "That's unfortunately true."

The brink of hope collapsed. Richard and Jim were now once again back where they started. They now assumed that Patrick could make a possible rebound and try again at his plan, being the relentless person he was. Jim wondered if it would make a difference if they tried to stop him this time. Both sat down.

"I think we both have tried way too hard to end his run," Jim said, trying to offer anything helpful. "After all, we can still put him down for good."

Richard thought and then said, "Yeah, you're right. Whenever he comes, we can put his journey to an end."

***

I stood only a mile from the office where the time machine, I hoped, still sat. I looked at all of the buildings that were still standing and thought that there were still a million people residing in this city, yet none of them showed their faces. They were all in those buildings, locked up, with no technology to help them. Tomorrow would be the day that humans and population figures would start to crumble. Even though I intended to kill off large numbers of humans, they hadn't done anything. They were just trying to live life. This only fueled my need to end this catastrophe as soon as I could.

So I began running away to prevent losing the remaining time. The end of time was approaching, and knowing that I wanted to reverse it was overwhelming. I passed block after block of old streets and buildings. Then, finding myself near the lakefront, I saw the blueish office building. I couldn't see ground level yet, but I knew I was close.

***

4:00 p.m.

"Are we prepared yet to get rid of this guy once and for all?" Jim asked, standing up for once and peeling around the sharp corner of the building.

"We have no electronics or weaponry to help us," Richard replied, also standing up. "We might just have to use our minds and our strength this time."

"But his time machine still works," Jim remarked. "It runs on an independent electronic server, supplementing its own electricity to just the machine. It's not in the cloud."

"Wait!" Richard said, tapping his head. "Remember when they installed military equipment and weaponry in US cities in 2039, just in case a nuclear war happened?"

"Uh...yes," Jim replied softly.

"Those vehicles run on independent servers!" Richard

exclaimed. "They still function! We could still use them to stop Patrick!"

"*Yes!*" Jim said, pointing a finger at him. "How far away is the base for that equipment?"

Richard had to think for a moment but then had an answer. "They're in an empty lot on the north side of downtown," Richard replied. "Don't know exactly where, though."

"Good enough," Jim said, with hope in his eyes. "Shall we get to it, then?"

"What if he returns?" Richard asked. "And just flees with the time machine again?"

"You go for the equipment," Jim said reassuringly. "I will attempt to fight him off for the time being. Plus, he might be dead already, if he was in 2005."

"*What?*" a voice screamed from the background.

Sound waves echoed through Richard's and Jim's heads, and they knew exactly who had screamed.

***

Richard turned. Jim turned. And they saw none other than Patrick foiling their plan.

"What about me being 'dead already?" I said anxiously, yet sounding determined.

"Go … *go!*" Jim whispered at Richard.

Richard ran off to the right, out of my view. Jim remained.

"Where is he going?" I asked. "What is happening? Did he use my time machine?"

Jim said nothing, but he stepped up and threw a punch right at my face. I was blindsided by the vile attack, and blood dribbled out of my nose.

Jim stepped back. "We plan to not let you use this time machine again. We do plan to kill you in the process. The damage you have caused this earth is unimaginable. We can't die without making sure you're dead first."

It would be harder than I thought to get into the time machine. I lifted the generator, swung it, and ran toward the machine. When I reached it, I threw the generator in there as fast and as carefully as I could. Soon after, Jim threw my face against the aluminum floor of the time machine, hitting my chest.

He was on top of me, grabbing my shoulders, in an attempt to keep me from time traveling. I swung as hard as I could, using pure force out of frustration in order to swing Jim around. Components to the machine were beginning to swing around. Jim was in a perfect position to do some damage to my invention.

I swiveled my body on the ground, putting Jim's and my legs facing forward. Jim poked through a gap between our bodies and saw that the control panel was right there in the open. He drew back his fist, swinging it high to five feet, and brought it down as fast as he could, taking it through the entire control screen for the time machine.

I heard wires snap. Glass broke and bounced on the ground. I had to look at my priceless invention. I pinned Jim and stood up, leaving his neck down on the ground. I then saw the entire control screen torn and broken, with not a single bit of it left. The controls to start this up were completely broken.

Oh, shit.

"You can't really time travel now, can you?" Jim asked furiously.

I was clearly enraged and punched the man down. His eyes shut. His heart slowed. It was clear he was unconscious.

"Good lord," I said, walking out of the time machine, which could no longer function.

I just needed to process that. I couldn't time travel anymore. *Oh no, this is one huge step backward.*

"This is a major waste of time!" I said to myself, nervously. I knew I could still fix it, but it was a major incident that would waste precious time. I could only run back to the apartment and gather parts—again. Horrible inconvenience.

Now they all had time to get to me and really stop me. *But you've made it before,* I told myself, *in similar situations.*

***

The apartment stood in a valley surrounded by other buildings. No words were heard from it, but words just kept pouring out, as this apartment spoke for itself. The building was absolutely dead, crumbling and dismantling by the minute.

Outside was an alley—an open cave that presented the lows of life. No one had been outside since December 20—except one. Krystal was there, sitting. There was nothing she could do. The only thing on her mind was pure frustration. No hope was there to back it up.

She was so shocked that she remained expressionless. No one could have guessed what she was thinking. She was only waiting. Waiting for death to come, to take her away from misery and bring her one last blessing in heaven. It was as simple as that.

Krystal had no idea that any sort of hope would come her way ... but one would.

A few rumbles and tapping of feet shook the quiet scene. Krystal could hear them well. She peered into the alley, looking in each direction, and saw someone sprinting down the bleak road, directly looking at Krystal. Krystal squinted at the figure.

Who is that? she wondered, without her normal sense of jubilation.

The person rushed into Krystal's field of vision. "Hey!" the person said, breathing heavily. "Aren't you Patrick Shields's sidekick or assistant or whatever?"

"I was," Krystal replied calmly. "Aren't you Jen, from earlier?"

"Yes," Jen said. "Let me talk to you for a minute."

They walked together into a dark alley nearby, enclosed between two white brick walls, with cobwebs and dirt scattered around, blocking all noise of the surrounding population.

"So anyway," Jen whispered, "I have been tinkering with things in the city, looking for any sort of aid to save our world."

There was only silence for a few moments.

"Point being?" Krystal asked assertively.

"I found an electric chair in a nearby police station," Jen said with an increase in excitement. "And get this—it still works. It could kill anyone with ease."

Krystal rolled her eyes in disgust. "Is there any reason I should know this?" Krystal asked, leaning on one of the walls.

"Well, it depends," Jen said. "What are your thoughts on Patrick?"

Too many thoughts erupted once again. "I can't believe I trusted him twice and for such a long time," Krystal said. "He and I had the same beliefs about our world. I never thought it would include a terrorist attack on our planet and such a crazy theory. It all fell apart in the end, and the biggest mistake I made was believing in him for a single second."

Jen nodded. "Look what he has done to this earth!"

"I have seen enough of it already."

"Killing countless lives, innocent lives, all because of how they were happily living?"

"I guess."

"Would not such an evil, unorthodox worldwide terrorist attack be enough reason for Patrick Shields to die?"

Krystal's eyes grew wide. She now knew the only reason Jen had come to her. She knew she should answer her question. After a pause, she did so calmly. "I guess you're right. No one in his right mind would ever leave someone like that alive. There's just no way to kill him before we die."

"But there is!" Jen said. "Electric chair!"

This was the other reason she was there. And Krystal thought about it and came to a conclusion similar to everyone else's.

"Yes. He should die in an electric chair."

Jen was a little shocked but tried not to look surprised by the answer. "Right. So shall we find Patrick and give him what he deserves?"

"Right," Krystal said, relaxed.

Jen smiled as Krystal stood up, and they ran to the west, out of the alley and down the street.

***

Running tirelessly through the city, I followed streets I couldn't remember back to my apartment, where my car sat. It was my only resource until the time machine underwent a quick fix. I flew past buildings as fast as I could. The last bit of energy within my body was nearly gone, but I sustained it with my focus on potentially saving the planet. It was enough to keep me going.

Soon enough, I was following Prospect Avenue. My apartment tower, which seemed deserted, was in sight. A spectral sight.

With continuous progress toward the northeast, my tower got closer, and within five minutes, I was back at the main entrance.

The garage was toward the back. I raced there with no time left and saw the final wrapping in all its white glory. I felt for the crease within the wall, like a metal detector searching for money. And money was found, seconds later.

I lifted the door and heard the sounds of mechanics working together. The hidden garage door was raised, and there was my Caddy. But first, I needed even more supplies to fix the time machine. Luckily, new parts were stored in the garage.

I needed a new touchscreen, swinging screens, wires, and outlets off the shelves, and I'd bring them in the backseat of the car. I got in the Caddy and started the ignition for a hopefully quicker run back to the time machine. The air was already filled with constant noise, so it would be no trouble to push it to full blast.

The car spun its way out of the garage, with parts shaking around in the back. It whipped around the curb and raced down the street, back toward the time machine.

***

A blank area in downtown had been put to use back in 2039. Authorities and officials ordered that if a nuclear war or something like that happened, they must use this area to possibly sustain any strength, if a battle or world war happened.

Richard and Jim were sprinting hard toward it. The area was now in sight, outlined by tall black fences, with a control booth to the left side, blending in with gray clouds. Of course, no one was in that tower. All the electric guards were turned off.

This could lead to science experiments.

"All right," Richard said calmly, yet out of breath. "What do we have in here?"

"I see a helicopter," Jim replied, putting his face against the barrier. "It seems to be military grade, with twin rotors, and a camouflage color scheme."

Along with a helicopter were cars, gun racks, and other equipment that would apply to their current situation.

"What should we use to stop him?" Richard asked urgently. "We only have so long before he fixes the time machine. You know how surprisingly quick he is with technology."

"Obviously." Jim thought for a moment. "We'd better use the helicopter. Something quicker than whatever he has."

As Jim was talking, he heard a vague noise. Then, two shadows appeared under the condemned buildings and became two people. Those two revealed themselves to be Jen and Krystal.

"Hey! You guys!" Jen shouted, eventually getting closer. "Krystal and I have figured out a way to execute Patrick."

"Krystal?" Richard asked, raising an eyebrow. "I guess you changed sides."

"I guess so," Krystal replied with a devious smirk. "I came to my senses, I guess."

"Does this mean that Patrick will start to come to his senses too?" Jim asked.

"Oh God, no," Richard rolled his eyes. "He's locked up in the looney bin and is there to stay."

"If that's the case," Jen said, "Then we should go stop him."

The four agreed and ran to the big black fence, which they all crossed over easily and safely—there was no electricity to operate it—and ran toward a military-grade, twin-rotor helicopter graded with carbon fiber in black.

***

December 27, around midnight

I slammed tirelessly throughout the eastside neighborhoods. I didn't know if people could hear me, but regardless, they might thank me later. My CTS-V was louder than any these people had heard in a long time, and it didn't make a difference if they woke up or not. They had no tools to stop me.

I had time to spare, now that I had a car to run away with. And even if Richard came after me, he would assume I'd take the fastest route. Ah, but no. I might just take some convoluted detour to spread us apart and eventually lead myself back to the site of the time machine.

The time machine was at Wisconsin and Prospect, and I was currently at Prospect and Brady, around one mile north. If I took

Brady and followed it to other streets, I could confirm a win at
my expense.

I turned the corner as fast as I'd ever been going—it didn't
seem like too much of a big deal after a week of running.

Five minutes past the hour

Silent night.

Holy night.

Holy shit, this machine was loud.

This machine, being the only sound heard in the dead of
night, in the dead of *this* night, was eerily beautiful. Perhaps being
the last sound recorded by mankind, even I couldn't comprehend
the roar this car produced. At this time.

Looking at street signs with their green and white faces,
slashing my vision with a knife, I could process the names of
Water and Kilbourn. I only needed to get to Wisconsin via Water,
and I'd be on my merry way.

As I cruised along at around forty mph for good safety
measure, I noticed a subtle rumble in the background of the loud
V8. It sounded like a little whir. Electric. I worried it was the
engine, perhaps out of gas or something like that, but I obviously
couldn't check that.

Then, in my rearview mirror, I saw a white light coming up
from behind. *How is this possible in these circumstances?*

I pulled back the sunroof, and above the panel of glass, I saw
that white light and the outline of a helicopter. *A helicopter can't
work without electricity*, I thought. *This must be a ploy.*

That helicopter could only be flown by Richard Clark and
his gang.

Oh, I'm laughing inside my head right now.

Chapter 23

The helicopter squatted to a mere two stories above my level. The big, two-rotor military helicopter barely fit inside the tight block of Water Street. I'd already passed Wisconsin Avenue without knowing.

Then, I heard a voice come through a loudspeaker, like the pilot would speak to a robber or car-chase criminal. I glanced at my speedometer; I was going thirty-five now.

"Shields"—I instantly knew it was Richard's voice—"are you shocked at what we have here?"

I prepared to make a snappy comment but hesitated just before speaking. "How, exactly?" I asked, peering up for a second and then focusing back on the road.

"There is a nuclear weaponry airbase at Sixth and Brown," Jim said. "We found that these weapons, such as this helicopter, run on independent electronic servers off the international grid."

Woo. Smart. It seemed that one of my ideas prevailed back in the 2030s. But it was no longer to my advantage.

"We believe that your run will end here, once and for all," a female voice said. "And will end possibly with your death."

It sounded like Jen for a minute. Then it didn't, really. It had to be someone I knew.

Krystal? Is this a joke?

I squinted at the thought, blocking out everything but the headlights of the car. I knew it might have happened, and why would it have not?

Oh well, add fuel to the fire.

To those above, it was a signal that I was trying to escape. And it was factual. I slammed the gas pedal down on Water Street, and eventually fled under a deserted freeway to Saint Paul Avenue.

The helicopter rose with a bit of a weave out of the street block. As it went upward at a thirty-degree angle, it just skimmed some buildings, but the powerful rotors were unscathed. The overhangs of the oldest buildings in the city, circa 1860s, were broken off, and rubble landed on the street, along with my hood. With lights like a disco ball pointing in all directions, outshining the starry night above, it created activity that everyone could hear, but it seemed nobody did. Engines and rotors and everything else created something that only we could ponder.

As I raced by Jefferson Street, I was only half a mile from the site of the time machine. Getting there was a little confusing, though; it seemed like I should remember it.

Doesn't matter, I thought as I swiped at the steering wheel, pointing the nose the north and turning left. I was getting closer by the second, with a huge military helicopter following me from behind. With its rotors ripping in the wind, it was hard to hear anything outside of that realm, but I did hear a noticeable cough coming from under my hood.

What is it? I have no idea. I took a quick glance at the dash and found the fuel gauge registered on empty.

Empty! Are you kidding me?

The car came to a complete crawl on the slight incline of a hill.

Richard slowed the rotors down continuously, and the helicopter prepared to land. I let go of the steering wheel in anger. Out of all the things that could have gone wrong while running away through a barren city and being chased by a military helicopter, I ran out of gas? The simplest but least predictable situation.

What a funny day.

The Caddy came to a standstill. The military helicopter slowed down at the same rate, taking its protruding body and laying it to rest on the street. The wind from the rotors blew the trees in a whispering yet noticeable manner, swaying like my mind.

The wheels deployed and kissed the ground. The rotors came to a standstill as the entrance on the left side cracked open. Out came two people I knew very well. One I expected; the other was a bit of a shock.

Richard and Krystal walked across the concrete with their shadows following them. They approached my dead Cadillac, probably thinking that after all the chances they had to stop me, they finally had.

And I might say, once and for all, that they were right.

Richard knocked on the window. I pressed it down to the bottom and then turned off the key. He pointed at me to get out of the car. His expression and demeanor said it all.

I unlocked my door, opened it slowly, and stepped out. He grabbed my shoulders very firmly and walked me over to the helicopter. He took me to the opened door, threw me inside, and shut the door. He then stepped into the cockpit, and I saw he was flying the entire heli.

Inside, it was a typical helicopter, with supplies and gun racks on the side. Two of them watched over me—Jim and Jen.

They didn't say word to me. And I didn't speak to them either. I had nothing to say. I was handcuffed, as the two watched me, and the military helicopter took off into flight, the rotors brushing grime and dust everywhere.

I didn't know how to react, as I knew my time could be up once and for all after this month. They had captured me; all my tools had been used up. Knowing what was happening to me, I simply kept a straight face.

***

December 27
1:30 a.m.

There was only silence during the entire trip to wherever I was flying. The only thing I could hear was those big black rotors whipping in the wind.

Where am I going? Best to ask.

"Where are you taking me?" I asked.

Jim and Jen said nothing, but Richard replied, "We are taking you to the county courthouse." He seemed angry. "And we plan to give you the death penalty in the electric chair."

Oh … oh no. I never thought that would happen, especially something like that. Knowing about electricity, I knew how much those hurt.

I sank mentally. The death penalty … it was a huge shock to me. My run was over. I would not go on to save the world but to kill it, like a hunted animal.

I frowned.

"We will be landing in thirty seconds, everyone," Richard called to the back.

I looked out the window and saw that we were landing in that field they had talked about. It was filled to the brim with equipment similar to that on the helicopter. Why did I never know about it?

The courthouse was two blocks or so to the south, and it was not visible at all. The entire ground below was pitch black, with buildings and skyscrapers, making a maze in the sky, difficult to navigate. The only lights were the natural ones in navy-blue star-studded sky.

The helicopter then began to touch the ground once again and rolled along the ground a few feet to the north, surrounding various equipment similar to this.

The rotors stopped. The engines died down to a halt, and so did the movement of the aircraft. The pod door whipped open outward, letting the cool December breeze infiltrate the inside.

"All right," Richard said casually, seeming pleased. "I am impressed by how easy this has been."

Jen and Jim pushed me out of the side of the heli onto the soggy, muddy grass. My hands were cuffed behind my back, so I really couldn't escape.

Krystal and Richard came out, with one pleasantly looking at me with a devious grin and the other happy to stare away. The other two picked me up on my feet and pointed at me to walk toward the south.

Krystal and Richard marched behind, as Jim and Jen watched over me so I wouldn't try to escape.

We proceeded in a quick manner toward the fence, and I saw the hole they cut out in the middle of it just hours ago. We all slid through easily.

Out in the open now, the courthouse's menacing gray structure appeared in the distance.

I was heading there to my death.

2:00 a.m.

The courthouse was now just feet away; the four still tirelessly dragged me there.

Along a slight incline were three sets of front doors. Three arches atop them completed the entranceway.

Richard chose the middle one. "We have to get the door down somehow."

Jim walked up and found the screws loosely holding the door. He took an electric drill and removed the screws, one by one, until the door could be pried off.

The door shed some shingles of wood to the ground, and Jim set it under dim white lighting. Jim stepped in; Richard and I followed; and the rest were behind.

When I entered the gigantic building, a whole new setting appeared. Dark. Blank. Black. I couldn't see anything, and nothing could be turned on. Not one single human body was inside the complex of a building. Did any of the others know where the room was that held an electric chair? I wasn't sure they could find it.

"Where is the room anyhow?" I asked assertively.

"Shut it," Richard responded, feeling triumphant. "Where is the room anyhow?"

"Probably on the second floor or something like that," Jen replied. "Most courtrooms are on the first."

All kept walking once again. The only lighting was from the bit of the sky outside. Evil. Jim felt for a stairway or a hallway, and a railing was there. He began to walk up the staircase like a blind man, using his touch for navigation. He did so successfully, finding a short, seven-step stairway raised from the granite tiling by four feet.

He went up first, and Richard and I followed in order. The only thought in my mind was that I would finally lose my battle after all this time.

Jim kept going, finding the same number of steps to the left. He steadily walked up them, and the rest of us followed.

With little light to show what was inside, Jim said, "I believe this is the main hall to each courtroom," and then his echo bounced off each Grecian-esque pillar that supported the giant roof.

Tapping cautiously along the tile for twenty feet, Jim led us through the hallway to the supposed room. It appeared he now knew where it was.

As for the history of the electric chair, lethal injection sort of replaced it. But as technology advanced, like usual, it became more efficient and worked so humanely that a more modern variant was now used. It was even approved for the entire country.

Later, the hall was coming to an end, with two smaller hallways spanning left to right, forming a T-shaped intersection with a painting of Milwaukee at the end. We approached the wall with smooth tan wood that I felt with a stroke of my hand.

Richard looked both ways at the signs above the hallways. One read BATHROOM. The other read JAIL CELL NETWORK.

Getting closer ...

Jim walked up to the door to the right and felt the golden door handle below. He began to pick the lock with a paperclip. It worked somehow, and he slowly pulled the door open.

When we entered, a whole new setting appeared. A curved white hallway, like bright, blank canvases, led to the left. Almost nothing was in the hallways, just twenty-inch perimeter screens mounted on the walls as maps and prisoner info, all turned off. After proceeding along cold gray tile in the absolutely pitch-black scenario, another door appeared to the left. It had a window to the left of it too.

This isn't looking too good, I thought.

This time, Jim handed Krystal the paper clip, but she declined it. Instead, she found the window nearby and broke it to pieces, with some glass falling into the room. This revealed what was inside.

And what sat inside was an electric chair.

The window opening was large enough to fit a human, and so we climbed through the broken window slot—and saw blood on the floor and walls. There was a viewing room to the left and a jail cell to the right. It had one light that was able to light up the entire room. There was a steel bucket filled with water with a cloth hanging over it. Next to it was a stand with sanitary gloves on it.

"What happened here?" Krystal asked Jen.

"Killings happened in here a long time ago," Jen replied softly.

Everyone was now inside the small room, except for Richard and Jim, who sat outside the shattered window, ready for the show to start.

The chair was white and modern, with sort of a half-cup portion to keep the person inside. There were no straps or anything. You just sat on there. And I just sat on it, laying my head on the shocks built in, like it was acupuncture. Sort of like lying on a deathbed, just waiting there, looking in the black sky and praying to God with little hope left. *Let me die, let ... me ... die.*

But I sat up with confidence. Why did I do so? Because the thought occurred to me: *how can an electric chair work without electricity?*

"How will this work?" I asked, faking my depression.

Krystal leaned over the control booth and looked at the wiring down below. She was a tech expert like me.

"Huh ..." she said, standing back up. "The chair appears to run on an independent server, which means that the electricity is developed right from the booth and not from the wireless cloud. It was designed before the wireless cloud became a standard on appliances. *It still works.*"

I then lay back down in the same solitary manner as before. *It truly will work this time, and there is absolutely nothing that can be done with it now.*

"Turn the system on, Krystal," Richard called from the outside. "We got ourselves here right now. Let's see it happen."

My time was up. Most say it should have been ten years ago, especially Richard. I tried so hard. So goddamn hard. I built a time machine that was on the other side of the city. It didn't work. I traveled far back in time to see the Mayans. The ancient cities. To travel across China. I did more than most dare to wish. It wasn't that bad.

I simply couldn't save the world. Everyone doubted me, and I couldn't prevail just as humans could not help themselves. This was the saddest thing I had ever dealt with in my life. The saddest thing I would ever deal with. I wished to go into wherever death would take me. *Just get me out of here. Out of planet earth. It's been a disgrace to me.* When it all was built up, the humans that hated me wanted to tear it all back down to nothing. *God, I wish you could just tell me what to do, because I messed up on you.*

God, take me away.

Death will be the best thing to happen to me in my life.

Krystal hit the button with a slight push; she got up and watched. I could feel the tension building up in my spine and my head and my legs, like needles raining on a windy plain. My palms started to sweat and shake at the thought. My entire bottom side was electrified with no electricity. The burn started to become a ghastly wind, getting hotter, and hotter, and hotter—a burn that could not penetrate any more. It happened with all of its might, and I just braced for it to be all over. Rising, rising, rising, I clenched my eyes shut. I squeezed my palms.

The rest watched with no feeling whatsoever. This was it.

***

Bam!

A sudden explosion of fire beneath caused the chair to explode into many pieces, and I flew into the air and against the back wall. Jim, Jen, and Richard stood back to avoid being hit. Krystal ducked under the control booth. I was free from the electric chair.

I was still alive.

Wait … it didn't work.

It malfunctioned?

I opened my eyes wide, gaining confidence. I wasn't aware that I had to grab at the reins. I had new feelings coming up, and all new confidence building.

The machine had malfunctioned. All eyes, including mine, were as wide as saucers. I couldn't comprehend what had just occurred.

Cool!

I was free as a bird flying above. A sudden surge of all new power established itself within me.

I have all the time now to fix the time machine. I just have to get out of here first.

As the smoke cleared from the explosion, which at the moment was the only thing producing any light, I trembled my way through darkness and rubble at my feet. I swayed my arms through the air, feeling for the opening in the broken window, with air passing through my fingers. I did so without any of the others being able to see me. I crawled through the window effortlessly. I knew now that the hallways led in both directions, so I ran to the left and sprinted hard. I couldn't hear anyone following me—no running footsteps—but it didn't matter. I had to get back to the time machine, which was ten minutes away, because I knew they were all still alive.

This hallway seemed much lengthier than I first thought, and I was losing energy, the quickest I ever have. But I kept going and that was when I heard footsteps following me.

The first thing to do was look for an exit.

There ought to be a door to the outside somewhere. I saw nothing, and felt nothing but jail cell bars. Then I saw the wall—a great big gray concrete wall in front of me. Both doors to each side were locked, and Krystal was getting closer. There was nothing I could do but surrender.

"Wait!" she called out. "I have to talk to you!"

It didn't sound encouraging until she said that. She slowed down and got within inches. "You don't realize!" she exclaimed, putting her hands on her knees, out of breath. "I hacked into it so you could survive and keep going."

I raised my eyebrows in surprise; she was now the reason I was still here.

And I was disgusted too. Why would she join their side? *Maybe it helped. I don't know what to say.* "Thank … you?" I spit out under my breath. I collected my thoughts. "This actually helps my case a lot. Now I have another chance to save the planet."

We looked at each other one last time, and I ran to the left to escape out the door. It appeared to be quite old and falling apart. I cleared the rubble of the decrepit door and made my way back to the gloomy, extremely dark outside.

I knew where the time machine was. And I had to get there, fast. If the others were not dead, they were still hungry for me to die, now more than ever before.

I looked back once more. Krystal was still running fifty paces behind.

2:40 a.m.

At Cass Street and Wisconsin Avenue, I was now only one hundred feet away from the time machine. The physical stamina was at an all-time low, but the mental concentration was at an all-time high. It balanced out quite nicely.

I passed the deserted buildings on the left and right; only the moon to the east gave my direction. The curve along the bluff was approaching fast.

And at last, there it was, shining alone in the moonlight at all the vertices and edges. The time machine was still there, and there also were the supplies to fix the touchscreen.

I made it a few seconds later, opening the pod door and looking for supplies and damage. It wasn't too bad.

I took a screwdriver and a high-tech seal lighter (a welding machine that uses light) to fix the touchscreen. As I began, I saw Krystal jogging outside.

"I'm here!" she said, seeming certain that I needed her.

In the end, I probably did. I needed to break out as fast as I could.

"Do you want to help?" I asked calmly.

Of course she said yes, and I let her in.

***

3:00 a.m.

Replacing the glass and getting the wiring correct again was very strenuous, but it took less than twenty minutes. Most likely, it would work again.

"Wait!" Krystal called out. "Can I come with you again?"

I took my time on this one before I responded. "No," I said. "I need to do this by myself. This is the entire earth. You understand that, right?"

"Yes," she replied softly and seeming saddened too.

I walked back into the time machine and decided to give a send-off before leaving.

"Thank you," I said. "Thank you for sticking with me and helping me when my case seemed lost. If I don't come back, I just want the world to know that I was only saving it and that the medicine was never intended to hurt."

She smiled, and I smiled back. She teared up, and I did as well.

I shut the pod door. I turned it on. It worked.

Krystal backed up.

I set it to 1901, New York City. It worked efficiently, as usual.

It rose off the ground, and I braced myself to go back in time.

And it did, successfully.

CHAPTER 24

December 28, 1901
New York City

> I threw a whip into the burning sky
> A cry to god once more
> Beg for mercy, it's all a lie
> beg for mercy with all in yore
> But what I see is melancholy
> blessed with alchemy
> A beautiful sight to my eyes
> All galore
> In time it was I
> Who bled
> On the death bed
> To see
> What has become no more
> The earth has become no more
> But deep inside the sleeping shadows
> Far away where no one goes
> Lives a place of freedom space
> And after all I had been through
> I was almost there only to what I succumbed to

I awoke to a chilling wind creeping on my spine. I braced my arms on the cold aluminum floor and picked up my weary body. Where was I in New York now?

I peeled my eyes open and looked out the window to the right. Outside was dark, no light showing. I couldn't see a thing. I could only feel where I was.

I unlocked the capsule door and pushed the heavyweight open. It sounded like it was pushing branches and tree limbs back, a bending sound. I assumed I was in yet another forest of Central Park.

Okay, I'm here. Nobody sees me. Nobody can see me. I'm good to go. Ready to save the future of our earth. How exactly am I going to do that?

Originally, I wanted to kill off any sort of technology—the exact stuff that shaped our very lives. But it turned out to be a lot harder than I thought.

This was the supposed end of the book. All I needed to do was finish the story. But how?

I was in territory where I was wanted. I was wanted in every time after 401 BCE. I was wanted now because of my amazing technology. I was wanted later because of my wrongdoing. My goal was to destroy technology in the past for a safer future.

What made the future so ridiculous? Was it all the advancement through life that was part of nature?

My time machine was part of advancing through tools and nature. After the world started to fall apart, physically and virtually, in December, it seemed that this progression was sped up, but not naturally. Who did it? Was it the people who kept making money off their products? That was only because the public accepted the fate. Was it the public's fault that they accepted the fate of modern technology consuming their brains, virtually? Oh yes, indeed.

I breathed deeply as I thought. I let more air get in, to think clearer.

Whose fault was it; who created an uphill journey to a landslide? You know whose fault it was? Mine. It was all my fault.

Why?

It was because of my time machine. It was the thing that I thought would save me, while it was ripping every other being apart. It was a horrible cause. Some might view it as selfish. I literally brought more technology into the present because of human curiosity. When they saw that shiny, ahead-of-its-time device, of course they wanted to learn as much about it as possible. To them, it was a good thing. *We could get so far ahead with this invention*, they said to themselves and each other. Why didn't I know that?

I was too focused on the cause at hand. I wanted to get rid of what they already had and eliminate all the ideas they had to head into eventual modernity.

I finally figured myself out and what went wrong in my plan. What should I have gotten rid of in order to save the earth?

I needed to eliminate the idea of a time machine. There are people who are crazy enough to literally get rid of everything for a different lifestyle. A safer lifestyle. If I got rid of those two factors, there would be no forward lifestyle. And there would be no technology, exactly what I was trying to get rid of. If someone saw the evidence of what we were dealing with, they would not end up like this. This plan would work. I thought it was almost foolproof. Almost. I'd said that the first time though...What I had to do was get rid of the time machine. And what I really needed to do was get rid of myself.

I needed to die.

It was a simple statement. Because that simply was what it meant. Richard and Krystal and everyone else who was affected by my wrongdoings were right. I had to be gone in order to save the planet. If I was gone, the idea of *me* would be gone. Because I was also in the past, time would progress on, and no one would know that I was there once to abolish the idea. That there would be this deadly uproar in our technology. But didn't this mean that it would just be like it used to be?

It didn't, actually.

It's not because I once existed. Once. Someone would know, somehow. And because someone would know, that one person would also know that I was right about our future. That would mean they would fix it over time. Except I wouldn't be there. What I unfortunately created actually allowed me to destroy it.

***

I sound absolutely crazy. Really? This is what I have come to? After all of this, I end up dead? How can it work if I no longer exist? Nothing might happen. It might end up like how it is currently—a sad, slow destruction. There is a one-in-a-million chance of this working, and if it doesn't, I will live in hell for the rest of time.

I guess I have sounded crazy this whole time. But I was sort of right, so far. I just couldn't fix it.

My mind is blank. No thoughts. Just a memory of what horrible things I have already done.

***

A few minutes later, still in thought
It can't hurt to try.

I must do this. No matter how it turns out, I need to leave this plane, knowing I at least tried.

I have to leave this plane for the sake of others. I was never a selfish person. If such a sacrifice is what it takes, then I am up for it.

I still have my doubts. If this doesn't work, the only person I am saving from this atrocity is myself.

***

As I pondered these deep thoughts, I found myself in the same forest in New York as last time. I peered out of the fence and looked at all the old buildings and cars on the streets, like it never changed.

I had always loved the designs of these buildings. Such thoughtfulness and uniqueness and creativity in an exterior wall. Beautiful. I loved these designs more than what we had in the present. I always thought this became simpler, to the point where it just lacked creativity.

But I never would have appreciated these designs if there were not others.

You don't love something to its fullest until it's gone. Will this include the planet? No, because it won't be gone.

I needed something to kill myself.

That's right.

I felt motivated to do so, for my sake, and for the sake of the rest of the world.

Like a poison or something—a painless death.

Perhaps there is something at a local pharmacy, I thought.

I crawled out of my rest area and peered over the wooden fence to look at all the businesses. I found a pharmacy at the far end of the street, almost near the Flatiron.

How was I supposed to get there when I looked so different from everyone else? Calhoun would find me and probably was still looking for me.

I needed to fit in. *Funny how that needs to happen,* I thought. *Never have.*

Looking around on the forest floor, I found nothing except for sticks and the path I'd made myself. As I crunched twigs beneath my tired feet, I stepped on something quite soft.

I looked down, and it appeared to be a jacket from this era. Black, plush, well crafted.

From its position and from what I remembered, this could be Calhoun's coat. It was in the same position. Maybe he was looking for his coat.

Do I dare wear this to get over there, even with him on watch? Eh, it's better than whatever the hell I'm wearing.

I put on the coat—it was a little small but it sufficed as a disguise. I then crawled past the time machine and crawled quietly along the deep forest path and across the fence. I hopped onto the cobblestone sidewalk and walked on it, just like anyone else would.

I figured it was afternoon; few were out on the streets, and the ones who were didn't seem to notice me. I kept walking, not forgetting what I was about to do as a cold breeze moved the trees slowly.

Getting closer, I approached the intersection. Sitting there in the cold was a man with a gray beard, wearing a similar jacket to mine and a hat. He stood next to me and looked at my attire with a critical eye. He seemed to notice my trashed blue jeans right away and then looked in the other direction.

"Jesus Christ, whatever happened to decent attire these days? Yeesh," he muttered through his stained teeth.

"I know, right?" I replied, not really knowing what to say.

"Ugh," he groaned, rolling his eyes as he crossed the street to the east. I went to the north.

I approached the pharmacy, which was to my right across the street. Every single building was black and white; but they seemed more colorful than they really were. All were dressed in a cream, with white and brick-red accents, along with displays of clothes, flowers, and classic furniture in each front window.

The pharmacy was white, so it was easy to see. It was a relatively small building along Fifth Avenue.

I traveled across the cobblestone street, clutching my coat together to block the cold wind. Each tap of my foot against the gray cobblestone came with a shiver up my leg.

This pharmacy better be open ...

I looked at the front door, and the entrance had an OPEN sign, so I walked inside. A bell atop the door rang as I came in, and the door shut on its squeaky hinge.

"Good evening, sir," the clerk greeted me.

"Yeah, hey," I replied, out of breath, looking around. *Oh, poison ... where? Does it even have any?* "Do you have any types of poisons in this pharmacy?"

The clerk pondered this for a few seconds and then said, "Why, yes, we do." She looked a little perturbed by my presence. She seemed like a middle-aged woman. She then walked over to an area on the right, saying, "We have it but it normally doesn't sell too well—because it's poison." She walked behind the counter and showed me all the options. "Which one would you like?"

I wasn't good with this stuff. I never thought I'd need poison. I wanted a painless death, if anything at all, to save the future.

"Can you describe them for me?" I asked.

"To the left we have insecticide, pesticide, and the typical germicide," she said. "To the right we have more deadly poisons, including arsenic, which can kill any living organism in a short time if enough is used." She paused for a moment and then added, "It is our least-selling drug, very deadly."

I decided to go with the arsenic pills or whatever she'd just said. *Sounds deadly and instant,* I thought. "I'll take two bottles," I said casually.

"Are you sure?" she asked.

"Yes, I am."

"But why?"

Oh really? I have to tell her why? "Ma'am, I'm in a hurry. I need that, please."

She shrugged, bagged it, and walked back to the register. "That will be two dollars," she said.

I put my last two dollars on the white counter, and the clerk stuffed it into the old black cast-iron register.

"Have a nice evening."

I walked out but looked back for a second at the inside. She was just standing there, staring at me, clearly confused about why I would buy such a poison. The door shut with a slam.

I sprinted across that street, hoping that the time machine was still there. *If it's not there, that's it for all of us.*

I ran with a determined look on my face along the wooden fence and the Central Park forest, looking for that path I'd made. This made the pharmacy seem much closer to it than it really was.

I looked to my right, found the path, and leaped across the fence as fast as I could so no one would get suspicious. Someone probably already was—that clerk.

I looked for the time machine, and thankfully, it was where I'd left it. I slowed to a stop and just stared at the time machine.

I have to destroy this creation, I thought, *but I need someone to know it existed at one point. They just can't use it.*

I walked into the machine, looking around, trying to figure out how to preserve it.

I decided to simply destroy the control screen. I walked out of it, and slowly but surely picked up a thick branch. With one long, hard swing, I smashed the control screen into millions of glass shards that tapped the ground like snowflakes.

A tear dripped from my left eye as I did this. I dropped the branch. Now I had one thing left to do—the hardest part of this ... this unlimited feat to change history for the better.

I hesitated. I wanted to see my accomplishment, and see that

I could be right in the end, and see how much happier everyone on earth would be.

I slouched down and sat against the wall of the time machine. *Is it really too much to ask for me to see this new world? I'm the only one who wants to see it.*

I looked at the sky and saw nothing but tree limbs hiding me from the gray sky. *It's like a metaphor for the situation I am in,* I thought. *The world does not want me to see outside of what I am already encapsulated in.*

That was it. Maybe my results would be even worse than what I could imagine. Maybe that's what it was telling me.

Perhaps I should not defy expectations anymore and just deal with what I am right now.

I decided that I needed to go.

Yet another tear.

A tear in my eye. A tear in our world.

I was the only one who could switch it back.

"Okay, goodbye, world," I said aloud, while grabbing the bottles I had just purchased.

I had seen this before—it was a deadly poison that could kill within five minutes depending on the dose. It was a black hole of poison to dive into and stay in for a while.

I then wrote a short note. My final signal and goodbye, if anyone should care.

As I chewed and swallowed the poison, I finished the note. My emotions, whether dark or light, channeled through tears, to ink on the paper.

> By the time you read this, I will be dead. I have been to the future and the past, and just let me tell you, it was amazing. I was the one who defied

all and the one who tricked this planet. I have lived through doubt and the constant blasphemy about my soul. I would love to live on but I know too much now. The little machine I kept in my pocket would have let you time travel. I failed my mission and got rid of its power. Don't let anyone get to this.

This is what messed me up, messed the entire world up, and now we are like this. But luckily, I have a drawing of 2050. I will put it at the bottom of this note.

I hope you all have a better life. And remember—the future holds a lot of scary things.

The mindless don't appreciate the mindful.

But the mindful care about the mindless.

That's what messed up our world.

And now we've lost.

Lost the game.

The game we were all forced to play.

Win, next time.

Forever yours,
Patrick Shields

Man, what feelings, such an edge with this experience. I actually enjoyed it, trying to get my message out there. Such feelings of shock. Rhapsody.

Can't go on forever, though.

***

At that moment, Patrick let go of the paper. As the paper floated down, Patrick's body continued to drop faster as seconds whizzed by. As his body hit the floor, a loud thump erupted on the floor of the machine. His soul released through the cold-water vapor of the December breeze and lifted out of the trees, and separated it from his body, after being together for over forty-seven years.

Patrick Shields was now gone.

Another soul in the wormhole.

Chapter 25

December 28, 1901
8:00 p.m.

Darkness had fallen in New York City. Every street was still lit up, with building lights and street lights shining along Fifth Avenue. A light fluffy snow drifted slowly from the black sky, creating a thin layer of white along the cobblestone streets. Schools and businesses were finished for the day across Manhattan. Everyone was almost content tonight. Yet, even after Christmas, a sense of melancholy was in the air. A presence that felt slightly uneasy.

In the local pharmacy, the clerk, named Ruth, was closing up shop for the day. She had to get back to her brownstone and eat dinner and catch up with her family. Her last duties included cleaning off the counter and organizing the drugs and medicines.

Normally happy to walk back through the cold to her home, which was a mile or so south, she was clearly still baffled about that guy who had taken some of her poison inventory.

"That is one of the first customers to purchase any sort of poison from here," she said to herself, shaking her head. She took one last look at the counter, which was completely dust-free, and walked across the slightly shaky wooden floor. She put on her black coat and hat, and then picked up a lamp from the ground. She opened the creaky door and walked outside.

She locked the door, put the key in her pocket, and made her way across the cobblestone street as quickly as she could, while being careful not to slip.

She held the lamp in front of her coat as her guide through the dim street lighting. A few carriages were parked along the street, their roofs slowly becoming covered in snow. Ruth walked as fast as she could while using her hat to block the cold snowflakes.

Passing by building after building, she had the same thoughts she did every night. She missed her children, who were home, with a neighbor keeping watch over them. She missed her husband, who was farming for the family in northern New Jersey, providing most of the food for his family. They were healthy with the medicine and food from both jobs, but the wages weren't very high.

She constantly tried to replace the thoughts of the man and his poison with these thoughts.

She had nothing to do but walk and look at each lamppost. *How dim each is.* She walked carefully, squinting her eyes against the snow, which was falling faster. She continued walking past the lamps, looking at each one. Seldom was anything attached to the cast-iron lampposts, so when she saw a piece of paper attached to the pole, swaying in the wind, it caught her eye. She ripped the paper off the post and began to read it.

"I wonder what this is about?" Ruth asked to herself.

What she read was shocking. She read something about a deep depression in the stock market and that the person reading had to prevent it to help shape the future. She couldn't process it all at once. And when she got to the part about two time-travelers writing the message, she was in complete shock. She dropped the note and held her head.

"Two time-travelers?" she asked herself, confused. "Isn't that what that Calhoun guy was disturbed about?"

She had to tell someone about it. She didn't know what to think about this but considered that Calhoun wasn't so crazy after all.

"Finally, some proof for him," Ruth said, slightly worried. "I thought he was totally insane, confronted by those two time-travelers." Then, giving it more thought, she said, "Calhoun probably wrote this letter. You can't trust anyone in this world."

She thought it would be useful for her well-being and her business to get this reported for whatever it was. Maybe bring in some customers. It might help.

She instantly picked up the paper, dried it, folded it, and put it into her pocket. She looked up and then in all directions for anyone else out on the streets; she found no one.

She looked around once again and spotted a gap in the row of trees. Trees were everywhere along Fifth Avenue, but right there was a one-foot gap. She picked up her lantern, shined it against the trees, and saw it appeared to be a path.

There was literally no one out, so she then became focused on the path.

"More to the story?" she asked, raising an eyebrow.

She would have to wait to share what she'd just found, so Ruth decided to check out the path.

It's most likely for deer or something, she thought, walking closer to the path.

Once she got there, she found a fence ahead of her and a gap between numerous trees.

This path appears to be pretty wide and to go very deep, she thought. *Much too wide for any deer.*

She then picked up her lamp once again and shined it a foot in from the fence, and it instantly reflected on something much brighter, in a metallic color, much too bright and large to be a reflection.

"Whoa," Ruth gasped. "What in God's world is that?"

Totally focused on the end of that path, she took a huge step over the low fence and walked onto the path, crunching branches beneath her boots. She tried to get a better glimpse of what was there, and that silver reflective material just kept getting brighter and bigger. She figured she had to be close to the object somehow. Crunching even more branches and dirt and snow, she then nearly ran into the object, which was a material like she had never known, sort of like cast iron but lighter.

She swung the light around, completely oblivious to what this object was but curious to find out.

She swung the light lower to look for an entrance. What she would find then would be absolutely shocking.

Her lantern shone on a head, with eyes closed, mouth open, and then a body, leaning against the wall of the shining object. Ruth instantly knew he was deceased.

Ruth was shocked and dropped the lantern onto the snowy ground. She then picked it up again and collected her thoughts. Ruth was a naturally caring person, but she had never been confronted with anything like this.

"I need to find out what happened here," she said to herself, determined but worried. She cautiously uncovered the body from the snow; she didn't recognize the man. She carefully walked around the object, crunching across branches and two inches of snow. She looked for an entrance into the object, which was over two feet taller than she was and appeared very modern.

She shone the lantern along the ground and along the wall of it, and soon found that tree bark nearby was burned.

"This is so appalling!" she cried, trembling now in the snow.

She eventually got to the other side of the body and continued to shine the light along the ground, trying to find more details.

And she did.

Next to the body, Ruth found the empty bottles of arsenic tablets she had sold earlier that evening.

"Holy …" she gasped, picking up one of the bottles. "This has to be the bottle I sold to that man—I recognize the wrapping. I sold him a poison … to commit suicide."

She felt horrible now, knowing that this was the reason the man had wanted the poison.

No wonder why he wouldn't tell me, she thought, setting the bottle down. Right next to the bottle, she found yet another note, which was small and appeared to have a drawing on the bottom.

She picked it up, assuming it was probably the suicide note.

She shone the light very close to it and read it, word for word.

What she read was even more shocking—this man seemed to claim he was from the future and had failed at a mission; everyone hadn't believed him or his ideas. Ruth could not take it all in at one time.

The man's name, signed at the end of the note, was Patrick Shields. But none of this mattered to her after reading this suicide note. What stuck out for her were the words *time machine*.

"If he had a time machine," Ruth said to herself, "then this giant object must be the time machine!"

She continued to look for an entrance into the time machine. She eventually found it on the other side and walked in.

It was nothing like Ruth had ever seen before. Inside it was bright, minimalist, and more confusing than anything she had ever known.

"Is this the control area?" she asked, looking at the broken screen. It was totally destroyed and dismantled, much like it was described in the suicide note. "This has to be the time machine!" she exclaimed. "And that man has to be Patrick Shields, one of those time-travelers!"

The picture was becoming clear now. This time-traveler clearly killed himself for an unknown reason—at least it was unknown to Ruth as of now.

"Why would he come back in time to kill himself?" she asked

herself. "Something is very wrong with this situation. Calhoun was right; they do exist. He was most likely right about confronting them. But where's the other?"

So many questions without a single answer.

"I need to tell everyone about this," she said to herself. But then she realized he'd asked in the note that no one but the reader should find out. "Why wouldn't he want anyone to find out? Someone will find this eventually ... like me."

What she now realized was that the time-traveler, Patrick, meant that no one should

get ideas from it or use it in a bad way. She had to adjust the story a little to justify this.

She was then distracted by the time—she was over fifteen minutes late for her kids. She gasped, looking up at the clock on the street corner in the distance.

"I need to get home." She jumped over the fence, stuffing the suicide note into her right pocket. She began to jog toward her brownstone, which was up the street, around five blocks away along Sixty-Third Street.

She nearly slipped on the cobblestones near Sixty-Sixth but managed to make her way to Sixty-Third Street within three minutes. Trees and lampposts lined Fifth Avenue all the way down past her field of vision.

She turned to her left at the corner of Sixty-Third and Fifth. Third street was also lit up with buildings and street lights but was dimmer than Fifth.

Her home was near Park Avenue on the north block. It looked like a typical brownstone, with steps out front, a lamppost, snow-covered garden, and a few inside lights on.

She walked toward it along the slippery sidewalk, now covered with a thin layer of ice.

She walked up the same small staircase and unlocked the door with keys from her jacket.

"Whew," she gasped, tired but thankful she'd made it home safely. She hung up her hat and coat on the bronze rack and brushed the snow from her legs.

As she walked in, her kids, Charlie and Anna, came running up to her, delighted to see her for the first time in twelve hours.

"Mother!" they both cheered, hugging her. "Why were you so late tonight?"

She didn't how to explain what had happened to two young kids. "It's a long story," Ruth replied, thinking about the situation.

Looking around in the kitchen, there wasn't much left to eat, especially for three people. Ruth could tell her kids were hungry, but Ruth didn't have an appetite tonight. The kitchen had a simple, modern style and was small in size, being stuffed into a corner on the first floor.

"What would you guys like tonight?" Ruth asked, nearly falling asleep. "Please make it quick; I need some rest after what I've been through today."

"More ham!" Charlie exclaimed, excited to finally eat.

"Okay, got it," Ruth replied, slicing it on to two plates. She served it to Charlie and Anna and put the rest back into the freezer.

"Thank you, Mother," they both said with bright grins. Ruth gave a smile and then headed upstairs to her bedroom.

As exhausted as she was, Ruth still thought about how she would break this news to the public—and the sighting of that body who had been her last customer.

"If I say this the wrong way, Calhoun will instantly protest against it," she debated with herself. "I have to do this without interfering with his theories or giving him any sort of idea."

Her bedroom had a neoclassical style, with small details and intricacies in every corner, from the bed frame to the curtains. Ruth turned on a light atop a cabinet and lay down on her bed. She looked around, anxious to get the word out about her experience.

She glanced at her bookshelf, which had many types of reading material, from encyclopedias to novels. One particular novel was *The Time Machine* by H. G. Wells. It stood out like a lightning bolt to her after she supposedly had found *the* time machine.

She pulled that book off the shelf and began skimming through it, looking for something. She didn't know what, exactly. It was one of her husband's favorite books, but Ruth had never bothered to read it.

"Does it look like a piece of silver cheese in here?" she asked to herself. She kept skimming fast through every page but eventually gave up and set it down on her bed.

Ruth turned off the light and thought more about the situation. *I'm glad John's not here today*, she thought. *He would think I'd gone insane.*

She soon drifted off into the first stage of dreamy consciousness. Her thoughts from today penetrated her mind and would be injected into her dream.

***

December 29, 1901
6:00 a.m.

Ruth awoke at six o'clock, as she did every morning. This time it was not to go to work but for a much greater feat—to tell everyone of her discovery.

She threw off the covers and hopped out of bed. Her kids were up too, excited for one of the only times they got to see their mother.

"Why is she in such a rush today?" Charlie asked his sister.

Anna shrugged. "I don't know."

As the sun steadily rose, carriages and people began passing by. The first floor rattled a bit with all of the traffic just outside.

Ruth, now dressed, went to the kitchen to make breakfast

for her children. When she got there, her two kids were waiting for her.

"Can you play with us for a little while?" Anna asked, tugging on her dress.

"Sorry," Ruth replied, somewhat saddened. "I have to tell the news about what I found yesterday."

"Tell us about that Mother," Charlie begged.

"It's too complicated," Ruth said. "Perhaps we can talk about it later."

She poured out bowls of warm cereal for all three of them and ate hers as quickly as she could.

"Where are you going so early?" Anna asked.

"To tell the *New York Times*," Ruth said, heading straight to the coat rack. Ruth checked for both notes she'd put in her pockets yesterday. Both were still there. She buttoned her coat and put on a matching hat in charcoal black. As she was walking down the cold stairs to an even colder sidewalk, she wondered where the newspaper office was, exactly.

She wandered, looking east and west. "I feel it is not too far out of my way."

When she reached the corner to the south of her brownstone, she tried to remember where it was located. Then she remembered that it was a mile or so to the south. She instantly turned east toward Park Avenue.

Park Avenue, being one of the busiest streets in Manhattan, was filled with horses and carriages and with many pedestrians on the sidewalks. Traffic maneuvered slowly through the thick December snow. Ruth stood on the northwest corner of Sixty-Sixth and Park, getting slightly impatient to reach the *New York Times* office. She walked carefully across Sixty-Sixth and followed Park Avenue to the south.

As traffic increased near Grand Central Station, Ruth looked around her for the newspaper office. Surrounded by tall buildings designed from brick and stone, it was difficult for Ruth to find the correct building from afar.

Ruth thought it had a red brick facade and numerous white-clad windows. She looked to the south and finally recognized it. Ruth began to run through the traffic ahead, pushing her way through the people on the sidewalk. Within a minute, she had reached the entrance through all of the hustle and bustle. The door was unlocked and open to the public.

The *New York Times* office was on the second floor, but first she had to explain herself to the doorman, dressed in blue and standing behind a silver-topped counter.

"What is your business here?" he asked.

"Um ..." Ruth thought aloud. "I need to report something to the *Times*." Ruth was afraid she wouldn't be let in any farther than she already was.

The doorman thought for a few seconds and then said, "All right," he responded, rolling his eyes. "The *Times* office is on the second floor, ma'am."

"Thank you," Ruth replied with much enthusiasm. She followed a sign pointing to the stairway. Once she'd climbed the thin staircase, she reached a second-floor hallway that led to many rooms and doors and was dimly lit. Still, she could read the sign on one of the doors: NEW YORK TIMES.

She knocked and waited for a response. An answer did not come back right away. Ruth was about to knock again when the door swung open.

"Hello," Ruth said softly to the man who opened the door. "I am here to report some very important news."

The man scratched his head for a second, thinking. "Come on in," he replied brightly. "We will report any news that's relevant."

"This is really important," Ruth explained, walking inside the office. "At least to me."

The man, evidently a reporter, took a seat at an old chair near the door; another was organizing news stories. Ruth took her own seat next to the first one.

"I am Henry Sawyer, and over there, that's Charles Winthrop."

"Nice to meet both of you," Ruth replied, shaking Henry's hand and then Charles's but not really happy about wasting time with greetings.

"What is the news you have to share with us this morning?" Henry asked, seeming eager to listen.

"You no doubt have heard the rumors about the time-travelers who were here a week ago," Ruth said.

"Correct," Henry replied.

"Well …" Ruth hesitated and then said, "I found one of those time-travelers next to the time machine. He was clearly deceased. It was in Central Park. It was all shiny and modern and quite odd. I couldn't believe what I saw."

Henry took one long breath but said nothing. He looked at Charles. They both seemed skeptical, and Ruth wondered if they would refuse to believe her.

"Do you remember how much you drank last night?" Henry asked.

Ruth gave Henry an angry look, but Charles snickered once and then started laughing.

"Are you joking?" Ruth asked angrily. "You have the audacity to think I drank to excess?"

Charles and Henry were now both laughing at the story.

Ruth then pulled the note from her coat pocket. "Here, Mr. Sawyer," she said. "Read this." She handed him the suicide note.

He began to read it and as he did, he stopped laughing. He focused on it, reading it aloud, and raised his eyebrows at words like *time machine* and the sentence "the future holds a lot of scary things."

In the end, however, Ruth was disappointed with his reaction.

"Anyone could have written this," Henry said, shrugging.

"Hey, now, don't come to conclusions so quickly," Charles interrupted. "Let me see the note."

Henry handed the note to Charles, who read it again with a straight face. When he finished, he dropped the note on his desk and began laughing again.

"That's ridiculous!" he said.

"I'm afraid it is," Henry agreed. "I don't think this is worth reporting, to be completely honest, ma'am."

Ruth held her head high. "You don't understand," she said. "I don't drink … and I'm not making this up."

Although it was obvious they didn't believe her, the two reporters gave her their attention once again.

"I saw the machine. It's near Fifth Avenue." She smiled. "I can take you to the location and show you what I've seen, if you—"

"I don't know," Henry replied.

"Please," Ruth said. "Could you at least report it as a rumor?"

Henry and Charles thought about it for a few moments. The quietness of the room became a portal to the sounds of the street and other nearby rooms. Carriages driving past and muffled voices could be heard, ringing in Ruth's ears. Both reporters finally came to a decision.

"All right. Fine," Henry said to Ruth, rolling his eyes. "We will report this."

Ruth was delighted to hear this. "Oh my goodness, thank you!"

"If we hurry, we can get it in the second edition," Charles said from the other side of the desk.

"Can I use the notes as part of the article?" Henry asked.

"Of course, sir," Ruth replied.

Ruth sat back down timidly, as Henry and Charles worked together to write the report. When they finished, they handed it to Ruth. She accepted it and began to read. Under the byline of Henry Sawyer and Charles Whitman, the news report read:

Today is a rather unique day in the news. Indeed, the news story pertains to the ongoing theory of two time-travelers supposedly coming here and attempting to change history. Now, a week later, we have a report of a rather disturbing sighting. A witness has told us that a time-traveler, just one, was found dead with the time machine next to the body. It is reported to be shiny and modern-looking. If this is true, it would confirm that it is a suicide because the time-traveler left a suicide note. We intend to publish this note, below. In retrospect, it is an interesting read.

They'd printed the note in the report and then added additional comments:

We feel this note is genuine. It is heartfelt and honest; it sounds like a goodbye that only this specific person could have written. The witness also believes she saw the time machine somewhere along Fifth Avenue. We plan to investigate the specific location and will report our findings in the next edition of the *New York Times.*

Ruth nodded as she finished reading and returned the report to Henry.

"Hey ... uh ... what's your name?" Henry asked politely.

"Ruth, sir," she replied with a bit of a smile. "Thank you for publishing the story. I have to get to my job along Fifth Avenue now."

"We will check for the supposed time machine later today."

"Thank you."

Ruth stood up and buttoned her coat in preparation for the long, snowy walk to the pharmacy.

Chapter 26

Ruth followed along the north end of Park Avenue, which had much less foot traffic and activity than southbound.

I hope I didn't keep anyone waiting at the pharmacy this morning, Ruth thought.

With a ten-minute stretch of brick buildings, snowy ground, and cloudy sky, she finally made it Sixty-Sixth Street.

She decided not to return home to see her children; time was dwindling. No time whatsoever to ramble about. Now, within a mile from her house, Ruth began to question how she would get the word out about the dilemma. Should she tell her customers? Or even show them?

They'll think I'm insane, she thought, staring down at the red and gray sidewalk. She could now spot her pharmacy from Fifth Avenue. She looked closely for any customers outside the door.

She gasped once she got a clear view. She rubbed her eyes with her snow-covered gloves. "God, there are at least ten people there!"

She increased her pace and began to jog the rest of the way. The waiting customers could now see Ruth.

"There she is!" a man called out, pointing to her.

"What was the cause of this delay?" a woman demanded.

"Uh … it's a very long story," Ruth said. She slid past the group, unlocked the door, and let everyone inside.

The crowd entered in an orderly fashion as Ruth took her place behind the counter. She wiped it off swiftly and glanced at various sections of the small shop to make sure everything was in place. Within a couple of minutes, a daily shopper named Anne was ready to make her purchase.

"Ruth," she said, "you are never late to work. You always show up on the dot. You're always organized. What happened today?"

Ruth calculated the cost and wondered how to explain the situation to a patient Anne. "You really want to know why? You'll never believe me."

"Yes, I do," Anne replied with certainty.

Ruth took a deep breath and then said, "I was walking home last night, as usual, and I noticed a gap or path in the woods. When I went to investigate, I found a ... dead body. It was a time-traveler, along with his time machine in the woods. It is the craziest thing I have ever encountered."

Anne didn't exactly know how to reply. "Have you developed a drinking problem?" she asked cautiously. "My husband used to have one, and he fixed it by—"

"Oh, for the love of God, I don't drink!" Ruth shouted, clearly agitated. She slapped the counter, and the attention of the ten or so customers was suddenly directed toward Ruth.

"My apologies for shouting," Ruth said, contrite, trying to collect her dismantling thoughts. "A *New York Times* reporter suggested the same thing to me."

"This travesty was reported to the *Times*?" a man dressed in black asked. "Are you completely serious about this time-traveler or whatever?"

"Yes, I swear," Ruth replied. "I have the suicide note in my coat pocket." She walked out from behind the counter and headed toward the coat rack. This bewildered crowd was now intrigued and followed and surrounded Ruth.

She had the skeptic read the note aloud, as all the others,

including Anne, shuffled back and listened attentively. It took the businessman, named Harold, about a minute to read this note. Afterward, the small group was left in disbelief. Silence fell on the pharmacy.

"This is astonishing," Harold said.

"Blasphemy," Anne concluded, with slight emptiness inside.

"I swear, it's all true," Ruth said. "Would you like to ... see the machine and the man ... Patrick Shields?"

The crowd thought about it collectively.

"I think it's worth it," Harold replied, nodding. "I find it an absolute necessity to spread the knowledge of this conspiracy nationwide; there has to be a reason for it."

"Yes, let's head out."

Ruth put on her coat and pushed the creaky door open. She led everyone out to the sidewalk. On this cold and damp day, they bundled up and headed southward, following Ruth in her every footstep.

"I believe it was along Seventy-Fifth Street," Ruth reminded herself. She peered around in the same direction, looking for the gap the path had created. The group that trailed behind continued to follow nervously, wondering what they were about to witness.

"Wait ... I think ... there's the gap!" Ruth pointed excitedly at a southwest angle. The crowd of ten instantly looked and then cross the old cobblestoned Fifth Avenue as quickly as they could.

The path had since become snow-covered. Ruth stepped over the wooden fence, brushing snow off the top. One by one, Anne, Harold, and others soon followed and walked along the path to the fence.

"It's still densely forested here," a woman in the back said.

"The path appears to be well worn," Harold noticed.

It was very dim within this path, and by the last time the last person climbed over the wooden fence, two more witnesses had arrived behind them.

They appeared familiar only to Ruth, as they were the reporters from the *Times*.

"Is Ruth here?" Henry called out to the last woman.

"Yes, sir?" the woman replied, a little perplexed by his forwardness. Both reporters waited in line behind her.

Ruth and Anne had reached the specific area, with Harold behind a few feet.

"Behold," Ruth said in a calming matter. "Here is the machine, and over there is Mr. Shields, who is, unfortunately, deceased."

Anne, Harold, and the rest looked once and then stood in paralyzed shock. It was all indeed true.

"This *has* to be the machine," Harold gasped, wiping cold snow off the door. "What else could it be?"

"It doesn't look like anything described in the Wells novel," Anne pointed out.

"Clearly and obviously, it has to be from the future, as told," Ruth added.

Suddenly, the two reporters rushed up to Ruth, calling her name.

"Oh!" Ruth said, turning toward them. "It's the reporters from the *Times*."

"Henry and Charles?" an elder pointed out with a distaste. "I read their damn papers every day."

"This is … just … incredible …" Charles gasped, observing the entire area with eyes the size of the moon.

"You were right," Harold said, looking at Patrick's dead body. "This is a suicide. He took an overdose of arsenic, for God's sake."

"Look at this." Anne picked up the other empty bottle. "This has the Fifth Avenue Drugs label on it. Did it come from your pharmacy?"

Ruth held her head in shame.   "I knew I would admit this eventually," Ruth said sadly. "I sold that man those products."

"Oh my goodness … really?" Harold asked in pure disbelief.

"He seemed like a normal man at first, but he was wearing those odd blue denim pants, as you can see."

"Oh God, give me strength to handle this hot press!" Charles said with a gleeful smile, writing down every last detail upon a small notepad.

"Why would he want to kill himself in 1901 but not in his time?" Anne wondered.

"I don't think we will ever know for sure," Henry replied. "So many countless theories could be generated."

"This is unprecedented, haunting, cold …" the same old woman said, a little muffled. "I'm becoming slightly—but I would say reasonably—frightened."

"I feel like Patrick is attempting to convey a message about something. Something pertaining to his experience with his time. Who knows what that could be?" Ruth pointed out.

"Uh, Ruth?" the elder said, pointing.

Ruth's eyes widened. "Fifth Avenue is filled to the absolute brim with people." She walked halfway back down the path and found a crowd of people in both directions.

"Holy …" Ruth gasped. "We grew from ten to at least … two hundred!" She headed back to the same area.

"There absolutely *has* to be a message in here, in the suicide note," Henry said.

Nothing was beginning to look the same, as everyone crowded around the site of the machine.

"It's like he was too depressed to explain it," Anne suggested. "Just what could it be?"

Ruth nodded her head in agreement. "He did talk about 'constant blasphemy upon his soul,'" she said, remembering the note.

"Perhaps the *inside* of the machine holds some information," Harold suggested. He headed into the machine and took notes on some rather interesting stuff. "Whoa ... check this out! Come in here."

Anne, Henry, Charles, and two others went inside the disabled time machine.

"So advanced!" Charles exclaimed.

"Does this still work?" Henry asked.

"We would probably never figure this out anyway," Anne said, pointing out the destroyed control screen.

"All those inside," Ruth exclaimed, stepping out of the machine, "we have no time to waste just looking at this machine."

Harold's mind was suddenly struck. He developed an idea, a unique one nevertheless. "Time ... time ... that's it!" Harold instantly bolted out of the machine and back to Ruth. "I need your notes!"

Ruth nodded. "You can have the market one too."

Harold took both and headed down the path to stand atop a three-foot tree stump. *"Everyone!"* Harold shouted. "Would you please direct your attention this way!"

Whether Harold didn't speak loudly enough or the snow muffled the sound, it was hard to get everyone's attention, especially because the crowd had now grown to head four blocks back.

Ruth looked up, along with the first ten and Charles, along with the now seven hundred others.

"I believe time is the reason!" he explained at the top of his lungs.

"But why would he come here?" Ruth asked.

"Hold the reins," Harold whispered to Ruth.   " T h i n k about it, the time goes by ... we are humans—"

"No shit," the old woman added for context.

"We are continuously evolving. Where will we be in one hundred years?" Harold paused a moment for effect and then said, "If we keep on evolving, eventually, there will be inventions to replace us."

"That's crazy!" a man shouted from a block away.

"But just think about it. The reason this time-traveler was supposedly changing history was because humans—us ... our future families—might no longer be in control two hundred years from now." He waited for a response from the crowd, even if it was broken up, but nothing would come until Ruth decided to speak up.

"So what I'm trying to get out of this is that he was not particularly fond of our evolving as a species."

"That's merely scratching the surface," Harold replied. "Perhaps there is such a thing as taking it too far?"

Ruth thought some more and came to a conclusion shortly after. "So the reason he came to 1901 was so he could ... warn us about what is happening in the future?"

"Could be," the elder agreed. "But is there enough information to solidify this theory?"

"According to the *other* note Ruth had," Harold continued, "they are warning us about the supposed depression in the stock market." He looked for some reaction, which was seemingly continuously growing, along with profound sounds of gasping at the realization.

"He also talks about the future holding a 'lot of scary things.'"

Ruth, whether willingly or not, had to agree.

"Patrick Shields wanted to let us know that the future will be controlled by something greater and that he came to an end because of it. He was warning us about the uncertain distant future; he killed himself because he couldn't take our evolution anymore."

A silence. A long pause to put things into perspective.

"Does that ... make any sense to any of you?" Harold asked.

Everyone took their time to develop a collective answer. Someone had to.

"I agree," Ruth shouted with confidence. She stood atop the same stump. "It sounds at least a little logical. Where were we one hundred years ago, you ask? And where will we be, one hundred years from this moment?"

"Dead."

"The world could dive into an abyss of inevitable chaos if we know too much," Ruth added.

"Patrick did say he knew too much, after all," Harold chimed in.

"Who agrees with us?"

The crowd chanted a slurred *yeah* right back at them. The ones who didn't were either confused or in complete disbelief.

"How the hell did we just agree on this?" A woman held her head.

"In conclusion, we develop the theory that this future in our hands is going to become too powerful, if it hasn't already."

"I damn near knew it!" a man absurdly shouted back seconds later. He then pushed his way through the crowd toward the tree stump, where Harold and Ruth were standing.

All seven hundred pair of beady eyes were on the man, along with some directed toward the man directly next to him.

"All right, he whispered the same exact thing to me the whole time," the man said, defending his pride.

"How are you, sir?" Ruth asked cautiously.

"Who even is that?" Harold wondered.

Henry instantly had a response. "I think that's the man who witnessed both time-travelers a week ago."

"That's correct," Calhoun Clark, dressed in white, replied, taking center stump. "This is exactly, precisely, what I knew would happen; they were simply against human evolution."

"That's just the surface of the situation," Ruth respectfully argued. "Something must happen to change that situation for the future."

"You can't prove that," Calhoun replied sternly, in blatant disagreement to the entire problem.

"But why else would he want to kill himself?"

"I haven't a clue. We can't just ignore what we have or assume the future is bad. We can't hold on to our past; we need to make room for our future."

"But without the past, there is nothing to base the future on, is there?" Harold wondered. "People—no, society—can't ignore the weaker past and just loosely base the future on whatever is current, like you, Mr. Clark."

"We have to do something; we have to choose a theory and put it into effect and thus help the future, hopefully," Ruth said, attempting to come to a resolution.

Calhoun continued to disagree. "You are simply wrong."

"I found another note inside the time machine," Anne added abruptly, pulling it out of her pocket. She walked out of the woods near the stump and handed Ruth the note.

"Another? Wow ..." She read it quickly. "This note states that Patrick Shields must be killed in order to save our future ... that he is trying eradicate Manhattan and we must stop him—signed, Calhoun Clark."

Those seven hundred eyes again shifted to Calhoun, along with Ruth's.

"Was this killing your idea?" Ruth investigated.

"No, okay, I didn't do that," Calhoun said. "It appears he took care of that himself. It was a suicide!"

Everyone took a moment to understand the information.

"Okay ..." Ruth said, seeming uncertain. She slowly turned her eyes away from him.

"Let's take this message and make what Patrick Shields wanted to happen come true. Who's with us?" Harold asked the crowd as a final note.

Nearly everyone, except an enraged Calhoun, shouted an encouraging *yeah* back to Ruth. She smiled and looked back at the deceased body of Patrick Shields again.

"We are listening," she whispered. She stepped off the stump; Harold followed, and the impromptu speech had concluded.

***

The New York Times
December 30, 1901

Time to Change: The solution behind Patrick Shield's time-travel conspiracy

> New York—A cold Wednesday morning awoke to
> an urgent discovery by a pharmacist along Fifth
> Avenue.

The report issued a week ago by a man who supposedly was confronted by two time-travelers appears true. The *Times* reported the discovery of a suicide- a male time-traveler and his time machine parked against the decomposing body.

Word was quickly spread yesterday morning, with the same pharmacist showing disgruntled customers the evidence of it. Once released to the public, the crowd quickly grew from ten to over one thousand Manhattan citizens, lining several blocks stretching from Sixty-Third to Eighty-Third Streets. The speech, impromptu at best, was given along the Seventy-Eighth Street block.

A solution to the current situation, which was why Patrick Shields would go back in time to kill himself, was instantly developed with the public's input.

Unfortunately, the solution was just as complicated as the problem itself. A businessman came up with the final quote, noted here:

"But without the future, there is nothing to base our future on, is there?" People—no, society ... [in the future] can't ignore the weaker past, and loosely base the future on whatever is current ..."

The pharmacist also added:

"The time-traveler is attempting to warn us [that] the future will become too powerful."

Society realizes that no one will probably ever know the exact reason why, but to many—not all, but many—the solution sounds viable.

At noon yesterday, news of this occurrence quickly spread nationally, and by 1:00 p.m., it was nearly worldwide. This message became the only thing on people's minds, and in the end, it was universally accepted. Of course, it caused controversy, with many disagreeing on why Patrick Shields ended his life.

By now it was three in the afternoon, and the country was deciding how to address this warning. What seemed to be striking was the thought of humans evolving so much that we would take ourselves out of control; it is all up for speculation.

It was clearly confirmed, so much, in fact, that the government got involved. With public opinion taken into account, Congress decided to form a unique primary for the nation.

This primary involved voting for brand-new proposed laws, approved by President Roosevelt, who decided to address the issue right away. These laws, which were based off the theory of the warning, included three options:

1. To uphold development that conflicts with the human mind and then leads to an easier situation in which the problem pertains.
2. To boycott anything that could eventually lead to an absence of the human mind taking place within an activity.
3. To progress slower in order to delay or stop the evolution of humankind that would lead to absence of human activity or mind while portraying the action.

The public was asked to vote for which option would be put to substantial law, in order to do something to address the message. Many wondered if this would even help, but they were scared out of their wits by the thought of humans out of control, so they decided to vote.

Voter turnout was great; at least 98 percent of the country voted. Urgent to address future status and issues, the vote was instantly counted, and the results were finally in this morning.

Law proposal #1—34%

Law proposal #2—20%

Law proposal #3—44%

Citizens voted for the third law in a tight race with the first proposal. Meanwhile, the second law was aborted because according to many, this would take things a tad too far.

Congress does intend to put this law into effect by the end of this week.

What does this mean for us? Well, this discovery of someone more than one hundred years into the future will most likely go deeper than anyone should know. What the law means is that technological advancements and development will take more thought than previously noted. Companies will address more issues, which include whether this will change the perception of a human's mind affiliated with it. It sounds difficult, and complaints have come out of numerous companies already.

Will this help us as a society? Will this address Patrick's message? Nobody can know for sure. There has never been such a journey through human perception. Only the future will tell us.

Story will be updated after more companies address it.

Chapter 27

Coalition
December 31, 2050
Milwaukee, Wisconsin

A cold, haunting breeze caused everything loose in downtown to sway. It was pitch-black outside, and everywhere else for that matter. The only object shining was the distorted, bewildered moon and its dim yellow reflection along the pixelated, musky water of neighboring Lake Michigan.

Not a single sound could be heard. Not a single one.

And Christmas had passed.

The population of the earth, undocumented yet certainly profound, was dropping by the thousands every hour. Every single remaining human, trapped under invisible shields of regret and remorse, had given up attempting to go on. They were slowly going through the notorious motions of pain and suffering, until souls and death parted ways.

Every alley was empty. Every street was deserted. Yet humans still abounded, trapped inside buildings, just waiting for the pain to lift away and for them to go to heaven, where they could do no wrong, for they did no wrong. At least they thought so.

Yet there really was nothing they could do. Absolutely nothing they could do.

Strangely enough, nothing appeared to have damage in downtown. It was the complete opposite of the distorted faces of the people it held, strangely innocuous. All property was still; nothing was moved or decayed. A normal sort of temperature. Remaining thermometers read a cool fifty-seven. It's like this damage was virtual, not physical, but no one could run away from it or disconnect.

Invisible winds.

It was on the verge of dawn. The sky above, predisposed to fall, was turning from a dark midnight blue and getting steadily brighter. The sun was approaching the horizon, a sparkle of white switched between dark clouds and darker water.

At a lonely intersection, lined by four borders of glass and four crosswalks of white, Krystal awoke to a bright light shining in her eyes. Her eyes sunk back in her head with remorse and fear, yet her eyelids still cracked open at the sight of it. She lay right in the middle of the intersection. She picked her head up slowly and opened her blue eyes slightly; she remained facing to the east, down Mason Street. Between a dark glass tower with the address of 777 and a disabled yet still perfectly clear Northwestern Mutual tower, the sun was now slowly rising above the lake, shining directly down upon the building's facades and reflecting off Krystal's eyes. A melancholy yet euphoric, meticulous atmosphere was suddenly thrust and propelled with the bright, radiating shades of the sun. It was like a sad song that released all emotions, and the tears collected filled the lake below.

Krystal struggled to lift her dehydrated, starving body from the concrete ground. She was still in a fight to look for Patrick. She couldn't manage to see anywhere, only directly east. She was desperately looking for a fix to the situation, if there was one still remaining to be found.

For these new moments, she found absolutely nothing, no signs at all of anything working.

She frowned; a tear rose and fell off her cheek. She began to rest in the same spot, with nothing to do except wait through the anxiety of death by watching the sun slowly rise.

She slowly shut her eyelids, making no sound. Ears ringing was a sound unique to everyone, but it was also the only thing anyone could ever hear. For the rest of time.

Her still eyes remained peeled, just a tad open. She couldn't see anything but a bright spot called the sun.

Dim stars above were still shining, thriving like civilizations that were simply and seemingly too bright to die.

It got her thinking, whether it was a mere coincidence, or this was meant to be. Patrick had actually shown what was going to happen, yet he never had the strength or the support to change it and make things right.

More tears began to fall … to open, musky air, and they would dribble to the pavement, dampening the asphalt to a darker gray.

Suddenly, with ignorance of expectation, the tear reflected and shined in Krystal's eye. The scenario would get a little brighter. Just a little.

She noticed the tear, reflecting off the light. But it was far off to the right side; it could never, ever be the sun. The sun was shining toward the left.

She opened her eyes once again, wider than previously. She would set out to find the source of light. She then lifted her head off the ground and looked up to the right.

What she found was something new, something unusual for this time. Inside a glass window pane, just one light was on. Just one LED, flowing white light.

She was then lit up. A sudden, provocative burst of happiness shot into her soul like a paintball. She stood up quickly, embracing hope.

"Is … is that the power coming back on?" she wondered, rubbing her eyes.

She was very wobbly and quite tired, being barely able to stand. But alas, this discovery was holding her up.

Suddenly, to her left, another white, LED light turned on. She managed to pull off an underwhelming grin and took in what was happening.

She cautiously thought to herself, *Did this convoluted plan work? Is he coming back?*

Anything in retrospect was up for speculation. She was obviously not 100 percent. She was afraid to be, as it hadn't gotten her very far in the past few weeks.

Lights were turning back on everywhere. It seemed as if her hopes were coming true. One by one, bright white lights of all shades were flashing back on. Some flickered, some went back off, but most stayed consistent. What seemed to have been lost was hope, with the entire human race ceasing to exist, with the entire planet ceasing to exist; it was almost like nothing had ever happened. It was almost—not too profound, but almost—turning back to normal, whatever normal was. Krystal was shocked, and shocked even more than the lights turning back on, for she could absolutely not believe what she was seeing. Her heart was palpitating out of her chest; she couldn't help but smile. It seemed as if the entire earth got brighter with a flash.

Even though her eyes were directed at the flashing lights, her eyes transitioned to an innocuous object suddenly moving. She squinted for a closer look, and it turned out to be an autonomous car. A normal, aged, worn-out-looking one, since it has been sitting in the same parking spot for a week. Looking closer, it suddenly began to shift. The color, as bland as it was, began to change. The shape was changing, the year and design of it, morphing out of its previous shell and smoothly transforming into another. Krystal gasped at the slightest look. What in the hell was happening? It seemed entirely unnatural. Krystal began to doubt the change; worry after a week of desperate for food or water. She thought the cause was simply a hallucination. She thought that she was probably right.

A hallucination it was. One for all to witness.

The car kept on changing appearance, with a spectrum of colors flashing instantly and slowly disappearing. Shortly after, cars parked all around started changing. They were changing their colors, looks, shapes, and Krystal's perception on what was actually happening.

She held her head in despair, dazed and confused about what was happening. She was waiting for it to stop, if all turned out to be a hallucination.

Krystal then lay slowly down upon the gray pavement once again, shut her blue eyes, and waited out the supposed hallucination.

As she covered her eyes, the whole appearance of downtown Milwaukee seemingly began to change. Buildings were suddenly fading, until they were eradicated to no existence, right out of thin air. Their colors disappeared; they were rearranging before they suddenly fizzled and faded into nothing.

It seemed as though everything was becoming increasingly older, as time moved forward.

It was now time for the whole sun to rise above the horizon. Three-quarters above the lake, it provided a light and an emphasis on the changes that were occurring so rapidly.

Everything was morphing. These freeways, deserted and barren, that lined the entire city, were shrinking; cars that were once autonomous were now drivable.

Buildings were falling without sound, transforming to the historic counterparts that had once resided there.

It was indeed a sight to behold, but no one could witness it right away.

The sun was bright enough to now get people to take a glimpse.

The sun had shone into a man's house, who was currently just waiting … waiting like everyone else … for his pain to go away.

The man was awakened by the bright sun, a polar opposite to the melancholy, somber atmosphere that was undeniable.

The man, middle-aged and with death imminent, like everyone else, peered out his front door. The front of his house was located directly southeast of downtown, near an abandoned apartment tower.

He peeled his eyes open, slowly but surely, and looked outside, not sure what he was looking for. He usually woke up to a kiss and then be on his way, but this kiss would be missing this morning.

He'd still be on his way.

He knew that the sunrise was absolutely, eerily beautiful; he guessed it could be his last one.

He looked closer for detail because this sunrise on this December morning was quite vibrant. What else did he have to do?

Watching across the Hoan Bridge in the distance, he saw something flashing. He also thought he was beginning to hallucinate and that it was simply the beginning of the end.

But no; it seemed continuous and quite clear, not nearly shaky or disoriented. At all. It was, at least to what this man was capable of seeing, that a seven-hundred-foot apartment tower was vanishing. It was fading, coming back, and turning into a clearing, hiding in the crystal-clear blue sky.

This man had no words. If it wasn't a hallucination, it was the strangest thing he had ever witnessed.

He then decided to take a positive spin on it.

Perhaps the earth was changing, returning to its normal stance.

He could only hope so.

Numerous smaller buildings were now changing, and it was a sight he could not keep for himself.

Soon enough, the sun was bright enough to penetrate any window facing toward the east. Countless people emerged out of their shells, out of their homes, and walked up to the brighter-than-usual sun and stared into the downtown's soul, reflecting off of it.

To the man's surprise, another person near him walked out of her house. She also noticed something different about this sunrise.

"You!" the man sputtered with a weak voice. "Have ... you noticed these changes as well?"

"Yes!" she replied with a noticeable grin. "Could everything be finally returning to what it was, what it should have been?"

"There isn't any way to tell for sure," the man named Jason replied, slowly grinning. "But what it does tell me is that I am not alone."

"We have to get a closer look," Morgan, the woman, replied, pointing northwest.

The two departed their neighborhood street and proceeded northwest, up toward a boulevard named Lincoln Memorial Drive, a ghost of its former illustrious self. It connected to the bridge with two ramps, which gave access to the north. An absolutely perfect, wide view of downtown and the surrounding neighborhoods was ahead, around a mile away. It would give the two desperate, curious, and apparently adventurous citizens a better look at what was happening.

They soon reached the entrance ramp to the abandoned viaduct; it was very worn out, quite deteriorated. It wasn't like this before.

"Well, at least to me, the freeway has changed as well," Morgan observed, looking down. "It hasn't deteriorated this much since ... you know what, I don't even recall. Wow ..."

She turned around, looking at the precarious damage. She picked up her head and, much to her surprise, a group of twenty were behind her, slowly walking but anxious to reach the top of the bridge.

She pointed them out to Jason. "Look behind you."

Jason turned around and his jaw dropped at the sight of the crowd growing by the second, all with the same goal in mind. Jason knew that this was actually taking place.

"Holy … shit. This is amazing!" he yelled with profound joy. He then looked into the primary direction once again, swinging his head fast. He and Morgan headed north, along with the rest of the crowd that was continuously growing.

The exit ramp came to an end and merged with the bridge, as this crowd was just beginning.

It grew to completely take over all six lanes in both directions along Interstate 794. The viaduct was old and tiresome, shaking with every step every person took, but the crowd continued and insisted that they would have a better view of all that was changing.

The bright sun was shining in their eyes, buildings reflecting it, and it reflected the feelings, thoughts, and sights of the two-hundred-person crowd. Everyone knew this wasn't a hallucination; to dismiss it was serious. Was it better or worse for society? That was the primary question.

No one knew for sure.

They kept trudging up the steep incline of the Hoan, which rose to 120 feet above the cold Milwaukee River. Jason and Morgan, leading to group, were around seventy-five feet from that noticeable point.

The sun was fully risen now, and it was simply a race to the top. The crowd was tired from lack of resources, but a persistent desire was strong enough to pull them to the very top of the Hoan Bridge.

Morgan, Jason, and the many others stopped right at the end of the crowning yellow arch to finally see what was changing in downtown.

Half of the crowd jumped over the concrete divider down the middle to get a better look, providing most with some sort of view. Everyone looked northwest. Not a single eye was directed any other perceivable way.

They looked.

And they were stunned.

The crowd laid eyes on the entire city in absolute amazement. A coalition of ghostly yet vibrant colors were washing into and out of each other. Like the brainwaves of the people looking on, mesmerized. A translucent metamorphosis. The colors were fulfilling to the eyes but still physically empty. Everyone felt like they were floating. Like perhaps nothing had even happened. The sight was the pinnacle of anything they had ever witnessed, the most beautiful thing they had ever seen. They heard nothing, but the absence was deafened by the enigma presented forth. The everlasting feeling of notorious lust, the everlasting feeling of euphoria, and desire, and hope had risen out of the ashes and had resurrected itself for a renaissance of revolution. The magnificence of the sight became illustrious, almost as illustrious as the past had been for these people.

They could see the artist in the sky, painting a picture of reality and reflecting mortality, for he was merely taking his time with the swift whisks of his brushes. It seemed he was almost done. The bigger changes had stopped. Only small flashes were found in corners and pockets, like fireflies in a backyard, flashing at the precipice of the approaching dawn. But these innocuous minds were still flashing, comprehending what they had just witnessed. It was as if these changes of life itself were transparent, invisible. All could see, but something invisible was filling any gap that proclaimed the blood of a more modern time.

Silence. The most deafening sound. This entire experience, whether physical, virtual, or just mental, was a song. A song that only the eyes could hear. Whatever it was, whatever it turned out to be, was destined to be over imminently. It was like the atmosphere leaving and returning the earth, creating a whirlwind of emptiness, spinning the planet, and having the souls of the people—desperate for anything—return to each and every one. It was intoxicating.

The sun was as bright as ever, perched in the bright sky. It was merely a clear blue. Transparent. But in retrospect, none of that truly mattered because every single thing residing in downtown—once inanimate, then animated, and back to inanimate—was different. Noticeably different.

"What in God's name … happened?"

Nervous to give any answer, the two-thousand-person crowd lining all six lanes of the Hoan Bridge were shocked, to a point where they realized how small a part of the world they were.

"Did the whole world … return to normal?" a man asked in the middle of the crowd, audible to some. He sounded reluctant but then became outspoken once again.

"There is literally no way to tell; don't ask me!" Jason responded. "We have to find out for ourselves."

"What do ya mean?" a younger man in the southbound lanes asked.

"Something could have happened. We need to split up and see exactly what."

Shortly after that provocative statement was passed on, the large crowd began to disperse. Some headed south, back to their homes and apartments in Bay View, while others headed north toward the epicenter of the city. They all had the same goal, if with different resolutions to it, and that was to figure out and put an end to the debate of what the hell happened.

Jason took the exit for Lincoln Memorial, running toward

the Couture, the complex he once worked at. His car was parked out front.

After walking a long half mile off the bridge, he ran right at Clybourn Street and proceeded through the middle, where no cars were ever driven but where they were parked.

His car was a blue autonomous Toyota Prius, which was a stand-out in the pool of bland gray cars.

He approached it as fast as he could, out of breath, as he was so delighted to see it was still there.

"Yes! This is it!" he cheered. He opened the driver's door right away, surprised that it wasn't locked. There was no time to worry about a key or lock; he was opening a much bigger surprise.

He looked around, and what he saw wasn't familiar.

On the dashboard he saw a steering wheel with a silver Toyota logo slapped on it, along with two pedals directly underneath it.

"Wait … what?" he asked to himself, perplexed. "Do … do I actually have to drive this car?"

He noticed there was a start button in glossy vermillion in the center console. Wondering what would happen, he pushed it out of pure curiosity.

The Prius turned on with a roar of a noise, louder than any other surrounding sounds.

"This car, my car, actually has to turn on?" he asked. His excitement was beginning to boil. His car actually functioned. "Are we legit back to how we should be? Normal?" he wondered. His excitement was at its peak, but he still felt that something was wrong. As doubt persisted, he pushed the steering wheel to the left. Suddenly, the car's front wheels turned left as well.

He now knew what had happened.

"This is one of those old Priuses you actually have to drive!" he shouted with confusion and slight anger. "Have we gone back in time or something?"

He opened his door, walked out, and glanced at all the cars

parked nearby. They were all quite old, seemingly almost thirty years of age. And yet not one, not a single one, was autonomous.

"Tech works again," Jason explained to himself, denying how great it really was. "But has it receded?"

He attempted to learn how to drive again. The last time Jason drove was in 2035 on an old riding mower. A car—he hadn't driven one in forever.

He pressed the gas pedal cautiously and slowly made his way out of the parallel parking spot.

"Accelerate, dammit!" he shouted at the dashboard, cautiously continuing to press the pedal. Within fifteen seconds, he was at Van Buren. He ignored the stoplight, due to the streets being deserted. He forgot his turn signal and headed north on Van Buren, looking for more proof and answers.

All the lights in the buildings were turned off but only because the sun was out and bright.

He made his way along the trashed asphalt and was soon at Wisconsin Avenue. He stopped at the light, which was also functioning as an LED red. Anticipating a green signal, he suddenly saw another car drive by at thirty miles per hour.

"So … cars work, but they aren't automated," Jason figured. He then decided to proceed back home to see if anything in his home had changed or morphed.

He headed south on Broadway, steadily gaining his reins on driving. He then took the Hoan Bridge back to his house, instead of the long, disjointed First Street lining the south side.

Once he reached it, a GPS was not necessary for him; he saw from down below that people still remained to exit the bridge and go back to Bay View. He obeyed the fifty-miles-an-hour limit and kept his eyes open.

Within two minutes, he got to the car ferry exit, which was a straight, long, relatively large exit ramp. It was filled to the brim with the public heading urgently back home, dazed and dizzy. They didn't even notice the shiny blue Prius approach them.

Soon enough, though, a man looked around and was instantly shocked.

"Everyone, look at this!" he shouted, getting everyone's attention in the crowd along the slim, one-lane exit ramp. Those closer surrounded the Prius.

Jason rolled his window down and revealed his face to many.

"Does it work? Does it?" Numerous questions flooded Jason's head from a variety of those nearby.

"Well, yes ... but it isn't autonomous," Jason responded, hitting the innocent dashboard. "All of the cars parked near me weren't autonomous either. So strange."

"Really? As long as they work at all ..." one person said.

Jason drove through the crowd, which kindly opened up the lane for him, and eventually exited the freeway, heading south on the boulevard.

His house was located near the lake along Russell Avenue. He got there within a quick minute. The Prius was still the only car on the road.

He parked in between two SUVs in front of his house. He stopped, got out, but didn't shut his car off. He entered his house.

Due to force of habit, he flipped the light switch on. But this time, nearly after a week, it actually worked.

"Wow ... it has to be everything, not just the car!"

He soon found that nearly everything in his house worked— but at the cost of everything being brand new, yet seemingly thirty years old at the same time.

He decided, "I have to address this one way or another. I must have a summit downtown."

People confused, yet presented with hope, had entirely cleared from the Hoan. He got back on the freeway as soon as he could, with the view of downtown in the horizon—but more so of what it looked like thirty years ago.

He proceeded across an empty, worn-out viaduct, below the sky and above the river. He was planning on taking the Milwaukee Street exit but found another car traveling along it in the wrong direction.

He got off and headed for the Sunburst sculpture in front of Wisconsin Avenue. The roaring Prius was a shock to most, who looked out of windows of older buildings and picked their heads up and went down to the street.

People who saw him started following, and as soon as some did, he parked at the corner in front of the Mutual building and got out.

He decided he would address this meeting or summit via the sculpture.

He found the focal point but then wondered how he would get everyone's attention.

Surely they must be awake, he thought. All the lights have turned on again.

Looking west, he found that the group was still following at Cass Street. He decided, after ignoring them, he would reach out.

"Hey! All of you!" he called out to a mixed twenty-person group. "Everything works again!"

"Yeah!" someone said. "But it's all like thirty years old! The cars aren't autonomous!"

"I don't get it; trust me," Jason replied, hands out. "It's terrible! Everyone forgot how to drive!"

Soon, more and more people came out, from the north along Prospect Avenue, from the south along the Hoan once again, from the west as well, all feeding into one street and all feeding into Wisconsin Avenue.

Jason then realized he could pull off a collective speech.

"There's at least fifteen hundred people coming—holy!" he shouted, pleased. "We have to come together in this situation."

The separate groups got closer, yet they still seemed confused and worried, and doubt continued to persist. Fortunately, there seemed to be less of an emphasis on the pure negativity that bled throughout Milwaukee, for a gate had opened.

One of these groups included Krystal, who seemed to be centered in the mob that stretched along Wisconsin Avenue and the square in front of the Mutual building.

He waited for the majority of people to stop moving and began to fabricate a unity speech in his head. Jason stood atop a nearby stairway and elevated himself approximately fifteen feet above the rest of the surrounding downtown, in between two nearly dead trees.

The crowd could see him above and within the scenery in central Milwaukee. Jason began to address something incomprehensible.

"Well, everyone," Jason began, pausing every second, nervous on his feet. "We all can tell, and it was important for us to realize, that what occurred was extremely bewildering and strange."

"Are you trying to sound formal? It isn't working at all," a man called out.

Knowing how rude everyone was, Jason politely continued. "What this means for us is that everything technological, everything mechanical, virtual, and digital, now works again properly."

Everyone, unaware of the negative circumstances, began to cheer, but it was instantly broken up and interrupted.

"*But*," Jason continued, "at what cost to society?" He paused to let the thought sink in. "It seems that everything current—everything from autonomous cars, to entire wind farms, to a goddamn blender—has been replaced with their thirty-year-old counterparts. Cars now have to be driven. We now have to do things."

A collective gasp of shock shook the street; some booed, some professed hate and anger, and some rolled their eyes. But all were still left to wonder how this could happen.

"Everyone, focus, get together with these thoughts," Jason said as loudly as he could without exactly shouting. "Before we go and be all upset about having to do things ourselves, just be thankful that we are now able to survive in the first place."

Silence was the reaction.

Krystal smiled.

"We can live our daily lives again! Great, right?"

"But we actually have to *move*!" a slightly angered man shouted at the top of his lungs.

"I'm aware, and I may even agree, but I can't exactly do anything about it," Jason replied softly. "We need to figure out how this event happened. Does anyone have any ideas?"

People seemed like they wanted to take a jab at the subject but were reluctant. To Jason's surprise, no one wanted to leave or perhaps carry on.

"What we just saw was purely magical. It seemed to have shifted the earth back in time. I wonder if we actually have!"

No answer.

"This large event has changed the course of history forever, if it isn't the most iconic thing to ever happen to the planet, whether for better or worse. We need an answer."

He looked at his smartwatch that he'd picked up at home and found the date remained in line—December 31, 2050.

"Date is cleared; it is indeed the final day of 2050," Jason stated. "I say that this is virtually unexplainable. I believe that God finally found us suffering—after billions of prayers across the world from each and every one of us—and he lifted our spirits and gave us exactly what we desired but with a cost of less modern technology. I think it might have to do with that. God finally saved us when we were in desperate need."

Everyone paused in complete, utter shock. Like a lightning bolt in the middle of July.

Was this the solution—just God's work? Just a painting masqueraded by blood and the world simply a shell of its former self?

Nah.

"No," Krystal mumbled, gaining traction. "You are wrong." She decided, with her remaining strength, to push her way out of the crowd and up Wisconsin Avenue, with all attention—all three thousand eyes—staring down at Krystal.

She proceeded to take Jason's place and talk on the elevated parking garage. "It was not this 'God' who saved us ..." She spoke loudly but out of breath. "It could not have been anyone else but Patrick Shields."

The crowd's reaction to this statement was yet another thunderous gasp but with booing and anger very prevalent.

"He did not!" they all shouted.

"He betrayed us! How could he have fixed it?" others wondered.

"Please, please, I have a decent explanation," Krystal continued. "I witnessed him escape from prison and head back to the year 1901 to save us and give us back our technological resources. He felt so damn bad when he realized that what he did was wrong. He must have fixed it. *He must have!*"

"But ... but why is it all so old?" a young woman complained. "Like my dad."

"In the end, that was his ultimate goal. He thought that the reason we were all on the verge of death was because the earth had become so overrun with technology, and humans had become so defiant. And when it failed and turned off, we forgot how to live. How to survive. In order to even have a chance at saving us, he thought it would be best to push it back thirty years and make humans once again perform tasks in their daily lives and not to have them automated. He believed this would cause us to live a better life. He literally went back in time so people could receive his message and change this future back. It's the only conceivable way. To live. To survive."

Everyone out in the distance had no words. Yet Krystal, amazingly confident, begged them to still wonder whether she was right or not.

"But after all the harm he has done, how could he save us?" a person asked.

"Like I said, he was a caring person; he simply carried out his actions in the wrong way. He was trying to save our planet all of December, and it took him until now to finally do it. We have to appreciate that we are now able to grow food again, but like we did as children. It is literally the best solution to come out of many in this rancor. That's what went wrong, and we all need to stop being selfish and finally appreciate what we have in the first place- just as he stated previously."

A pause. Perhaps, the last one they found necessary.

They then smiled at each other.

That hadn't happened in the longest time.

"This is great!" someone shouted. Suddenly, to Krystal and Jason's surprise, the crowd began cheering and roaring with excitement, finally realizing that they could live freely again.

"We are all human," Krystal said enthusiastically. "Look at us. He tied us all together and unified us when everything looked the bleakest. We can manage to live this way. We can—no, we will—live this way. We need to do so, first and foremost, as of right now!"

The crowd erupted with cheering, hugging, and chanting of happiness. They had not felt this way since they were children. They could now not only survive but live a better life than they ever could have before. It was simply stunning. It was simply amazing, a complete metamorphosis of a mentality that scarred the entire human race. It was similar to a dream, but it wasn't. And the fact that Patrick Shields saved everyone was an even bigger emphasis on the dramatic irony that somehow saved all of earth. It was too surreal to be written down, to be a dream.

Completely incomprehensible.

Within an hour or so, the crowd had completely dispersed, and the rehab, physically and mentally, had begun. Everyone dispersed with bittersweet happiness. But a dense layer of insecurity was still prevalent, a feeling that no one deserved this due to previous selfishness or selfish actions.

Yet it didn't really matter to Krystal. Her bright blue eyes shone as bright as ever.

She was pleased.

EPILOGUE

New Year's Day

I stare out my sealed, three-glass-layer apartment window, watching the snow blanket the cold ground and trees, cars whirring by, and the great lake down the hill by the name of Michigan slowly freeze. I relapsed in memories of childhood.

I haven't felt such feelings in a long time.

I am simply being patient with myself, to slowly comprehend how Patrick saved everyone, but—to my despair, especially—he has not returned. He must have passed away trying to convey his message, as ridiculous as it sounded back in 1901.

I frown at the thought, as water drips down the window, as a pizza bakes in the oven. I guess I shouldn't be too ashamed; I got exactly what I wanted. I should be ecstatic.

Huh.

I am simply glad that the world functions again, and the earth is whole again. Hasn't been that way in a long time. It's amazing. I wonder how long it will last.

Through all my personal misery that I'm exaggerating, I get to start my life over because of Patrick. I get to carry on, wayward or not, without worry or stress. It's magical. It's magical how it all played out. From time traveling to a cop chase, to the biggest mistake ever created by anyone, to one of the most loved people on all of earth within a snap is simply astonishing. I do wonder if I am actually right sometimes. He would be so proud to see all of us begin to live in unity once again. It's fantastic, yet it still reminds me of him being missing. I think most of the city of Milwaukee misses him. Perhaps the whole earth. It's the craziest thing to ever happen in history. Not just modern history. All of history. Period.

But in the end, I can't help but try my best and not think about it too much. It's overwhelming and reminds me of who I miss so damn much. They may even want to change the boulevard out front to Shields Memorial Drive. I chuckle at the thought! I'd enjoy seeing that.

But, for now, it still remains the first day of 2051. A day for remorse that our sudden hero is gone and what he did for all of us at the same time. A melancholy start to the new year. A very new year—holy shit.

For now, it's over, to let something new begin. It's over, to remove these sins. It's over, to learn a lesson, and for the entire planet earth to come together, reconnect, and reunite once again.

Right now.

Patrick Shields, the supernova is over.

The godforsaken supernova.

And I am a witness for you.

> Something happened
> The day he died
> His repression
> Of depression
> Took a glide
> So he could do no more
> Damage to the norm
> Something happened
> The day he died
> When shaking ground shook
> He went ahead and took

Whatever he could
Whatever he thought he should
To feel right
Dim star
Shines bright
Something happened
The day he died
His spirit, arise
Without demise
With the better land
Speaking to the band
Of the better land
Warped in the face
Of singular planet place
Oh, he's not dead
He's only in space
Not merely a disgrace
Ashes to ashes, we now burn
Go ahead and take your turn
Your turn to burn
At what we all have learned

It's just a game
A game we are all forced to play
There were many ways to end the game
But only one could win it.

About the Author

Kristian Zenz is an aspiring author from the outskirts of Milwaukee, Wisconsin. He has had a developing interest in writing, constantly gaining more experience to the subject. He enjoys other hobbies such as basketball and soccer, and loves his hometown.